THE
BURIAL
TIDE

THE BURIAL TIDE

NEIL SHARPSON

zando
NEW YORK

The characters and events in this book are fictitious. Any similarity to real persons, living or dead, is coincidental and not intended by the author.

Copyright © 2025 by Zando, LLC

Zando supports the right to free expression and the value of copyright. The purpose of copyright is to encourage writers and artists to produce the creative works that enrich our culture. Thank you for buying an authorized edition of this book and for complying with copyright laws by not reproducing, scanning, uploading, or distributing this book or any part of it without permission. If you would like permission to use material from the book (other than for brief quotations embodied in reviews), please contact connect@zandoprojects.com.

First Edition: September 2025

Text design by Neuwirth & Associates, Inc.
Cover design by Christopher Brian King

The publisher does not have control over and is not responsible for author or other third-party websites (or their content).

Library of Congress Control Number: 2025934822

978-1-63893-202-4 (Paperback)
978-1-63893-203-1 (ebook)

10 9 8 7 6 5 4 3 2 1

Manufactured in the United States of America
MAP

*To Aoife, always together
through stormy weather*

THE BURIAL TIDE

1

Singing.
A woman's voice cooing gently to her in the darkness.
"Tá mé 'mo shuí, ó d'éirigh an ghealach aréir . . ."
The words were Irish. She couldn't quite find the meaning. Like her mind was fumbling for coins in the dark.
Abruptly, the singing stopped.
Where am I? Why am I here?
She forced her eyes open but saw nothing. Pitch black.
Hands flew to her face and the dry, rough calluses of her fingertips pushed at her open eyes and she hissed in pain. *So I'm alive.* She blinked away angry red and purple stars.
And not blind. Just in total, utter darkness.
Where am I? There was no sound except her own breathing and a strange, gentle rumbling. She reached out and hit soft fabric backed by hard wood.
No. No. This wasn't real. It couldn't be.
She was cocooned. Entombed.
A coffin.
As the panic rose, she kicked and punched and headbutted.
What's the worst thing that could ever happen to you?

This.
Buried alive.

She laughed, and the sound skittered around the wooden walls like a panicked rat. She sounded mad.

"FUCKERS!" she screamed.

Who was she screaming at? Whoever did this to her.

This didn't just happen.

The air was getting thick and fat with the sweat of her own breath, and she tried not to think of her brain cells slowly suffocating, her very consciousness rotting away like spoiled meat.

You've been buried alive. You've been buried alive. You've been buried alive.

If you're going to do something, do it now.

She yelled.

She kicked.

She punched.

Knuckles bloody.

Knees bruised and aching.

Toes broken and twisted.

You're going to die. You're going to die. You're going to die.

A crack. Something breaking.

Maybe the wood. Maybe her.

Exhausted, her hands flopped down beside her and her finger brushed against something solid in her pocket.

She didn't want to feel hope. It would just cut all the deeper when it proved false.

She stuck her aching fingers into the tight denim pocket and pulled it out. A phone. She screamed in joy, activated the screen, and winced as it lit up. The wallpaper was a picture of a woman with long dark hair kissing the cheek of a brown-haired man with a big innocent grin and slightly crooked teeth. They were standing on a beautiful beach, with clear blue sky above them.

The picture seemed to mock her, given the situation. The screen was fuzzing over with droplets of condensation as the air grew hotter and more humid.

A notification for a missed call popped up.

Mam. One minute ago.

She pressed Call, clamping the phone to her ear, and everything went dark again.

She could feel tears running down her cheeks.

The calling tone sounded weird somehow. Too harsh. Too metallic. Almost hissing. Or maybe she couldn't trust anything she heard. Maybe she was already half brain-dead.

Suddenly the tone ended and she heard a voice.

She expected that "Mam" would be a woman.

But the voice was male.

"Oh."

That was all it said.

But in that one vowel there was so much contempt. So much hate. So much indignation and shock that she'd even *dared* to call.

Oh. It's you.

With her last good lungful of air she screamed, "GET ME OUT!"

And then. And then, as if her voice was a clenched fist, she heard a crack overhead.

A drop of water dribbled onto her chin. And then another. It turned into a stream. Another crack. She realized what the strange murmuring sounds had been: Torrential rain. Raindrops falling onto the soil of her fresh grave.

The earth on top of her getting steadily wetter. And heavier. When she kicked and punched the lid she must have cracked the wood, weakening it.

Which meant...

The world broke open. She was drowning in thick, soupy mud. It filled her nose and ears, and tried to swim down her throat.

She managed to get her legs underneath her, onto the wooden base of the coffin. She pushed up, hoping to God that there was a sky somewhere up there, that there was air *somewhere* up there.

She kicked and clawed and writhed out of the earth like a maggot emerging from the rotted flesh of an apple.

And then she was out.

She lay there, spitting up mud, clinging to the lip of the grave as the rain poured down and washed the dirt from her body.

The coffin, like some hungry animal, wasn't ready to let her go, and she almost slipped back inside. But she dug in, fingers clamped to the earth, and she yanked herself forward until she was free of the trench.

The strangest thing?

Lying there, half dead, in a pitch-black graveyard with an ocean's worth of rain bucketing down on her, she felt only euphoria.

She had the only thing she needed to be happy.

Air.

2

She lay at the edge of the grave, this woman, shivering and alone. The rain stopped with a stunning abruptness. Absently, her pale fingers wormed through the filthy water as she sifted through her mind, trying to find her name, but all she could remember was the hatred of the man's voice on the phone, as if she'd done him some terrible wrong.

Her memory felt like a house that had been flooded and all the vital documentation, passports, and family photos were floating around in dark, murky water.

She could only hope that it would pass.

Slowly, trembling, rainwater and mud shivering off her arms, she got to her feet, and looked into her grave.

It was a strange feeling, to look into one's own grave.

There was no headstone. No cross. Nothing to mark her.

Perhaps it was too soon. Or perhaps she had not been deemed worthwhile.

She cast a glance around the cemetery. The clouds had cleared and the *reilig* was now bathed bone-white by the light of the moon and an ancient lamppost.

It was a seclusive and crouching little field, where stone tablets and Celtic crosses stood crookedly among the trees and brambles. A tiny church overlooked the graves and the whole affair was roped off by a white stone wall.

It was very early morning, almost dawn. She could taste that in the air.

The only sound she could hear was the hum of the lamppost, like damage in the ear, and the rustle of the sea tossing lazily in its sleep. She must be near the shore, she decided.

It is exactly the kind of place I would have wanted to be buried, she thought, *but I think that's been spoiled for me now.*

She looked down and felt a jolt of guilt. Her bare feet stood on another fresh grave, her toes penetrating deep into the soil shroud. She stepped off and saw that her own grave was but one of four.

Four newly dug graves. All unmarked.

For a second, she considered getting down on her knees and pressing her ear to the sodden ground, to see if she could hear muffled screams and fingernails raking pine.

But she didn't.

The ground was practically soup, yet that was not the reason. She was already as filthy as a body could be, but something in her blood warned her away.

Perhaps, she thought to herself, she was not a very good person.

But oh, her phone. She could call for help.

Plunging her hands into the open grave, she found the hard rectangle. She tapped it harshly with muddy, cold fingers but it refused to so much as flicker.

With a snarl of rage, she flung it at the stone wall and it splintered and skittered. But there was another sound, too.

THE WOMAN

She froze.

She *had* heard something. Something jostling in the darkness, startled by the sudden violence.

She was not alone, then. With a new fear, she ran through the graveyard, into the shadows of the chapel. She could feel eyes on her like fleabites, watching her.

But the darkness held flush, and no one emerged.

She decided that this was not a good place to be, soaking wet and filthy in a graveyard, in the early-morning hours, watched by persons unknown.

She resolved to find a new place.

Over the wall there was a little cobblestone path.

Carefully, she clambered out of the graveyard and picked a direction. There was sea salt in the air, and the ocean whispered to her.

Every road had someone waiting at the end of it, if you followed it long enough, she decided.

She would follow this road and find someone. Maybe she would find the sea.

Walking revealed that she had broken something in her foot when she'd kicked the coffin lid. The path was stony on her bare feet, and she hobbled as if on a bed of nails.

She suddenly realized that she was ravenously hungry.

Up ahead, she saw a glint of yellow light. A house. And where there was a house there would be food.

She broke into a run.

She wondered what kind of sustenance she'd find.

She needed to eat.

She had just crawled out of a grave, after all.

She felt she could eat anything.

3

Declan

It had been a mistake, Declan realized now, to come to the island.

It would teach him to put his faith in signs.

He had woken from a thin, anxious sleep to the skittering of broken glass on kitchen tiles and the unmistakable sound of footsteps downstairs.

I can't believe this. I lived in one of the dodgiest areas in Dublin for years and wasn't robbed once. I come to an island in the middle of nowhere and I get burgled.

Perhaps he would find it funny after he survived the night.

He remembered that he had found a hurley in the wardrobe when he'd first arrived at the cottage.

Creeping softly, he grabbed the handle and raised the hurl as he made his way hesitantly down the stairs.

He could see light from the kitchen doorway and realized that the fridge was open.

He took a deep breath, gripped the handle of the hurley, and stepped into the kitchen.

A figure, barefoot and filthy, stood crouched in front of the open fridge. There were empty eggshells littered around the floor, and the discarded plastic wrapper from a packet of ham slices. The figure held a large jar of mayonnaise in filthy hands, which she hungrily slurped into her mouth. He could not repress a grunt of disgust and she dropped the jar and looked up at him. He saw terror and confusion in her eyes.

She leapt back, colliding with the kitchen counter. Her hand snaked around, searching desperately until it found the handle of a carving knife.

She pointed it at Declan, the tip dancing nervously in the air.

By the light of the fridge he saw her face for the first time.

The hurley clattered to the floor.

They stared at each other in utter shock.

Finally she lowered the knife.

"Please," she rasped hoarsely. "Please help me . . ."

He stared back at her.

"Help you? How can I help you, love? You're fuckin' dead!"

4
Conn

"They've made a pill, so they have."

Conn glanced over the edge of his cards at his brother, who sat almost naked at the other end of the kitchen table.

Malachy took a sip from his whiskey, tightly holding the glass with the grip of a practiced and experienced drunk.

"They've made a pill, have they?" Conn said quietly, his voice barely audible over the racket of the storm outside. The rain was beating on the slate roof of the cottage like a violent alcoholic locked out of the family home.

"They have."

"What kind of a pill have they made, then?"

"A pill that makes you live forever, they say."

"Is that right?"

"That's what they say. Completely short-circuits the aging process. Bit late for us, course."

"Tell me something, Malachy," Conn muttered darkly. "Would this pill let you breathe underwater if you got swept into the sea?"

"No."

"Would it stop you being crushed if the roof fell in on you?"

"No."

"If I took my gun and shot you in the head with it. Would your pill fix that?"

"No, Conn," Malachy answered, reasonably.

"And when, in five billion years the sun fucking explodes, is this fantastic magical pill of yours going to make any difference to the proceedings?"

"I don't imagine so."

"Then it doesn't make you live forever. Does it?"

"I guess not."

"I guess not. Two threes." Conn laid his cards on the table.

Malachy's smile spread over his face slowly, like molasses. He set down his hand. A two of spades. And a two of diamonds. Slowly, he stood up and carefully and deliberately removed his underwear, exposing his genitalia to his brother, pale soft bean shapes in a briar patch of wiry, bristly hair.

Conn turned away in mild disgust.

He couldn't remember when they had begun this game.

When they had both been young men, it must have been. Their mother, God rest her, had drilled into her sons the dangers of gambling. How their father and uncle had almost killed each other over dice. How unpaid wagers had poisoned whole families on the island. So they never gambled with money. But they were two men on the most remote fleck of earth in western Europe and neither were good at making friends. How else were they to pass the time? So they had played cards for the sake of playing cards. And then, one evening, when they had both been drinking, it had become the game they played now.

It was not sexual. Or at least, certainly not for Conn.

But the tension of it. The risk of humiliation and exposure. It made a passable substitute for the thrill of gambling the month's earnings.

But recently, Conn had realized Malachy always played to lose.

He wondered why that might be.

Perhaps his brother simply enjoyed seeing him uncomfortable. Perhaps they were playing entirely different games.

Malachy gave a drunken wink and sat back down.

"Will you not give her what she wants?" Malachy asked.

Irritated, Conn began to shuffle the cards back into the box.

"If that's what you came to say to me, you can fuck off home right now," he said curtly.

"In that?" Malachy asked, jerking his head at the window, where the rain bubbled and broke on the glass.

"In that, aye. If that's what you came here to say. I thought we were just having a nice friendly game of cards. But if you're here as her fucking cat's-paw . . ."

"I'm nothing's paw, Conn. I just don't see the point? Is it worth ructions in the family, now? Gráinne wants a truce."

Conn said nothing, he simply pointed to the door and lifted a questioning eyebrow. Malachy raised both hands in a gesture of complete, amicable surrender.

And then, suddenly, the rain stopped.

In the silence that followed the brothers looked at each other in shock.

Conn, of course, moved first, running to the window and looking out into the now crystal-clear night, up the cliff, where he could just make out the broken, blunted steeple of the cemetery chapel. Malachy pressed beside him.

"It can't be," he whispered.

CONN

"I know," his brother replied. "It's too soon, Conn."

Conn half marched, half ran to the back hallway of his cottage.

A stuffed seal head, its mouth open in a furious scream, stared madly down at him from the far wall. He barely glanced at it as he lunged for the glass gun cabinet.

He opened it, considering and rejecting the shotgun, and instead took the old Webley. Easier to carry. Easier to conceal.

Then, he went into the kitchen and drew the carving knife with the ivory handle and the blade as old and jagged as a shark's smile.

"C'mon!" Conn barked, grabbing his coat from the rack and zipping it up so quickly the long white-brown hairs of his beard got caught in the teeth.

"Malachy, hurry!" he yelled angrily at his brother, whose hairy, bare buttocks winked filthily at him from under the table.

"I can't find me fucking jocks!" Malachy whined.

. . .

There was no talking on the way up to the cemetery. No whispering or chattering. They both knew well enough. They moved with a silence you would not have thought two drunk old men capable of. Not even their breathing was heavy from the hike up the cliff.

They stepped silently over the wall and hid in the graveyard.

Conn did not make a sound when he saw her there, out of the grave. He wanted to cry out and call her name, or maybe weep, but he did none of that. He and his brother simply hid among the trees, like rabbits watching a stoat.

When she had flung the phone against the wall, Malachy had almost broken, but Conn held him so tight that he felt his brother would snap in his arms.

For one terrible moment, Conn felt her eyes on him, but then she ran from the graveyard to hide by the chapel. She froze there, black as ink with the light of the lamppost casting her in silhouette.

He could have given chase and touched her, if he wanted.

But more, he wanted to live.

She tilted her head, like a cat hearing a mouse in the wall. He felt in his pocket for the knife. The handle met his palm and he prepared to stab her in the neck. And keep stabbing her until he was sure she would never rise again. Not from the grave. Not from the ground. Not from his dreams. She would be over. It would all be over.

But then, she turned and was gone, climbing over the wall and limping away down the rough path that glinted like a snail trail in the early-morning gloom.

Malachy gave a little cry and Conn held his brother close.

• • •

On the way back to the cottage, Malachy told Conn that he could see their mother's face watching from a tree. She was looking at them from between the branches, her teeth bared like a dog's, her eyes pale and gray like dull marble. Malachy planted his feet on the path until Conn had fired the Webley at the tree four times and his younger brother was at last convinced that she was gone.

Conn asked Malachy what their mother was doing in the tree, or how she had gotten up there.

CONN

Malachy replied that he had not been able to see her body, only her face. But he thought the body was that of a snake. So it made sense she would be in a tree. Where else would you find a snake?

They did not speak of the woman who had emerged from her own grave.

Upon returning to Conn's cottage, they made up the sofa for Malachy. After tonight, there was no thought of Malachy attempting the journey home through the darkness.

Conn laid a blanket over him, then went into the back corridor where the old black landline telephone hung. He picked up the handset and made a call, relating the night's sighting.

He returned to the main room to wish his brother good night.

"You were going to go at her with the knife, weren't you?"
"I was."
"Why didn't you?"
"Sure, wouldn't that be murder?"
"There's worse things."
"Aye. There's worse things," said Conn.
"We're in for a bad time, now," Malachy murmured, half asleep. "It's too soon."

5
Declan

He convinced the young woman to come into the living room and sit down on the couch with a cup of tea. He then considered convincing her to hand over the knife, but sensed that she was not quite there yet. It rested on the arm of her chair, in easy reach.

Her eyes followed him with a mixture of desperate pleading and deep suspicion.

As he stayed on the other side of the room, Declan could feel a tension in his chest, like the beginnings of an asthma attack.

He was aware that any sudden movement could cause her to panic and reach for the knife.

Be cool. Be calm. We're all friends here.

"I'm just going to call someone," he said quietly.

"Who?" she asked.

"I really think you need a doctor."

She nodded uncertainly.

He could feel her gaze on his back as he left the room.

What I need is a grown-up, he thought ruefully to himself.

DECLAN

He was twenty-three but right now he felt like a child, hopelessly out of his depth.

Growing up, adults had been in short supply.

His mother had been severely bipolar and lost the battle with her own demons when Declan was still a toddler.

The last he had heard of his father, he was living in Newcastle in a men's shelter and trying to get clean. That had been fourteen years ago, and there had been no further updates, so Declan assumed that the attempt had failed.

And so Declan had been raised by his grandmother. She had tried to shield him from all the cruelties that could be visited on a fat, asthmatic, sensitive child who liked writing songs and poems more than kicking a ball around a field. But she had died last year of a quick and hungry cancer. So vicious, in fact, that her doctor hadn't even bothered to hide his shock and morbid fascination when sharing the scans of the tumors groping her chest.

"Like fingers," the doctor had said, shaking his head in wonder.

After her death, Declan had become very depressed, and had tried to channel that depression into his writing, like all the great poets. But he found that depression was a poor fuel. Everything he tried to write, be it poem or song, came out stunted. Wrong and dead.

That was why he had jumped at the artist's residency. One of the innumerable writers' mailing lists he was on had informed him that there was an opportunity to live in a cottage on Inishbannock for four months, rent free, for the right artist.

A sign. Although born in Dublin, and with a Rialto accent as thick as cement, Declan knew the island. His grandmother was born there, and she had told him stories of her life on Inishbannock. The island always existed in his mind, sunny and simple and quiet. A place to flourish in.

It had felt so right. In his darkest hour, aching from the loss of family, he leapt at a chance to go somewhere that was both new and familiar. Inishbannock would remind him of his grandmother, but not his late grandmother. Not the aching, agonized, hacking, dying figure who haunted his dreams like a witch in a deep forest. His real gran. The warm loving figure of his childhood. His one good thing.

However, instead of the sunny idyll of his grandmother's recounting, he found the island wrapped in a purgatorial grayness, the trees on the skyline as black as bats' fingers against the clouds. The people were like that, too. Friendly. But just enough.

A woman named Gráinne, who ran the local pub in the village, and seemed to be a kind of island chieftain, had welcomed him. Her son Padraig, a giant of a man, but so quiet that Declan thought he must be mute, had driven him to his new home. His rental cottage was in walking distance of Ballydonn, the largest settlement on the island.

Alone on the northern shore of the island, Declan had become even more isolated and depressed. It got worse when he awoke one morning to the sound of a phone going off somewhere in the bowels of the cottage. He found the source after several anxious minutes, through a door to the basement, which he had simply assumed was a cleaning cupboard.

The black phone had been welded to the wall. He'd picked it up and listened in growing panic as he heard a woman's voice, obviously pre-recorded:

DECLAN

"There has been an outbreak on the island.
Several people are dead.
Please remain indoors.
Do not make contact with anyone.
Supplies will be provided."

Never one to listen to instructions, Declan had thrown on his clothes and half run, half jogged to Ballydonn. The village was seemingly deserted, like a film set about to be struck.

Gráinne, a towel clamped on her face, had appeared in the window over the pub and shouted to him that there was plague on the island, some terrible disease that Declan did not recognize the name of. She told him to go home and stay put. Food and supplies would be sent. Finally she yelled down that it was too dangerous to interact with any other human being and slammed the window in his face.

She did not say the words "you bloody fool." But her tone was clear enough.

In shock, he had walked back through the abandoned village, passing the church. Propped up against the wall were four photographs—victims of this plague, he had assumed. They had been solemnly arranged with wreaths and mass cards. One of the photographs was set a little apart from the others, as if it had been added later. He dimly recognized the pretty young woman with sad eyes and long brown hair. He was sure he had seen her around the island before. With a man. Her husband, he assumed. He looked through the photographs again and realized that very man was among the dead, as well.

Both victims of the outbreak.

He wondered what the effects of the disease were, whatever it was. He hoped to God it wasn't respiratory. With his asthma, he lived in horror of suffocation. Of waking up in the dead of night with an iron vise on his windpipe.

On the way back to the cottage, the skies opened and Declan was drenched to the bone.

Padraig arrived that evening, leaving a basket of essentials at the gate and driving off in the pouring rain.

Declan quickly learned that depression and terror were two spirits that should not be drunk together.

For the next day or so, Declan did not leave his bed. That is, until the dead woman broke into his kitchen and raided his fridge.

Now, he picked up the black phone in the basement and dialed.

"Hello?" a sharp voice echoed on the other end, clearly just having woken up.

"Is that Doctor Quinn?"

"Yes, who's this?"

"Sorry, we haven't met. My name's Declan Burke. I'm doing the artist-in-residence thing..."

"Oh yes. The man from Dublin."

"Uh, yeah. Listen, sorry to call you so early. Your number was one of the ones I was given when I moved in. I know you're in the middle of a crisis and everything..."

"What's wrong?"

"It's about the outbreak."

"Are you feeling unwell?"

"No. No, look. One of the people who died. There was a young woman, right? Long brown hair?"

"Mara Dunne. Yes."

"I don't think she's dead."

There was a long pause.

"What makes you say that?"

"Well . . . She's having a cup of tea on my couch."

. . .

The woman—Mara—looked up at Declan and gave him a weak smile as he entered the room, nervous and forced.

"Doctor's on her way," he said. He remained in the doorway, keeping his distance. "Do you . . . like . . . do you want to sleep? You must be tired?"

She shook her head. "I'm scared if I go asleep I might wake up back in . . . I don't want to sleep." Her voice sounded like she was asleep already. Slow, and uncertain.

"So you, you woke up . . . like, inside, like?"

She fixed him with a look and nodded.

He exhaled. "Fuuuuuuuuuck," he said. "Fuck me."

"Do you know me?" she asked. "You do, don't you? You recognized me earlier."

He shifted uncomfortably and leaned against the wall. "I saw you around. Once or twice. We're not, like, mates or anything. I'm only visiting the island. I got this bursary to come to Inishbannock and work on my art for a few months."

"You're an artist?"

"Yeah."

"What kind of art?"

"Poetry. Song-writing," he said. "I rap."

There was a long pause.

"Would you like to hear . . ."

"No," she said. "Sorry," she added. "Sorry. Just . . . not in the mood. Right now."

"Absolutely," he said, generously. "No bother."

"Declan?" she asked. "Why exactly are you wearing that mask?"

Unconsciously, his hand went to the blue surgical mask that was stretched taut over his broad features. "You don't remember?"

"Remember why you're wearing the mask?"

"Remember how you . . . how you ended up where you ended up?"

She shook her head.

"There was an outbreak. Just a few days ago."

"An outbreak of what?"

He spread his hands. "Something broke out. Really nasty. Really fast. Four people dead in one day. We've been told to shelter in place. They're not letting any boats in or out to the mainland. I'm starting to worry they'll never let us leave." He gave a snort of bemused laughter that had notes of real panic lurking in it.

"And you think I might have it?" she asked.

"Mara," he said. "I know you have it. I mean . . . that's how you died."

The look she gave made him immediately backtrack.

"I mean, obviously yer not. Y'know. Obviously. But, they thought you were."

A look of horror crossed his face. "Oh shite! You don't think anyone else was buried alive, too?"

She shook her head. "No. I think I'm the only one."

Declan did not feel comforted by that. But he wasn't going down to the graveyard with a shovel, either.

"So . . . you really woke up inside . . ."

DECLAN

She shook her head violently.

"Okay," he said quietly. "Okay. We don't have to talk about it."

He heard a sound, a low-pitched whine. It was coming from her. He needed it to stop. He could feel his patience shredding, fear taking over. The sound felt like the first sight of the coffin coming out of the hearse. A face lying on a white hospital pillow that had suddenly become too still.

"I don't know who I am," she said at last.

"That's the shock," he said lamely, trying to be comforting. "That's all that is."

She looked up at him, pleading. "What do you know about me?" she whispered.

Declan tugged at his mask. "Nothing really. You live outside the village, I think."

"Did we talk?"

"Not really, just . . . you know. Howerya. Nice weather. I didn't really know you, Mara. I'm sorry. I know that's not what you want to hear."

"My name's Mara?"

"That's what the doctor called you. But you really don't remember? I wish I could tell you more. I'm not . . . very good at talking to people. I mean, you can probably tell that?"

She smiled. "It's okay. Do I . . . have any family? Any friends?"

"Yeah, I've seen you around with some bloke."

"And who is he? A boyfriend?"

"I thought he was your husband, but . . ."

He almost said, "I think he's dead." Declan was fairly certain that man's photo was outside the church, too. But he wasn't completely positive. And that was the kind of thing you needed to be sure of before you spoke.

He simply gestured to Mara's left hand. Her thin, pale fingers wore dark bruises and crimson wounds from what he assumed was her desperate fight with the coffin lid. But they were bare of rings. "I wasn't really paying attention. I've been in my own head, a lot. Always have been. I'm sorry."

"Don't apologize," she replied. "I don't sound very interesting."

"I'm sure you were lovely. Are. Are lovely." He felt his large face flush pink under his blue mask.

Another awkward silence.

"How's the foot?" he asked at last.

She looked down at her bare feet. The right one looked like it had run up a gambling debt to serious people. On top of the bruising, the toes seemed to be at odd angles.

She tried moving them and was rewarded with what looked like a stabbing pain.

"Something feels broken," she said.

"The doc can look at it."

"Is she the only doctor on the island?"

"Yeah. I think so?"

"So she's the one who pronounced me dead?"

"I guess she must have been," he said awkwardly.

"Well. Maybe I don't want her to take a look at me?"

"Ah no, I'm sure she knows what she's doing."

"I was buried alive because of her."

"Well yeah," he said. "But in fairness to her, she was very busy. And look, three out of four ain't bad."

. . .

DECLAN

Not a good sign, to see a doctor terrified.

When Quinn arrived at the cottage, Declan was reminded of gauzy old news footage of large, shapeless figures ambling softly around the Elephant's Foot in Chernobyl. She was covered in red plastic, head to toe, and he couldn't even see her face through her mask.

But he could sense the fear in her. As she approached Mara, she looked like a woman being led to her execution.

Quinn's gloved hands rustled like Christmas tinsel as she laid them on Mara's face.

"It's not possible," Quinn whispered. "Heart rate's normal. No fever."

She reached out to brush Mara's hair to one side and Mara couldn't help but lash out in fear, slapping the doctor's hand away. Quinn sprang back.

"How did you not know I was still alive?" Mara asked Quinn, every word serrated.

Quinn pulled herself up to her full height and took a few steady breaths. She was a tall woman, and the suit made her look taller. She towered over Mara.

"Because you were stone-cold with no heartbeat. Just like everyone else who died," she said simply. "I didn't see the need to get a second opinion."

"Well maybe you should have," Mara snapped.

"I'm sorry," Quinn whispered. "Mara, I don't know how this happened. I can't imagine what you've been through."

"Been through?" Mara repeated. "It's not over. How did I . . . why was I buried?"

"We believe there was an outbreak of Marburg virus on the island. You and three other people died. Or so we thought."

"Marburg?"

"It's related to Ebola."

There was a silence that took several degrees off the already frigid temperature.

"Distantly related?" Declan asked, more in hope than expectation.

Quinn glanced at him and then back to Mara.

"It's incredibly dangerous. As Declan knows, we've had to quarantine the entire island. You were one of the first victims. After your burial the tests came up positive and we went into lockdown."

Mara buried her face in her hands, letting off that awful, unsettling whine.

"I . . . I don't remember anything . . . I don't . . . know . . . who . . . please . . ." Mara pressed her hands to her eyes.

"Okay. Okay," Quinn said soothingly, laying a sheathed hand on her shoulder. "I think Mara could use another cup of tea, Declan, thank you."

"No, I'm fine," Mara said.

"Tea, please," Quinn reiterated.

Declan, realizing that the words "tea" and "please" were euphemisms for "out" and "now," took the hint and closed the door behind him.

6
Mara

"I don't want tea," Mara insisted.

"Hot sweet tea. Best thing," said Quinn, as if Mara was a child. "You're in shock. It's to be expected."

"Is it?" she replied bitterly. "Is it one of the common symptoms of coming back from the dead?"

"Well," said Doctor Quinn. "At least the patented Mara Fitch sarcasm survived the journey back from the afterlife."

"Mara Fitch? That's my name?"

"It is. And it seems like you've had some brain trauma, too? Memory lapse?"

"Yes," Mara reluctantly admitted.

"Alright, let's see if we can help with that."

The red-clad doctor opened her bag and took out a large black felt-tip pen and a yellow sticky pad.

Mara watched in pensive silence as Quinn tore page after page off the top of the pad and wrote on them, one after the other.

Declan returned with the tea and looked curiously at Quinn working away.

"Thanks, Declan. Just set it on the mantelpiece and please close the door after you," Quinn said.

Mara caught the small, worried glance he shot her. She gave him a sad smile and mouthed, "Thank you," as he left the room.

Mara looked back at Quinn, who had placed three yellow pages in a row on the coffee table.

Mara read them one after the other: KATHLEEN, EMMA, DEIRDRE.

"Are you sure you're a doctor?" Mara asked.

"Why do you ask that?" Quinn replied.

"I can read your handwriting," Mara said.

"You've made that joke before," Quinn said, in a tone that implied it hadn't been funny the first time. "Now. One of these is the name of your mother. I want you to tell me which one it is."

Mara looked up and saw that Quinn was holding her phone up, recording her.

"What are you doing?" Mara asked.

"Trust me," she said. "Now, what is your mother's name?"

Mara leaned over, her brow furrowed. None of the names seemed to spark anything. Not a hint of recognition. "I don't know."

"Don't overthink it," Quinn reassured her. "Let your subconscious suggest the answer."

Hesitantly, Mara stretched a finger out and let it fall on DEIRDRE, then flinched as Doctor Quinn whooped with joy.

"Good!" she crowed. "Yes, well done!"

Mara looked into the phone and gave a smile that was as much from fear as relief.

MARA

They continued on. Her father's name. Her home county. First school. Birthday. Favorite color.

Each time she was given three choices.

Each time she chose at random.

Each time, Doctor Quinn promised her that she was right.

She held the phone up to Mara's face.

Mara saw herself—a young woman. She was dry now after a shower, but she looked pale, thin, and harried. Declan had lent her the use of one of his hoodies and a pair of tracksuit bottoms, and in his clothes she looked tiny and frail.

Her stomach clenched as she studied her own face, suddenly realizing it was the same face from the now-shattered phone wallpaper.

She was the woman who had been staring so adoringly at the man, standing on a sunny beach with white sands and endless blue skies.

"Tell me, Mara. Tell me everything you've learned," Quinn said.

"What . . . what do you mean?"

"What is your name?"

"My name . . . is Mara Fitch."

"What was your mother's name?"

"Was?"

"She's dead. What was her name?"

"Oh. Her name was . . . Deirdre?"

Quinn pressed stop and then made her watch the woman on the screen repeat the whole story.

"All starting to come back now," Quinn said. Not a question.

Mara nodded, uncertainly.

Was being told her history the same as remembering?

Suddenly, a thought occurred to her. "What about my husband?"

The figure in red looked at her. Or perhaps not. She couldn't see the eyes.

"Who said you had a husband?" Quinn asked.

Mara said nothing, but glanced hesitantly at the doorway Declan had vanished through.

"He must have seen you with Cian in the village," Quinn said. "Cian's your partner, you're not married."

Mara's eyes widened. "Where is he? Is he alright? Was he one of . . ."

"Cian's fine. He was on the mainland when the outbreak happened. He'll be back when the quarantine is lifted."

"Does he know . . ."

"I haven't been able to get in touch with him yet."

"So he thinks I'm dead?!"

"For now. And isn't he in for a nice surprise?"

There was a knock on the door and Declan re-entered with yet another cup of tea, this time in a mug bearing the crest of the Kerry Gaelic football team.

"All good?" he asked, setting it down next to the other cup on the mantel and backing away.

"Thank you, Declan," Quinn said. "I'm taking Mara back to my house. She's going to be staying in my spare room until I can run some tests to ensure she's not contagious."

"For how long?" Mara asked, even though she realized she didn't have much of a choice.

"As long as it takes," Quinn replied solemnly. "Okay. I need to get the car ready. Stay here."

She rustled out past Declan and the two were left alone.

"Sorry about all this," Mara said. "I'm not normally this much hassle. Or maybe I am? Who knows?"

"It was lovely meeting you all the same," he said. "I'm really glad you're okay. Will you come back to say hi? I don't really know anyone else on the island."

"Okay. Yeah. I'd like that."

As she walked down the driveway, Mara noticed that her limp had disappeared, her foot felt perfectly fine. Perhaps it had just been numbed, her body in shock. She wiggled her toes in her new shoes, fully mobile. Once in the car, Doctor Quinn handed Mara the phone and pressed Play. As they drove down the road, Mara took in the beginnings of a sunny day, and the sheep grazing in the green fields, and listened to herself haltingly regurgitate the identity she had been given.

"My name is . . . Mara Fitch . . . My mother's name was Deirdre . . ."

7
Mara

"A bath is exactly what you need," Doctor Quinn said. "A nice long soak."

Mara stood shivering and barefoot on the tiles of Doctor Quinn's bathroom. The doctor stood beside the massive black cast-iron bathtub as it slowly filled with water.

The bath was colossal, and was melded to the house like an organ to a body. It was big enough to drown in and looked like it weighed as much as a ship.

Quinn, still all in red, stood and twisted the tap, shutting off the water.

"Call me when you're done," she said, her voice artificial sounding through the visor as she closed the door behind her.

Mara stripped off and approached the bath. She lifted one leg and then the other over the lip and tried to sit down, but her heel slipped on the bottom of the bath and her head sank briefly beneath the water. That was enough.

She started to hyperventilate, water filling her mouth.

Her vision became a mad blur of brushstrokes as she reached out to either side of the bath. Her hands slipped on the smooth surface, frenzied and useless.

MARA

It was the sides of the bath, those great black walls, that did it.

Her feet down a long, narrow enclosed stretch. Like being back in the coffin.

As her vision burned into white stars, she slipped below the surface and began to breathe water.

Don't do it. Please don't do it.

She was screaming in her mind but she didn't know to whom. Who was doing this to her?

No one. She'd done it to herself.

Hands latched onto her neck and arm. A strong grip biting into her flesh and then an irresistible pulling to the surface, like gravity reversing.

She felt the fear burning away with the rush of light and air, and all that was left was rage. In that moment, Mara did not know who she was or where she was, but she knew, knew from her bone marrow to the tips of her hair, that she did not wish to be touched.

A shape moved in the blur and she lashed out.

She slipped and slid onto the bathroom floor, cracking her elbows and knees on the tiles.

She could see Doctor Quinn, lying crumpled by the base of the door—knocked clear across the room.

Mara crawled toward her.

"I'm sorry . . ." she wept. "I'm sorry, I'm sorry . . ."

She could now see Quinn's eyes through the visor, like stark-white pearls beneath murky water. The woman was terrified.

Then, slowly, the fear faded to something that might have been pity, or disgust, or some rank comingling of the two. Quinn got to her feet and draped a towel over Mara's shivering naked form. "It's alright," she said robotically through the mask.

"It's... it's... it's... it's... n-n-n-n-not... a-a-a-a-alr..." Mara stammered and stuttered as Quinn dried her.

"Just a panic attack. Only to be expected."

"Why... why... I just..."

"Yes. Showers from now on, I think. Showers from now on."

Quinn helped Mara to her feet and dressed her. She escorted her to the guest bedroom, where a plate of food awaited, and locked Mara in.

Mara sat on the edge of the bed and looked at her reflection in the bedroom mirror. She looked unreal. Candlepale. Ghostlike.

Mara Fitch.

What kind of woman are you?

She reached for the plate of food Quinn had prepared, and took large bites of cold chicken and undercooked rice.

The food tasted weird. Medicinal.

She's not drugging you. Don't be paranoid. Probably just a lousy cook.

She hoped that she would get used to it. She didn't.

Two days of tedium and Doctor Quinn's strange, metallic-tasting food passed without remark.

Forbidden from leaving her sick-room, she tried reading Quinn's collection of romance novels and filling in a journal that the doctor insisted she complete every day. Except there was nothing to write. She was in the middle of nowhere, doing nothing.

Sleep was her only release, and that felt too close to death to be a true comfort.

MARA

Quinn seemed to spend most of her days out on the island or moving about on the lower floor. They rarely spoke. The only consistent sound she heard was the constant bleating of sheep in the surrounding fields.

But on the third day, she awoke at five o'clock in the morning to the sheep screaming.

They screamed like people.

She race to the window and watched their white bodies running in the darkness. Something was loose in the field and it had sent the sheep mad.

A dog?

But there would be barking, wouldn't there? She had heard nothing except the screaming of the sheep and their hooves on the ground.

Then came silence.

Mara went back to bed and tried to sleep.

Before she drifted off she thought she could hear something else.

On the wall, beneath her window she heard a soft . . . What was the best word?

Padding.

A padding sound.

Like hands being laid on the wall. Dozens of hands feeling the walls.

Looking for a way in.

. . .

"Mara? Mara? Mara?"

She didn't know how long Doctor Quinn had been standing over her bed, quietly calling her name.

The room was dark with evening, except for a few shards of sunlight cutting through the thick dusty drapes. It glinted against Quinn's plastic suit.

She could tell the sheep still had not returned. Mara wanted to ask Doctor Quinn what had happened to them, but refrained, already knowing that she would only get a shrug and a verbal pat on the head.

But the morning after, she had been woken by the shush-shush of brush bristles moving over the walls of the house, as if a stain was being slowly and laboriously removed from the brick.

"Guess what tonight is, Mara?" Quinn's voice broke through her dazed thoughts.

Mara blinked and rubbed her eyes. She felt sick. A strange taste was in her mouth again, that slightly metallic, medicine taste.

She is drugging me, isn't she? And I can't say anything. She'll either stop feeding me or up the dose.

"What?" she asked dully.

"Tonight," said Quinn, "you get to speak to Cian."

Downstairs, Doctor Quinn's laptop was set up. There was a man on the screen and Mara did not recognize him.

Blond. Green eyes. Cheekbones that a girl could cut her heart on if she wasn't careful.

A very handsome man. Almost intimidatingly so.

She tried to recall the picture of the man on the phone. Could this be him? The memory had been made in the middle of a crazed panic and she couldn't be sure—but his face seemed too defined. His hair was the wrong color, too, but it could have been dyed.

Cian was shaking his head.

"I can't believe it. I can't believe I could be this lucky," he said. "Everyone thinks, when someone close to them dies, that it's not really happening. That they're still alive. But it came true. You're alive. You're really here."

"I'm really here," Mara said, as if she believed it.

He had a Dublin accent, but not like Declan's. It was suave Dublin. Affluent. Southside. *Rugby with the goys. You spilled prosecco on my focking chinos.*

She tried to remember everything Doctor Quinn had told her about him.

His name was Cian Morley. They had met at UCD. He had been studying engineering, she arts. They had moved to Inishbannock two years ago, when he had gotten a job overseeing the construction of the offshore wind farm on the northwestern coast of the island.

These are things I know. They are not things I remember.

She listened to Cian speak, hoping that the sound of his voice would flip some switch and she'd suddenly feel a love for him crashing over her.

The moment never came.

"Mara, did you hear what I said?" he asked.

She came back to Earth.

"Sorry. Sorry. No. Could you say that again?"

He looked at her like she had stabbed him.

"I said . . . when I heard you were dead I thought about killing myself."

She felt her bones shrinking in her skin from pure shame.

"I'm . . . Cian, I'm so, so sorry . . . I've just been very . . ."

Doctor Quinn rushed in to the rescue. "Mara's been through an awful ordeal, Cian. She's still in shock. She's having trouble focusing."

"Of course," he said. "It's fine, love. I shouldn't have even mentioned it."

She blushed in embarrassment, like a child who had made a terrible mistake but everyone would forgive because she couldn't know any better.

They talked. Cian cried. Mara listened.

He seems so nice. So kind.

And yet, the shell-shocked, animal part of her brain that whispered of Doctor Quinn slipping drugs into her food watched the man on the screen with its hackles raised.

He doesn't seem comfortable with me. He feels . . . rehearsed. Practiced. Like he's checking every word before he says it.

They talked about the quarantine. Cian said there hadn't been any new cases and that he expected to be allowed back in a few days. He said he'd make arrangements for the house to be ready for her when it was time to come home.

"That'll be wonderful," she said.

He gave her a big, loving, heartfelt smile.

Something in her shuddered, and turned away.

• • •

The next morning, Mara was awoken not by screaming sheep, but by a woman's voice—urgent yet controlled—through the windowpane.

"You didn't see Daithí pass here last night, Helen? Agnes is sick with worry. And at his age. . . . Anything could have happened to him."

Mara could hear the worried tone of Doctor Quinn's reply, but not the words.

MARA

"No, no. You're needed here," the first voice replied. "But keep your phone close, in case we need you . . ."

Mara looked out the window and saw, standing at the garden gate, a tall, older woman with silver hair tied back in a severe bun.

But it was the man standing beside her who held Mara's attention. He was huge, towering over the woman, who was hardly petite herself. And for a second, she was sure this was the brown haired man she had seen on the phone. But then he turned to look up, drawn by the motion of her appearance in the window, and the certainty faded.

The hair was right, and the face was not completely different, but it was not the same man. The eyes were the wrong color, and the wrong shape, and had the wrong soul behind them. Both the woman and the man were wearing blue surgical masks.

The woman was talking to Doctor Quinn, who stood, unseen to Mara, in the front doorway of the house. The man pointed to Mara.

"Oh, there she is!" the woman called out and Mara was completely taken aback by all the joy and excitement and *love* that she could hear in the woman's voice.

"Hello, Mara!" she called. "My God, it's good to see you, love! How are you? Open the window, love, open the window, let's get a look at you!"

She fumbled with the latch and swung the window open.

"Hello," Mara said, shyly.

"Do you remember me, love?" the woman asked.

She shook her head.

"I'm sorry. It's all . . ."

"Don't apologize! My God, after all you've been through, isn't it a miracle you're here at all? We know all about your memory, love. I'm Gráinne. I run the pub in town. And this is my son Padraig. We just came up to leave in some supplies for yourself and Helen. Isn't that right, Padraig?"

"It is, yeah," the large man mumbled.

Indeed, there was a large bag of groceries set at the end of the garden path, ready to be collected by Doctor Quinn.

"Thank you," Mara said. "That's very kind of you."

"Not at all," Gráinne replied. "On Inishbannock we look after each other. And when Helen here gives you a clean bill of health, you come straight down to the Temple, I think you deserve a pint."

"That sounds lovely," Mara said, and meant it.

Being literally anywhere other than Doctor Quinn's spare room sounded lovely. And a pint would only sweeten the deal.

They chatted for a little while longer, and when they left, Mara felt oddly relieved.

Doctor Quinn and Declan had been the only two human beings she had seen in the flesh since coming out of the ground. Now, it felt like the population of her world was slowly increasing.

She watched as Quinn hauled the heavy sack of groceries, which look like it contained enough supplies for a fortnight.

She wondered why Gráinne had lied to her. She had delivered the groceries, to be sure, but Mara knew that was not the only reason she had paid a visit to Quinn's house.

She wondered who the old man was, and if he was alright.

8
Padraig

"He'll be like Mother Teresa," Gráinne said, as they drove away from Doctor Quinn's house.

It took a few seconds for the words to register. His mother had a long-standing habit of carrying on conversations in her own head before launching them onto the marketplace and expecting you to keep up. But even for her, this was remarkably esoteric.

His mind was still back at the house, looking up at Mara as she stared at him, trying to place his face.

He was a little shaken. What a thing it was, to see someone you had helped bury, up and about among the living.

"What's that, Ma?" he asked, not taking his eyes off the road.

"Daithí Griffin," she said. "Who else would I be talking about?"

"How is Daithí Griffin like Mother Teresa?" Padraig felt completely lost.

"If he's dead, no one will care," she said quietly.

That was not how he remembered it.

"Did people not care when Mother Teresa died?" he asked.

"Oh they did, I suppose. But you see she made one terrible mistake. She died the same week as Princess Di. Completely overshadowed. If he's after getting himself killed so soon after the outbreak and the whole business with Mara . . ."

"That's all people will remember," Padraig said, nodding.

"Stop," she said. "Pull over here."

He stopped at the side of the road and watched his mother get out of the car. As the wind picked up, her hair whipped around her head like a slate-gray flame. She bent down beside a large blackberry bush that sprawled over the drystone wall. He got out of the driver's seat to see what she had found.

It was a walking stick, worn from years of use. The back of the handle was chipped, as if it had been flung roughly to the ground.

"They're strange, aren't they?" Gráinne murmured. "Walking sticks. They make you walk faster, but run slower."

"Is that his?" Padraig asked delicately.

"Aye," she said wearily. "That's Daithí's. So. He made it this far at least."

They found him, or at least, *enough* of him to be getting on with, on the other side of the field. But his head, with around a foot of his spine, was missing.

The bones had been picked clean, but the seagulls were not yet convinced and still investigated the matter.

Gráinne waved the stick at them and they flew off, angrily cursing her violation of their natural rights.

"Ah, poor Daithí," she said, tsking as she stared at the headless corpse.

PADRAIG

Padraig thought about everything he could remember about Daithí. He'd coached the school Gaelic football team that Padraig had played for. He hadn't been a great coach, but he'd been a kind one and all the boys had loved him.

Padraig took every memory of the old man that he had, and put them in a box in the back of his mind. He then went back to the car to get a black plastic bag and a rope. On the way back through the field, he found a large rock to use as ballast.

Afterward, they drove back down the road to Daithí Griffin's cottage on the south coast of the island. As they knocked on the door and waited for an answer, Padraig saw his mother glancing through the half-opened rolling door of the garage, where the prow of a tiny blue motorboat could be seen.

A woman opened the door, tiny and ancient. She looked at them with trepidation.

"Hello, Gráinne," she whispered nervously.

"Hello, Agnes," Gráinne replied with tender sadness. "Might we come in, love?"

. . .

They were invited into the Griffins' living room, but remained standing and both refused tea, which was enough for Agnes to realize that the worst had come to pass.

"Agnes," Gráinne said. "I'm afraid it looks like Daithí . . . well, it looks like he's no longer with us, love."

Agnes Griffin slumped on to the sofa. She was so light she barely made a sound.

She didn't cry or weep. She simply said, "Oh," more a croak of pain than a word.

"On behalf of all the Comhairle," Gráinne continued. "Our deepest sympathies."

"You're very good," Agnes murmured, like a mantra. "You're very good."

She looked up at them. "Where?" she said.

"Well, we heard from Doctor Quinn that something had been interfering with the sheep near her house, so we started around that area. And we found . . ."

Wordlessly, Padraig passed the walking stick to Agnes who took it in a tight, tremulous grip.

"How?" Agnes asked.

Gráinne glanced at Padraig.

"Well . . . We've been thinking about that. Daithí was seen leaving the Temple last night. And I suppose, would you say, Padraig, that he'd have had quite a bit to drink?"

"I would," said Padraig. "Yeah."

"So, we thought perhaps he got home here and decided that he wanted to do a bit of night fishing. You know the way the mood sometimes takes men like Daithí?"

Agnes shook her head uncertainly. "No. No, I don't think so. Sure Daithí hasn't . . . hadn't . . . fished in years. It's too much work getting that boat out of the shed. And he wouldn't have been confident enough to go out after all this time."

"Ah well," said Gráinne. "But in a way, doesn't that make sense? Maybe he decided to go out, and the effort of getting the boat out gave him a heart attack. Only when he was far away from the island?"

"Delayed reaction?" Padraig ventured.

PADRAIG

"The very expression. And he did it because he'd had a bit of a skinful in the Temple. Affected his judgment. And now that I think of it, Padraig, didn't you say you overheard him saying he missed fishing?"

"I think I did, Ma. He was talking to Stiofán and he was saying he was tempted to go out last night. And Stiofán told him it was a bad idea."

"Could you ask Stiofán and make sure he said that?" Gráinne asked.

"I'll ask him and make sure he said that."

"He must have taken the boat out, had a heart attack, and fell into the sea. I would lay good money that we'll find the boat floating out there near the island."

"I'll go look, Ma," Padraig said, rising to leave.

"Hang on, pet," Gráinne said. She looked sadly at Agnes, who was still clutching Daithí's walking stick. "I don't think he would have gone without his stick, though," she said soothingly, taking hold of it and gently but firmly prising it from the old woman's fingers before passing it to Padraig. "But I'm sure we'll find it. And return it to you. He was a wonderful man, Agnes. And I promise you, he'll be remembered."

Padraig left the room without another word, heading to the garage. The rusty door shrieked as it opened, and with a few grunts of effort, he was able to wheel out the boat trailer and began to head down to the sea. It felt like such a waste, leaving such a fine boat out here, abandoned.

The swim back took longer than expected and it was lunchtime when Padraig finally made it back to the Temple. His mother had made him his favorite: bacon, cabbage, and mashed potatoes, and a glass of ice-cold cider. She laid it in front of him, fresh from the pot, the steam still rising.

She kissed him on the cheek and gave his shoulder a loving squeeze.

"Thanks, Ma," he said.

"Thank *you*," she replied. "Amn't I lucky to have you? Eat up."

9

Cian

The sheep's head had been laid so perfectly on the little jetty that Cian could only imagine it had been left there for him and him alone, to welcome him back to the island.

It was the head of a full-grown ewe, big and weighty, with a perfect, snow-white bob of wool on the crown. Cian's eyes looked over the pure, spotlessly clean fleece until he saw the place where the head had been messily severed from the body. Pristine orderly white suddenly giving way to shredded red. Not a slicing, but a tearing. A ripping.

He took a step back, his hands still jammed in his pockets against the cold.

The sheep stared up at him with wide golden eyes, as if embarrassed by its lack of a body and not knowing what to say.

Cian looked around briefly, on the off chance he would catch the culprit scuttling under a rock. But the jagged naked cliffs overlooking the concrete jetty were still, except for the ever-present seagulls, who swarmed over the rock.

Stiofán, the boatman, had finished tying up the small ferry and was tramping up toward him.

Cian knew Stiofán hated him, as he hated anyone who dared live on the island who'd not been born here. For a moment, he seriously considered that the boatman had left the sheep's head for him as a welcoming gift. He raised an eyebrow at the bearded old man.

Not an accusation, exactly. Simply a question. Was this you?

But Stiofán's expression shifted to fear at the sight of the head, which told Cian enough. The boatman spat and took the sheep's head by one ear and kicked it into the sea with a practiced swing of his foot.

Former Kerry player, Cian remembered.

"So, how've things been since I've been gone?" Cian asked him, pointedly not looking at the wisp of bloody wool clinging to the toe of the ferryman's boot.

Stiofán turned and stood just close enough to make Cian's fists twitch instinctively. The older man was a good foot taller than him, and Cian found himself looking at a mouth full of teeth half blackened from tobacco.

"Oh, it's been only awful," Stiofán growled. "People dying of plagues and God knows what. And then we have poxy fuckers coming from Dublin and sticking windmills all over the place. Isn't that right?"

Cian smirked and looked around at the pale overcast sky and the choppy, iron-hued sea.

"Stiofán, do you ever ask yourself, 'What am I doing here?'"

"I do," the boatman replied and turned away. "I ask myself what you're doing here all the fucking time."

First port of call was the Temple.

Gráinne handed Cian the keys to his car.

"As promised," she said coldly.

"I'm honored," he said with a smirk. For many years he had been trying to wean himself off this particular smile, as he knew people never reacted well to it. But now, he indulged himself.

"Thanks, Ma," he said. She had called while he was in the hospital on the mainland, claiming to be his mother, so she'd be put through. He had found that very funny at the time, but he had been on quite a lot of painkillers.

Instantly, he recognized his mistake. She would not have seen the humor in that. Not now.

A look of venomous fury in Gráinne's eyes told him he would pay for that.

Stupid. That was stupid, Cian. If there's anyone on the island not to make an enemy of . . .

He was stunned, then, as he saw her expression change from hatred to (could it be?) actual concern.

"Are you sure you're up to this?" she asked, gesturing to his stomach. "Should you be walking about?"

"As long as I don't try to run any marathons, they say I should be fine."

"You're on your way up to her now?"

"I am."

"But you've spoken to her?"

He gave her a skeptical look and she smiled innocently. *As if you don't know everything that happens on this island, old woman,* he thought to himself.

"Have you?" he asked.

Gráinne nodded, pursing her lips contemplatively. "She's been through a terrible shock, Cian. This shouldn't have happened. I can't believe what she's gone through."

"What has she told you she remembers?"

"Nothing. Nothing at all. She's going to be relying on you, Cian, for everything. It's going to be a very hard road back. If you need help. If you need anything. My door is always open."

"I know that, Gráinne. Everyone does."

"I mean it. My family has been through its fair share of difficulties. I want you to think of me as a resource."

"I already do," he promised.

The car was nothing special. A secondhand Volvo hatchback, around eight years old with a decal of a Vietnamese flag on the back window. But driving it made Cian feel like a lord. There were only five people allowed to own a car on the island and he was one of them.

You're in now, he thought to himself with satisfaction as he drove across Inishbannock to Doctor Quinn's house. *In the Golden Circle.*

He probably wouldn't use the car that often. There was only one service station on the island, Harte's in Ballydonn, mostly used by the farmers for their tractors, and fuel was horrendously expensive. His bike would still do on most days.

Ah, but to be able to drive down to the jetty and beep the horn at Stiofán and watch the hate crease his face in half. That would be something to savor.

As he pulled up to the house, he felt like an actor who hadn't rehearsed his lines.

What am I supposed to say to her? How am I supposed to feel?

Helen opened the door and stood back to let him in.

He liked the doctor. One of the few people on this miserable rock who didn't remind him of a character from a bad John B. Keane play.

CIAN

It was just a pity that she didn't seem to like him much, these days.

There was a definite formality to the way she welcomed him into her house.

They were both Irish. Formality was as good as an insult.

"She's through here," the doctor said.

He felt a tightening in his stomach, stitches biting into his flesh, bruises tingling with bad memories.

But then he saw her, and his anxiety melted away.

She looked so . . . small.

Thinner than he remembered.

Mara was wearing a red dress and Helen had done her makeup. She looked up at him so expectantly, so lost and desperate for someone to guide her.

"Hi," she said.

He went in for the kiss.

She froze a little in his arms before returning it.

He pulled off her.

Her mouth smiled.

Her eyes stared.

10
Mara

The night before she had dreamed of a little white cottage with a red door, gray slate roof, and nursery-blue windows.

In the dream, she walked along a beautiful white beach beneath a stony gray sky.

The sea was black as oil, and she wore an old-fashioned dress that she had to hitch up to stop the hem dragging in the sand.

There was a cottage down the beach and she knew, the way you know in a dream, that someone was waiting for her there.

And then a voice called to her from the cottage:

"Run! The sea! The sea!"

And she turned to look at the black sea and it had teeth. And thousands of black eyes blinking up at her from the oily surface.

She ran. Of course she ran.

But here was the strange thing.

She didn't run to the cottage.

She ran to the sea.

MARA

• • •

Mara had hoped that Cian would take her to the cottage in her dream. If nothing else, it would mean that her memory was not entirely unsalvageable.

As always, she was disappointed.

The house was a glass cube, a new build overlooking the sea. As she stepped through the door, the first thing that struck her was how unhomely it felt.

It felt like walking into a brochure.

"I had it cleaned," Cian said. "All ready for you. Top to bottom."

Mara nodded appreciatively. But it didn't feel "clean." It felt sterile, like they were the first living things to ever set foot in it.

"Are you okay?" he asked.

"Yeah, I'm just really tired. I might lie down."

She glanced around uncertainly.

"Upstairs, sweetheart," he said. "Second on the left."

In the stark bedroom, in a perfectly made-up low-slung bed, Mara fell into a deep dreamless sleep.

When she awoke and came back down, he had made a pasta dinner, lit some candles, and poured some wine.

They ate in silence.

"Penny for your thoughts," he said at last.

She smiled sadly and shook her head. "I don't think they're worth it. Bit shop-worn."

She looked around her. "My God. This place. How did we afford it? Are we rich?"

He shrugged like a man too rich to worry about whether or not he was rich. "We get by."

"You're an engineer."

"I am."

"And I'm . . . ?"

"You're Mara."

"You know what I mean. What do I do?"

He sighed and took a sip from his wine.

"You're still figuring that out."

"I'm unemployed?"

"You worked remotely for a tech company in Dublin. You got laid off. You'd been looking for a new job before all this happened."

She felt a pang of guilt.

"I'll start looking again," she assured him.

He reached out and took her hand. "The only job, the *only* job, Mara, that I want you to focus on, is getting better. Like I said. We're doing fine."

"That doesn't seem fair to you," she said. "I can at least start searching . . ."

"Doctor Quinn doesn't want you going online," he said. "And I think she's right."

Oh. Well if Doctor Quinn thinks that and Cian thinks that, I guess that's the opinion of everyone who matters, she thought.

"So what am I supposed to do all day?" she asked him.

He gave her a smile that stayed below his nose.

"Just get better," he said. "That's all you have to do."

He poured her another glass of wine and asked quietly, "How much do you remember, Mara?"

"Bits and pieces," she said.

"You don't have to lie. I know you don't remember me." He smiled.

That should reassure me, shouldn't it? Mara thought to herself.

But it doesn't.

It feels like we're playing chess and I've forgotten all the rules, and he's just told me it's checkmate in three turns.

II
Cian

After dinner, she said apologetically that she was still exhausted and wanted to go back to bed.

Cian soothed her, comforted her, told her it was *absolutely fine*.

He desperately needed to be alone.

He washed the dishes and listened to her bare feet padding up the stairs, moving around on the upper floor.

When he was convinced she had gone asleep, he went to the downstairs bathroom and from his pockets took out five different cannisters of capsules and tablets.

Painkillers. Antibiotics. Anti-inflammatories. He swallowed them in ones, twos, and threes, washing them down with water from the tap.

Then, he pulled off his T-shirt, finally allowing himself to wince. He was exhausted from the pain, and from hiding the pain. But he took a grim satisfaction as he surveyed the carnage across the right side of his torso.

A bloody, purple trail of stitches and bruises traced a course over his stomach and up under his nipple. A shark bite, he had told the doctors on the mainland.

What else could it have been, after all?

He gave himself a smile in the mirror.

It was the smile of a man who had survived the worst, and intended to take his prize.

He stepped out into the living room, still shirtless, letting the stitches breathe.

Something stirred in the shadows of the dark landing above.

Quick as a shot, he pulled the T-shirt over his head, wincing in pain as he did so.

Had she been . . . was she watching him?

He slowly, silently ventured up the stairs. The landing was clear, the door to the bedroom was ajar, open just enough that she could have come out and gone back in without it moving an inch.

Cian went into the bedroom, and called her name ever so softly, trying to make the shape under the sheets tense or stir.

But she seemed to be fast asleep.

Her journal was beside her bed, a pen lodged between the pages.

Maybe I imagined it, he admitted to himself.

He looked at the perfectly still, perfectly innocent figure of Mara lying asleep in the bed.

Or maybe I need to stop underestimating her.

12
Mara

The next few days were light, empty things that skittered away like dead leaves in a stiff breeze.

Every morning, Cian went to work and Mara would stay in the great glass house, feeling like a goldfish in an aquarium.

She didn't know if it was lingering agoraphobia from her quarantine, or just the fact that she still couldn't remember anything about her life on the island that kept her from going outside.

Finally, perhaps a week after Cian had brought her home, Mara was faced with the choice of eating dry cereal for breakfast or wrapping up in hat and scarf and walking to Ballydonn.

It was a cold day, and she was starting to suspect that there wasn't any other kind on the island. The overcast sky, another seemingly permanent fixture, hung overhead like a sheep's belly. But it felt good to get out of the house, the cold air on her cheeks made her feel more real.

You are here. You are Mara. You are walking to Ballydonn.

These were things she could be sure were true. Everything else was suspect.

As she walked on, she became aware of an incredible silence.

There was no sound of traffic, no sheep bleating. All she could hear was the low sibilance of the wind whispering slanders under its breath and when, at last, a crow cursed throatily at her from a nearby tree, she almost started.

She felt like a flea, wandering alone on the belly of a dead dog, unable to understand where all the other fleas had gone.

The whole island felt dead.

Inishbannock was shaped like a bow tie and Ballydonn was nestled on the southern side of the knot. This meant that, although her house was on the northern tip of the island, it only took twenty minutes or so before she could see the village rising in the distance.

Strangely, the village seemed more silent than the country road.

Mara stopped to catch her bearings at a large red water pump that stood in the town square.

On her side of the road, there was a tiny church, a village shop, the post office, and a quaint little cottage that she realized was the local Garda station. Sitting outside the station, an old guard sat in his chair, wearing full uniform, playing with a purple Game Boy Advance.

He did not look up at her approach and seemed utterly unconcerned with her existence, to a point that she felt vaguely insulted.

I'm a stranger who's just shown up in town unannounced. What if I'm dangerous?

I might be dangerous.

Ah, but maybe he knew her? Maybe they were old friends. Maybe she and Garda Nintendo had teamed up to solve a string of murders across the island? But in that case, why hadn't he said hello?

No, the only real conclusion to draw was that she wasn't worth his attention.

She looked across the road. There was a grocers, the pub, and a bakery with a lilac shop-front and an electric bike parked outside. The place had a weird vibe. Very traditional and also somehow trendy and gentrified. It was also empty.

Not just of people, but of meaning. She had the weirdest sensation of being an actor on an empty stage, of being watched and not being able to see the audience in their darkened seats.

On a childish whim, she gripped the handle of the pump and tried to make it work.

The handle was stiff, but gave a little, and Mara pressed harder and then felt a snap ricocheting through her bones and off the walls of the nearby buildings like a gunshot. She had broken the handle clean in half.

Fuck. Must have been rusted right through.

She glanced around anxiously, but the guard hadn't so much as looked up from his screen. Hastily, she stashed the broken handle in a nearby flower pot and walked on, trying to look nonchalant.

Great first day, she thought ruefully. *Visit the local village and wreck their most important landmark. Hugely important historically, no doubt. Queen Maeve probably used it to wash her hair or something.*

There was a sign on the grocers' front door saying BACK TEN MINUTES, scrawled with thick black marker.

MARA

There was a chill in the air, and Mara didn't like the idea of standing outside in the street being licked to the bone by the Atlantic wind, so she decided to step into the pub.

"Ah, there she is. I see you've come to collect, good woman. Sit down there, now."

The pub was dark and smelled of old varnish and leather. The stools were all arranged upside down on the tables, like fat little toddlers with their legs in the air.

Along the wall were fishing nets and oars and, over the bar, a truly magnificent stuffed marlin that must have been seven foot long from snout to fin.

Below it, she saw Gráinne cleaning glasses behind the bar.

"So, this is your pub?" Mara asked.

The landlady put down the glass, threw the rag over her shoulder, and spread her arms like a circus ring-master.

"*Fáilte go dtí an Teampall!*" she said effusively.

"*Go raibh maith agat,*" Mara replied, unthinkingly.

I speak Irish, apparently, she thought to herself.

Obediently, she sat down at the bar and Gráinne began to pour her a pint of stout.

"Bit early, isn't it?" Mara asked, hesitantly.

Gráinne's eyes flashed mischievously at her. "Trust me," she said. "You'll be grand. You have the constitution of a whaler."

She set it down and Mara watched the bubbles sink in the three-fifths-full glass. Then Gráinne took the glass and gave the final pour, topping it off with a big creamy head. Mara waited for it to settle and then raised it to her lips. The taste and smell were overpowering and she felt an instant rush of familiarity. It was like nostalgia, but without any memory of what she was being nostalgic for. It was a good pint, regardless.

"So. How's the head?" Gráinne asked.

"Perfect," Mara said. "Tastes great."

"Not what I meant," the older woman said with a maternal smile. "I meant, how's it up here?"

She tapped her brow with a long, thin finger.

Mara sighed, and shook a "no." She could have lied. But she had a feeling that Gráinne would see through that instantly. She didn't seem like an easy woman to lie to.

"Well," Gráinne said softly. "Is there anything I can do to help?"

"What were we?" Mara asked.

"How do you mean?"

"You know me. What were we to each other?"

Gráinne looked at her with real pity. "We were friends. Are, are friends," she corrected herself.

"Good friends?"

"I like to think so," she said. "You'd come into the pub with himself, most weeks. I was always glad to see you. You were great for the atmosphere. We'd always have laughs. You're a funny woman."

"Am I?"

"Savage craic altogether."

"I don't think I'm much craic anymore," Mara said glumly.

"Well," Gráinne said reasonably. "Being buried alive would take the craic out of anyone. Still. You're here now. And that's the important thing. Things will get back to normal soon enough."

"Yeah, well, it seems like things are already back to normal," Mara said bitterly.

Gráinne frowned. "How do you mean?"

MARA

Mara struggled to find the words. "It doesn't . . . feel like there was an outbreak here," she said at last. "It doesn't feel like there was a terrible tragedy. It doesn't feel like anyone died. It feels like everyone's just fine."

Instantly, she regretted it.

She could see pain in Gráinne's eyes, and not just pain. Anger. But then she looked away.

"I know it must feel that way to you, Mara. But you have to remember you were in quarantine. You've missed a lot. A lot of mourning. A lot of weeping. We're just trying to carry on now as best we can. Put a brave face on things."

"I'm sorry," Mara said.

"It's not you who should be apologizing," Gráinne replied.

"Did you lose someone. In the outbreak?" Mara asked.

Gráinne went very quiet. And then gave the slightest, merest nod.

Mara was about to ask her the question when a voice came from the back room.

"Ma! Which of the taps did you say needed to be cleaned again, it's gone out of me head!"

"Hang on, Padraig, I'll show you!" Gráinne called. And then she was gone.

Mara sat alone in the bar, nursing her pint. She looked at the pictures and newspaper clippings on the wall, and the old tobacco advertisements with charming cartoon jungle animals happily selling cancer.

And then, she heard whispering. Angry, tense whispering like beetles scuttling under crepe paper.

For a second Mara thought it was coming from behind the bar, from the doorway Gráinne had gone through. But then she realized it was coming from her left, behind the glass-and-wood partition that divided the pub in two.

She picked up her pint and went to take a look. On the other side of the partition there was a tiny performance area, a little stage with enough space for maybe three people, and chairs and tables arranged in a semi-circle. There was a man standing on the stage, punching the air faintly and whispering angrily to himself. She could only catch a few words here and there under his breath.

". . . Lose me . . . never thought . . . all you do's abuse me . . ."

He looked up and he saw her and his face went wide, first with shock and then with joy.

"Hey!" he said and threw his arms wide to give her a hug.

"Declan!" she said with a grin. She was, she realized, very happy to see him.

"Can I? Is it okay to . . . ?" he asked, uncertainly, his arms open like a very large seagull coming in to land.

"Come here!" she said and she hugged him so hard she heard him gasp in pain.

"So, what are you doing here?" she asked him.

"Rehearsing. Doing the open mic night here, tomorrow. Fuckin' brickin' it," he said with a nervous smile. "You should come!" he added, a little too quickly.

"I'd love to," Mara said. "That sounds . . . yeah, that sounds amazing."

"So. How've you been?" he asked gently.

She shrugged. "Ah, you know yourself."

"Sure, sure," he deadpanned. "Buried alive. Back from the dead. We've all been there."

"Sorry," she said with a wry smile. "Shouldn't complain."

"Suck it up, Dunne," he said. "You're not the only the one with problems."

The smile vanished from her face.

"What did you call me?" she asked.

"Dunne? Isn't that your name?" he said, frowning.

"No," she said. "It's Mara Fitch."

"Oh," he said. "Sorry, I thought Doctor Quinn . . . never mind. Doesn't matter. I'm actually really glad to see you, Mara." He leaned in and lowered his voice. "I've . . . eh, I've been worried about you."

"Why?" she asked.

"Just . . . could we go somewhere and talk?" he asked.

"Declan, if you want that lift, Padraig's going now!"

They both looked up. Gráinne had come around the partition.

"Oh cheers, thanks, Gráinne," Declan said, flustered. "I'll be right out."

There was an awkward pause before Gráinne returned to the bar.

Declan whispered to Mara, "Could I get your phone number by any chance?"

"I don't have a mobile," she said. "Sorry."

"Landline then?"

"Do you know your landline number?"

"Fair point. Look, I'll talk to you after the show, yeah?"

He gave her a nervous nod, and then he was gone.

She returned to her seat to finish her pint. She caught Gráinne looking at her with a trace of concern.

"Everything okay?" Mara asked her.

"What were you two talking about?" Gráinne answered.

Mara shrugged. "Just catching up."

"Right so," Gráinne said with a sour note.

It felt as if Gráinne was trying to warn her about something, but couldn't put it into words.

Warn me about Declan? Why would I need to be warned about Declan, of all people?

She finished her drink in silence and said goodbye to Gráinne before making another try at the grocers.

The sign was gone from the shop door, but it looked no more open. Thankfully, the door gave way and Mara stepped inside. It felt like a jungle. The light was murky and string bags of small children's footballs, and buckets, and spades hung from the ceiling, like garish yellow and blue fruit. The air smelled of plastic and rubber.

For a second she thought she was alone, but then the shadow in the back room got up and shuffled toward her.

This man was preceded by the strong stench of cigarette fumes. Mara instinctively brought her hand to her mouth and nose. He looked to be in his seventies, bald except for a thicket of black, filthy, unkempt hair that encircled his lower scalp, thick and stiff as a toilet brush.

He was incredibly thin, and his eyes stared at her palely from a face that was brown and leathery from the sun, or from the tobacco, or both. Mara felt there was something reptilian about him, like he had the face of a great ancient turtle who'd seen whole centuries come and go.

He stopped dead when he saw her. Stared at her like he'd seen the ghost of someone who'd died, and they'd been on bad terms.

"Mara," he said at last. "Back again."

"I'm sorry," she said. "I don't know who you . . ."

MARA

I really should get a name tag, she thought bitterly. *Hi. I'm Mara and I don't know who you are.*

"Yessss," he said. "I heard. I heard. A dreadful business. You poor thing."

"Thank you . . ." she whispered.

"Malachy. Malachy is my name. Oh that's terrible, now."

She did not feel sympathy from this man. She felt . . .

Was sadism an emotion?

Whatever it was, she was suddenly very conscious that she did not have a clear path to the door.

"We knew each other?" she asked.

"We did, we did . . ." he said quietly. "Actually . . ."

Malachy looked around conspiratorially. His large hairy ears seemed to swivel like satellite dishes. It would have been comical if he didn't set her skin shivering. He gestured for her to lean in with a nicotine-stained finger.

Against every instinct in her body, she came closer.

And then she felt his hand clamp over hers, and his mouth opened with a blast of breath, black with tar, assaulting her nostrils.

"We were married . . ." he whispered lasciviously.

She snatched her hand back and almost knocked over a display of faded postcards.

His laughter sounded like whooping cough.

"Ah, I'm only codding. I'm only codding," he said.

For a moment, she imagined him dead on the floor, his face still grinning, but at a sharp right angle to the rest of his body.

"Hilarious," she said, through gritted teeth.

The smile vanished from his face so quickly that it made her doubt it had ever really been there at all.

He was showing his teeth now, that was all. And his eyes were burning in the gloom like green embers.

"Oh, did you leave your sense of humor in that coffin?" Malachy growled.

Mara realized something, with absolute certainty.

This man hates me. And I don't know why. And I really shouldn't antagonize him while it's just the two of us.

"I'd just like some milk," she said, quietly.

He hissed in irritation, and took a carton of milk from the fridge behind the counter, plopping it in front of her.

She felt a sliver of ice in her stomach as it hit her that, in all her excitement and nervousness around leaving the house, she had forgotten to bring any money.

"I . . . I'm sorry . . ." she mumbled, her cheeks flushing as she searched her pockets.

She found a few random coins, but they slipped from her fingers, and went rolling under the counter. Cursing, she got down on her knees to retrieve them.

Just as she managed to pull them out, she felt a shadow falling. She looked up and Malachy was standing over her. A thought entered her mind. Clear as a bell.

We are in the last few seconds before something awful happens.

"I'm sorry," she whispered. "I don't think I have enough."

His eyes seemed to harden, and then . . . suddenly he just looked tired.

Whatever he had been thinking of doing, the moment had passed.

He turned his back on her and shuffled away.

"It'll go on your account. Oisín can settle with me later." He sighed over his shoulder.

She stood up and took the carton of milk.

She walked as fast as she could to the door and could only barely resist the urge to sprint.

She pushed out, and suddenly she was back in the sunlight and clean air, and she could feel the door snap behind her with a reassuring finality.

It took a few seconds for the realization of what Malachy had said to settle in her mind.

Part of her wanted to go back in.

Just to ask him who Oisín was.

But that was one part in a million.

Every other part was telling her to get back home.

And never set foot in his shop again.

13
Mara

It took Mara a day to realize what she had been hoping to gain from her trip to Ballydonn, and what she had lost instead.

She had hoped to find a place to feel safe.

The house, the weird, sterile, showroom house was Cian's. She felt that instinctively. Even when he wasn't there, she felt his presence in the glass cube. The place felt wrong, and it only took a quick glance at the walls to show her why.

There were no pictures. No photographs of family. No boozy party snaps of her and Cian, with their arms draped around each other, eyes half-closed and big drunk smiles on their faces. Like everything else, she was simply expected to take it on faith that their relationship was what he said, and that the story of their life together was fact and not fiction. The details were too fuzzy around the edges. There were no inside jokes, no intimacy in the everyday. This house was not their home, but the place Cian kept her.

She had been hoping, in the back of her mind, to find a place in Ballydonn that felt like it had been hers. The Temple could be that, she supposed.

Maybe that's what she had done before.

What was it Gráinne had said?

You have the constitution of a whaler.

That had to be earned, after all.

Maybe she could become a barfly, knocking back pints and swapping salty stories with the locals, all the while wishing the clock to slow down so she didn't have to come back to the house.

But even the idea of going anywhere near Malachy's shop filled her with dread. And so her world shrank even more.

She could feel invisible walls closing in.

Perhaps she had simply crawled out of one box and into another.

Inishbannock was strange because it was normal.

How could an island that had just undergone a terrible outbreak have no trace of the trauma?

No quarantine signs.

No checkpoints.

No army and Civil Defence swarming all over the place.

Nobody *talking* about it.

And how did a living woman, who was not sick, and by all evidence had never been sick, get buried alive without anyone realizing?

The only real proof that the outbreak had even happened was that she'd woken up in a coffin.

And if the outbreak had never occurred, why had she been in the coffin in the first place?

It was the most pressing mystery, but not the only one.

Mara had also been thinking a great deal about Cian's wounds, which she had spied the night he brought her home. Although, that made it sound a lot more intentional. Really, she had gone back downstairs to ask how to turn off the bedroom light. But now the terrible lines of violence over his torso were seared into her mind.

The fact that he had not mentioned them, the fact that he had been keeping them from her, and the fact that he had obviously been in terrible agony that day . . . was enough to tell her that she had stumbled on a secret. Which meant she couldn't let him know that she knew.

But she had since seen him with his shirt off, coming out of the shower. And the wounds . . . well, they were still there. But only because she knew to look for them. They were just faint pink lines now, delicate little brushstrokes. No harsh purple bruises, no spiky black stitches. And he seemed to move without pain. Cian had winked at her, clearly happy to show off his physique and give her a show.

How had he healed so quickly?

But she couldn't ask him. After all, she wasn't supposed to know there was anything to ask.

Mara was still keeping her diary, for all the good it did. Far from jolting her memory, it simply served as a tally of everything she couldn't remember or couldn't understand.

Why was Cian injured? Why are there no pictures of us?

She had taken to drawing little doodles when she couldn't think of anything worthwhile to write. She was no artist, but as she sat at the kitchen table with the book open before her, it gave her some measure of satisfaction to draw waves on the white paper with the blue ink. Rows and rows of waves, cascading down from the top of the page to the bottom in neat little rows.

She snapped out of her reverie as Cian came through the front door.

MARA

He was home from work early, and she felt a little uneasy at that. Still so uncertain about everything and everyone, even small changes to routine spooked her.

He strode over to Mara, pecked her on the cheek, and passed her a meticulously wrapped package, flat and square.

Taking a step back, he stood with the expectant air of a dog waiting for a well-deserved treat.

"Open it," Cian said quietly.

Carefully, Mara tore off the paper and revealed a silver picture frame with a portrait of her, him, and an older woman, all smiling at the camera. She was wearing a dress that she didn't recognize, and her hair was in a different style, but it was her. Cian was smiling happily and his arm was draped affectionately over the shoulder of the older woman, who looked like she was in the middle of a massive guffaw.

"It's lovely," Mara said. "Who is she?"

And suddenly, the Cian she knew was gone. The cool demeanor, the condescending stare, the insufferable stain-of-a-smile that was always tucked in the corner of his mouth.

He seemed genuinely hurt.

"That's your mother, Mara." He gave a weary, deflated sigh. "That's Deirdre."

Mara felt the guilt hit so hard that her throat dried and she couldn't say anything. She simply put the picture on the mantelpiece, pride of place. Then she turned to him and said with genuine feeling, "Cian, can you please tell me about her?"

They sat down on the couch and he told her everything.

Mara's father, he said, had died very young and left her and Deirdre alone in the world. Deirdre had raised Mara alone, and had been the kindest, sweetest mother a girl could ask for. She had loved Australian soap operas and dogs. She had owned three small terriers, Larry, Curly, and Shemp (Moe had died and been replaced). Her mother had a small house and she always talked about winning the lotto and buying a mansion, just to have room for more dogs.

He said that when he and Mara had started dating in college, Deirdre had taken an instant liking to him and had practically adopted him.

She figured out something halfway through this story.

"You loved her," she noted.

He nodded. "I did. Yes."

"What happened?" she asked.

"Alzheimer's," he whispered. "No decent way to go."

She didn't know what to say. So she gave him a hug.

And for a moment, just a moment, it felt right. Like she'd been swimming for hours and finally, finally, she could see the waters becoming shallow with the promise of dry land ahead.

Maybe this was where she was supposed to be.

"Hey," she said. "I'm going down to the Temple in an hour. For the open mic night. Come with me, it'll be fun."

She'd agreed to meet Declan after his performance, and while it would be harder to have a conversation with Cian there, in the moment, it felt right to extend an olive branch.

But as soon as she said the words she felt him harden in her arms and the temperature in the room dipped.

"You're going out?" he asked "Tonight? Really?"

"Yes?" she said. "Why not? What's so special about tonight?"

"I told you," he said. "It's Deirdre's anniversary . . ."

"Cian, I'm sorry."

"I told you that."

"No you didn't."

MARA

"I FUCKING TOLD YOU, MARA."

She took a step back and raised a hand, just a gesture. He flinched.

There was something about his footing and stance. As if he was getting ready to dodge a punch. Or fire one off.

Okay, how did we get here?

She took a very deep breath and tried to stay calm.

"Cian. You did not tell me that."

His body language relaxed, but his expression didn't.

"Yes I did," he said, quieter but steely cold.

"I think I'd remember," she said angrily.

"Do you?" he sneered. "Do you really?"

It felt like a slap. She turned away in shock.

"Fuck you," she mumbled. "Fuck you."

"Do you have any idea what it's like?" he continued. "Every day I'm trying to give love and affection and support to this *fucking stranger* who's living in my house! You're a *void*, Mara. A black hole."

"I'm sorry," she said. "I'm not recovering quickly enough after being FUCKING BURIED ALIVE. I'm sorry I had to crawl out of my own grave!"

"Yeah," he said stiffly as he headed up the stairs. "I'm starting to regret that, too."

Mara stormed out of the house, slamming the front door behind her, and felt no remorse when she heard the picture on the mantelpiece fall and smash.

. . .

She had been walking down the road for five minutes before the summer night descended like a veil. She realized with a shudder that she was walking down a country road on a moonless night, in dark clothing, and that she should really go back to the house for a torch and a hi-vis jacket. Mara wondered if her pride was really worth risking her life, and found, somewhat to her surprise, that it was.

Damned if I'm going back to him. Let him lie in bed all night worried that I'm bleeding in a ditch. I hope the fear eats him alive.

But the longer she walked, the more her resolve weakened and Mara would have given up if it hadn't been for the dry stone wall, pale and glinting in the darkness like buried bone. She was able to follow the stone trail across the black, silent (always silent, always) belly of the island.

Her footsteps were the only sound in all creation, and the crunch of her boots on the gravel sounded oddly moist, like teeth crushing apple.

And slowly it crept on her, the paranoia of a country road, the sense that gray cold hands were reaching out from the shadows behind her to pluck at the hairs of her neck.

So it was the sight of the windows of Ballydonn, glowing yellow like welcoming fires on the horizon, that sent a jolt of joy through her, and she broke into a run.

She tried to push her way through the door to the bar, only to realize too late that someone was trying to come out. She heard a sharp cry of alarm and the sound of someone being thrown roughly to the floor.

Hurriedly, Mara swung the door open to survey the damage.

She found herself staring at a young mixed-race woman sprawled on her arse and looking up at Mara with a mixture of shock and anger. She was around twenty, with a large elegant nose decorated with a silver floral piercing, and her hair was a labyrinth of braids, some of which had come loose when she hit the floor.

"Oh God, I am so sorry!" Mara said and extended her hand.

The woman took it and Mara pulled her up. She was even slighter than she looked, and she looked like she needed to wear heavy boots in strong winds.

"It's alright," the girl said in a thick Cork accent, straightening her T-shirt. Her eyes met Mara and suddenly there was a flash of recognition.

"Oh hey!"

"Hey . . ." Mara said, uncertainly.

"How you been?" the woman asked.

"Good," said Mara, nodding politely. "Good. Good."

"Glad to hear it," the woman replied, nodding along.

There was a long pause.

"Sorry, do you know me?" Mara asked.

The young woman's smile curdled into a very uncomfortable grimace.

"Noooo," she moaned. "I thought I knew you from somewhere. And I'm just realizing that I don't. And now it's really, really awkward and I'm going to go for a smoke. Sorry."

"That's okay," said Mara as the woman walked down the sea-front. "Sorry for knocking you down."

"Oh, I think we're even" was the reply.

Mara felt a blast of heat and noise as she entered the bar. She heard a voice booming through a microphone, too close to the speaker's mouth.

"Alright, so a little background to this one . . . Oh hi, Mara!"

Declan was on the stage smiling at her. Everyone else in the bar turned to look at her, and the room was suddenly very, very quiet. She gave a tiny wave and looked around awkwardly for a free seat, but the room was too full. At last, she simply planted herself against the wall and tried to turn invisible.

Declan frowned. Apparently, he had not expected her arrival to kill the atmosphere stone-dead. He swallowed nervously and found his voice again.

"Okay, so . . . this one is . . . you probably don't know this about me, but, eh . . . well, my family's actually from the island. Well, my granny was. Anyway . . ."

Mara quickly stopped feeling sheepish for herself and started feeling embarrassed for poor Declan. God love him, he was not comfortable on-stage.

His words were getting quieter and quieter and his gaze started to be irresistibly pulled to his shoes.

She caught his eye and gave him a shy smile. And that was enough. He smiled back and his whole bearing seemed to relax. When he spoke again, his voice had found its grip.

"My granny used to tell me lots of stories about growing up on the island with her mother. My great-grandmother. And her mother really didn't want her to leave the island. But Granny wanted to see the world. Or Dublin, at least. And she left when she was quite young, and found work in the big city. Met Granda. But, years later she came back to Inishbannock. And, eh, well, her mother just refused to even acknowledge her. Acted like she didn't know her. Like she'd never had a daughter."

There were sighs and gasps and aws from the audience. Little puffs of sympathetic breath.

"And my granny left the island again. She never came back after that. So this is, this song is about that . . ."

He began his performance and Mara thought it was like there was suddenly a different man onstage.

He seemed taller, somehow.

The song he sang, or the story he told, for it was a song and a story, and it was sung and it was told, moved between the viewpoints of his grandmother and his great-grandmother. His grandmother's verses he spoke in rhyming English, his Dublin accent brash and aggressive, impatient with the stagnation and stillness of life on the island. And then he'd switch to singing in Irish for the older woman, an old keening lament of regret and loss.

He had a beautiful voice, and Mara felt guilty that she'd been dreading listening to him perform.

After Declan finished, the evening drifted on and Mara found herself at the bar.

"Will you be getting up yourself, now?" Gráinne asked her with a wink as she poured her a pint.

A three-person band, a fiddler, a bodhran player, and a piper, had taken Declan's place on the stage and were playing their hearts out. Mara had to lean in to be heard over "Drowsy Maggie" and the whoops of the crowd.

"What, did I use to perform at these?" she asked.

"You did. You used to sing. Beautifully."

Mara shook her head.

"Not tonight. Maybe some other time," she replied. "How about you?"

"Do I sing, you mean? No. I'm more of a *seanchaí*."

"A storyteller?" Mara asked, curiously.

Gráinne nodded.

"Keeper of the island's stories. And secrets. And scandals."

She gave a mischievous grin.

"Oh?" said Mara, returning the smile. "And will you be regaling us, then?"

"Not when the place is this packed. I'm needed behind the bar."

Gráinne looked at Mara and the smile was gone. It was not a malevolent look. But it was cold, somehow. Detached.

"One of these days, I'll tell you a story, Mara. I promise," she said.

"Then maybe I'll give you a song," Mara said, taking a sip from her pint.

"So where's himself? O—Cian couldn't make it?"

Onstage, the song came to a sudden end and the crowd burst into cheers and whoops.

Mara felt as if the chill of the pint in her hand had gone traveling, up her fingers and arms and down her back.

"What?" she said.

"I said, 'Cian couldn't make it?'" Gráinne yelled over the applause.

Mara stared at her. Gráinne stared right back, as blank and untroubled by her gaze as a portrait hanging on a wall.

And the lie didn't crack. She held her gaze with Mara as steady as anything.

She was so calm, so assured, Mara could almost (*almost*) convince herself that she hadn't heard what she knew she had heard. But it had been there. A soft little vowel sound before the hard, sharp velar stop of "Cian." Gráinne had been going to say "Oisín" and then corrected herself. She was sure of it.

Mara didn't say another word. She took her drink and began to move gingerly through the packed pub, looking for Declan.

MARA

The band had started another song and she could hear that the fiddle was now out of tune, and every time she turned her head someone glanced away.

They're all watching me.

The music was a manic jig and she could hear a ragged insistence, a desperate screech, running through the notes.

Dance! Dance! Smile! Smile! One two three! One two three!

She was suddenly struck by how sick it all was. These people, dancing, clapping, laughing in the shadow of the plague that had passed through, leaving death in its wake.

People had died.

She had died. The person that she had been, the life she had led, was still in the grave.

And no one cared.

The whole island must be mad.

She turned again and saw someone who was not afraid to meet her gaze.

Malachy, the shopkeeper, was sitting on a stool at the far end of the bar.

He gave her a filthy smile. Literally. The teeth were brown.

And he raised his glass to her health while his eyes wished her an early and cruel death.

"Y'alright?"

She screamed and almost threw her drink at Declan when he tapped her on the shoulder.

14
Mara

There was a soft green moon in the sky as they walked down the quay, past row after row of fishing boats. Idly, Mara noticed that the boats all seemed new and freshly painted. Three of them, blue, white, and red, formed a vivid, floating French tricolor. Evidently the fishermen were doing well for themselves.

She took a deep breath. It felt good to be out of the bar and in the night air.

She was still rattled from her fight with Cian and her panic attack in the Temple.

Declan was a calming presence besides her. Despite Gráinne's earlier half-warning, she instinctively trusted him. She had broken into his house in the middle of the night and he had treaded her kindly. And more important, *she* had found *him*. Which meant that whatever plot or scheme was surrounding her, he wasn't part of it.

"You were really, really good tonight. I mean that," she said.

"Better than you expected?" Declan asked with a smile.

"I didn't say that!"

"Nah, you didn't say it."

MARA

Mara turned to Declan. "Can I ask you something?"

"Sure," he said, with a certain hopefulness in his voice.

She laid out for him, in forensic detail, the circumstances of her fight with Cian.

He listened carefully and when she had finished he asked, "*Did* he tell you? About it being your ma's anniversary?"

"No." She shook her head. "I'm absolutely positive."

He shrugged dismissively. "Then he's being a moody prick," he said.

"Oh shit, look!"

They'd come down the quay and out on to a pier. Standing at the end, Declan raised his hand and pointed out over the sea, toward where the mainland slumbered on the horizon like a great black dragon.

"Do you see them?" he asked, excitedly.

Mara looked and saw two tiny doglike heads, glinting like new pins as they vanished furtively beneath the surface of the water.

"Seals," she said with a smile. Declan's honest, natural, city-boy joy at seeing wild animals was infectious.

"I've seen seals, I think, every day since I came here," he said, proudly, as if it was to his credit. "Sea around here is full of them."

"Declan, does the name 'Oisín' mean anything to you?"

"Absolutely," he said.

Her heart skipped a beat.

"Mate of mine back in Dublin. He's serving a year in Mountjoy for lamping a paramedic at Electric Picnic."

Common enough name, she supposed. She shook her head. "No. Someone on the island."

He thought for a bit.

"Doesn't ring a bell. Why?"

She took a deep breath. Ah, here it was. The moment she'd been dreading.

The moment where she had to put this thing into words, and then step back and see how crazy it really looked.

"Apart from the fight tonight, things have been . . . weird with Cian. Since I came back. It doesn't feel right."

"Like how?" he asked.

"I think something happened between me and Cian," she whispered. "Something bad. Maybe he did something. Or . . . maybe *I* did something . . ."

They stood in silence for a few seconds.

She was thinking of the look of fear in Doctor Quinn's eyes when Mara had knocked her away.

"And now," she continued slowly. "He's just using this to pretend that nothing ever happened."

Declan took that in and breathed it out heavily through his lips.

"Jaysus. That's pretty fucked up," he said.

"You saw us together, right?" she asked. "Me and him? Before the outbreak?"

"Yeah. In Kilty's."

"Where's Kilty's?"

He turned and pointed a finger down the coast. "Okay, you see that village there?"

In the darkness, she could just about see a little smudge of gray with yellow twinkling lights on the pitch-black far shore.

"Yeah."

"That's Farvey. It's the next biggest village on Inishbannock."

"I didn't know there were any other villages on the island?"

"Well, 'village,'" he said, with air quotes. "It's a couple of cottages, the campsite, and Kilty's hostel."

"Ah, so that's where they keep all you filthy outsiders?"

"Exactly," he said with a grin. "Safe from all you weird inbred island folk."

"I've only been here two years," she said. "I'm only slightly inbred."

"Really?" he said with genuine surprise. "I didn't know that."

"Why? Do I sound like a native?"

"You sound . . . yeah, I guess. You've a weird accent, honestly."

"Oh thanks."

"Weird is good. Weird is right. Weird works," he assured her in a growling American accent. "Anyway, Kilty's has probably *the* worst bar in Europe. One step up from cans in a basement. But, it's the only other place to get a drink on the island that's not the Temple. So that's where I usually drink."

"What's wrong with the Temple?"

"Nothing. Lovely pub. If you're a local."

"You don't feel welcome there?"

"They're perfectly pleasant."

"Ah."

"Yeah. And before the outbreak, near as I can tell, that's where you and Cian used to drink."

"So . . . we would walk across the full length of the island, pass a perfectly nice pub, and go and drink in the worst pub in Europe?"

"What it seemed like to me."

"Why?"

He shrugged. "Inishbannock seems like the kind of place where everyone knows everyone's business. Maybe you and he just wanted some privacy?"

"What aren't you telling me, Declan?" she asked.

He sighed.

"Whenever I saw you there, you looked scared."

"I looked scared of him?"

He shook his head.

"No. Both of you. You and him. You'd look up anytime someone came into the bar. You'd talk in whispers. There was something going on and it scared both of you. That's . . . that's why I tried to give you my number yesterday."

"Why?"

"Just wanted to check in, I guess. After Quinn took you from the house, I tried to find out whether you were okay, whether you were still sick, like. And . . . no one wants to talk about you, Mara. You might as well not exist. I was actually, it's stupid . . ."

"Go on."

"I was kinda worried someone had killed you."

"What?"

"It just . . . I dunno how to describe it. It was like you were disappeared. It feels like the outbreak, you being buried, coming back. No one wants to discuss it. It feels like everyone's . . ."

"Trying to pretend like it never happened?"

He nodded. "Yeah. I dunno. And then there was your clothes . . ."

She unconsciously looked down at what she was wearing.

"Nah," he said. "I mean, what you were wearing that night. When I found you in the kitchen."

She realized that she had no idea what she had been wearing, other than mud.

"So, when you had your shower, I took your clothes and put them in the washing machine. Not even thinking. And then I remembered about the outbreak so I called Doctor Quinn and asked her what I should do with your clothes. And she told me to burn them."

"Okay?"

"So I put on the gloves and the mask and I take them out of the machine and . . . they were already burned."

". . . What?"

"There was a T-shirt, jeans, jumper, and you . . . your other stuff. And they were all burnt. Scorched. They had been burnt before I put them in to be washed. And I just didn't see because they were so filthy."

"That doesn't make any sense. Why was I buried in burnt clothes? Hell, why was I buried in *casual* burnt clothes? They couldn't spring for a nice funeral dress?"

"It's got to be something to do with the outbreak. They were burning your clothes to stop the spread of the disease?"

"Why not just cremate me then? Why burn my clothes and not my body?" Mara asked, feeling an intense irritation.

More mysteries. Why not? Throw them on the pile.

"Not a notion. You avoided my question, by the way."

"What question?" Her mind skittered across their conversation and the many threads they had pulled.

"Who's Oisín?"

"That's what I want to know," she said, exasperated. "Twice now, people have called Cian 'Oisín' and then pretended like nothing happened."

"People get names wrong."

"The same name, twice?"

"Ah, you'd be surprised. I had a girlfriend, Orla. People kept calling her 'Aoife' and we never knew why . . ."

"Did you see me any other times?" she asked, cutting across him. "Other than with Cian in Kilty's?"

"Yeah, actually. That's the other thing I wanted to talk to you about. I think I might have seen you the night of the outbreak."

She stopped and stared at him.

He nodded. "Yeah. I think I saw you with Santa."

Mara stared at Declan and raised an eyebrow.

He laughed, as if realizing that he sounded crazy.

"Sorry, I mean, there's this auld fella who lives in a cottage, down the beach, near mine. Long white beard. I see him now and then but I don't know his name. I just think of him as 'Santa.'"

"And you saw us together?"

"Yeah. I couldn't sleep, so I was out for a walk to clear my head along the cliffs. And I saw him chatting with someone outside his cottage. Someone who I thought might have been you. But I was too far away to be sure. And I remember thinking it was a bit weird."

"Why?"

"Well, I'd only ever seen you in Kilty's with Cian. Or in Ballydonn. And now you were here, alone, on a completely different part of the island. In the middle of the night. So that just struck me as a bit, y'know, weird."

"And we were just chatting?"

"Looked a bit more intense than that."

"Arguing?"

"I don't know. Maybe? It . . . looked like you were pleading with him. Just from the way you were moving your arms. The way you were standing, it's hard to describe . . . and then he slammed the door. As if you'd said something he really didn't like."

"Declan, could you show me where he lives?"

"What, right now?"

"Tomorrow, I can come over and . . ."

Suddenly the world turned white. Mara put her hands up to screen her eyes and, through the harsh glare, could just make out a car moving slowly toward them down the pier, dousing them with the high beams.

It came closer and closer, and Mara suddenly became very aware that there was not enough space on the pier to get past the car. If it kept coming, it was either into the sea or under the wheels. Then, the engine fell silent and the car stopped around ten feet away. The door opened and a figure emerged.

"There you are," said Cian.

She couldn't see his face in the darkness, but he sounded like he was smiling.

"Cian," she said. Mara wished she could see his face. She wished she knew how scared she should be.

"I felt really bad about earlier," he said, and she felt his lie twist in the air. "So I thought I'd come down and give you a lift back home."

"Oh. Thank you," she said. "I'm sorry, too."

He might have believed it. He might not. She couldn't see his face.

"We'll say no more about it," he replied. "Who's this?"

It was a bright question. A friendly question. Of course it was.

"This is Declan," she said. "He was the one who found me after I woke up. I was just thanking him . . . I was *saying thank you*. To him."

Mara glanced behind her at the pitch-black water that shuffled restlessly a few inches behind her heels.

"Howerya," said Declan with a half-hearted wave.

"Ah, the man himself," said Cian stepping forward, his hand offering a handshake that Declan accepted.

"Thank you so much for all you've done for Mara. I mean that," Cian said. He clapped Declan chummily on the shoulder. "But I'll take it from here."

And then, suddenly, Declan no longer existed for Cian. He turned, his back completely cutting Declan off from her line of sight.

"Good to go," he said. A statement. Not a question.

"Yeah," she said, anxious to bring the scene to an end.

"Alright, let me just turn the car around," he said.

As the car reversed back up the pier, Declan leaned in and whispered in her ear, "Listen, Mara. Remember what I said about you and Cian drinking in Kilty's?

"Yeah?"

"Well, forget all about that."

"Why?"

The car stopped. She could see Cian looking through the rear-view window at her, waiting for her to join him.

"Because," he said, trying and failing to look as nonchalant as possible. "That's not the bloke you were with."

15
Mara

She had not slept a wink all night. In the morning, when Cian pecked her on the cheek and wished her a good day, she smiled, and the act of raising the edges of her mouth felt like lifting an iron curtain.

Getting into the car with him on the pier had felt like she was having an out-of-body experience. As if she was a futile spirit, hovering over her own shoulder, screaming, *You know he's not who he says he is*, don't get in the car, you stupid . . .

But . . . what could she do? If she had said, "Declan says you're not really my boyfriend, your rebuttal?" Cian had the entire island to back up his version of events.

Everyone on Inishbannock was on the same page except for Mara and, now, Declan. A *folie à deux* was better than a *folie à une*—but not by much. Still, she told herself, it was a start.

Now, with Cian gone to work, and a cup of tea and a bowl of cereal in front of her, her sense of gnawing dread began to fade and was replaced by something like grim satisfaction.

She had begun. She'd poked the first hole in the massive façade of lies erected around her. She felt like a prisoner in a cell who'd gotten her hands on a spoon. She was going to burrow her way out. No matter how long it took.

Time to dig.

First order of business was to meet up with Declan and look for "Santa."

But how to even find Declan? It was not, she quickly realized, the most promising start to an investigation. She had no money and no internet access. She didn't even have Declan's phone number.

She would have to find him the old-fashioned way, wandering around the island until she saw a familiar landmark and was able to find his cottage.

• • •

The day was heavy and overcast. As Mara trudged roughly in the direction of Doctor Quinn's house, she nested her hands in her fleece pockets to guard against the Atlantic chill.

As always, the dead silence of the island quickly became oppressive and she whistled to stave it off.

As she walked, she thought about Doctor Quinn's little memory-card game.

Was that really to help me recover my memories? Or was she just molding me into a convenient shape?

As if on cue, Doctor Quinn's house emerged from below the line of hedges. It sat up on a hill, giving the good doctor an excellent vantage point to watch over her patients and to see anyone approaching. While it was a perfectly lovely two-story farmhouse, the kind that you'd see over the logo on a bag of flour, to Mara, it looked implacably sinister, square and black as a cell door against the blank sky.

She hunched down low and pulled her hood over her head, keeping close to the dry-stone wall until finally she was out of sight of the doctor's house.

She passed the field still empty of its sheep, but where a great flock of crows, as well as numerous flies, croaked and shuffled over something that lay on the ground, obscured by their shining wings. Something told her not to look at it, to keep moving.

Farther along the road: a house skinned to the bone by fire. Most of the structure collapsed. The front wall stood alone with empty windows, like an eyeless mask.

Mara stared at the blackened wood and fragments of bubbled, melted glass and could almost hear the crackling of the fire and taste the smoke on her lungs.

And yet, she felt cold.

She had the sudden, inescapable sensation of walking on a grave. Someone had died here. She was certain of it. Some ghost lingered, screaming silently under its breath.

She shuddered, and forced herself to walk on, but was startled to come upon a tiny old woman whose hair was as white as a rabbit's tail. She wore bright-pink Wellington boots and a purple woolly hat, and as she sat on the wall outside the burnt and gutted house she kicked her legs like a little girl.

"Hello, Máire," she cooed as Mara went past, her shoulders hunched against the cold.

Mara stopped, mostly to assure herself the woman was not a ghost, but living flesh and bone.

"Hello," she said. "Do I know you?"

The old woman looked at her in shock. "Know me? Of course you know me. We played handball together last week and you cheated."

Mara smiled sadly. The old woman was clearly "away with the fairies" which was a nice Irish way to say "in the grip of advanced senile dementia."

"I don't think that was me. But if I did I'm very sorry."

The old woman looked huffy but then relented. "It's alright. I might have cheated, too."

"What's your name?" Mara asked.

"You know my name, Máire, are you playing a game?"

"No," said Mara shaking her head. "And it's 'Mara.' I had an accident. I can't remember anything."

"Ah," said the old woman with a nod, as if they were both on the same blank page.

She must have been in her nineties, but there was an elfin childishness to her.

"What's your name?" Mara asked again.

The old woman frowned. "What time is it?"

"Must be almost eleven," guessed Mara with a smile.

"Then I'm Bridie," she said.

"Does your name change depending on the time?" Mara asked.

The woman looked at her with a knowing smile.

"Course. All names change with time. Sure you know that, Máire."

"Mara," she corrected her.

"Here," said Bridie. "Would you like to see the gun?"

"What gun?" Mara asked.

Bridie pointed over her shoulder to a thick hedge in the garden where a faint dull glint could be seen peeping out from the base.

Curious, Mara swung over the wall and went to examine it. Bridie stayed where she was.

Mara reached down and, sure enough, found herself holding a large double-barreled shotgun.

"It's because of the sheep," Bridie called over her shoulder in a sing-song voice.

"Someone was shooting sheep?" Mara asked, confused.

"Don't be silly! It's because the sheep are getting 'et," Bridie explained with a laugh. "So the farmers came out and they were shooting at them, to scare them off."

"To scare who off?" Mara asked.

Bridie looked at her, genuinely confused.

"Is it a game, Máire?" she asked.

"Yes," said Mara. "So?"

"They were shooting at the Fomor," Bridie said. "To scare them. But they don't always scare. The bigger they are, the braver they are."

Fomor. Mara didn't know the word. But she remembered the sheep screaming and running in terror in the darkness outside Doctor Quinn's house. She remembered the sound of hands softly padding on the walls.

She looked again at the weapon in her hands. She knew next to nothing about guns, but she guessed that if it had been stashed here to be used again, the owner would be disappointed.

The weapon was filthy, and there was a dark-red patch that she assumed was rust on the stock. There were also dents here and there. She would have thought the weapon would need to be cleaned and repaired before it could ever be used again. Maybe it had not been stashed here. Maybe it had been disposed of. Maybe no one was meant to find it again.

"What time is it?" Bridie asked.

Mara clicked her tongue. "Just eleven," she said.

"I have to go," Bridie said. "My mam will be waiting for me."

The only place her mother could possibly be waiting for her was the hereafter, but Bridie was so small and delicate that it took Mara a moment to realize that there was anything amiss with what the old woman had said.

Mara ran back to the wall and watched the retreating figure vanish around the corner.

"Bridie!" she called. "Come back!"

"That's not my name . . ." was all she heard in reply.

. . .

Declan was not home.

She knocked on the door, walked around the house, called out. Nothing.

Irritated, Mara kicked a stone against the wall and decided to wander down the dirt path to the beach.

The sand, white and fine as salt, stretched out before her. The ocean seemed bluer on this side of the island, somehow.

Far out in the sea, two or three black heads glinted in the sunlight. She waved to the seals, and one of them bobbed its nose, as if nodding a greeting. Mara slipped off her shoes and socks, and hitched up her jeans, and stepped into the crystal clear water.

Her toes went instantly numb from the biting cold, but she didn't care.

She closed her eyes and took a deep breath. For a moment, she felt at peace.

And then suddenly the undertow pawed hungrily at her feet and pulled her farther into the water.

MARA

The icy current scalded her ears, and her vision became a mad blur. Mara tried to right herself, but her arms and legs were cold iron. The water was freezing and she suddenly felt a sharp dagger of a cramp in her stomach.

And then she felt arms around her, pulling her out of the water and dumping her onto the sand like a sack of coal.

Mara lay there gasping and glanced over to see Declan, keeled over on his knees and elbows, breathing roughly as if he was in pain. For a terrible second, she thought he was having a heart attack. He fumbled in his pocket, took out a blue inhaler, and took two puffs.

"Y'alright?" he whispered between shuddering breaths.

"Yeah," she gasped. "Thank you."

"No bother," he said, but she could tell he was trying to be calm. He was not calm.

Slowly, he pulled himself to his feet and extended a hand to her and pulled her to standing.

Her teeth chattering, Mara spit out, "How did you— I mean, did you—"

She cast her eyes around. There wasn't a single human being other than the two of them for miles around. If he hadn't been there . . .

"I was coming back from the shop," he said. "I saw you from the cottage."

She looked up. "You ran all that way?"

He smiled and wheezed proudly, "Faster than I look."

16
Declan

Say this for her, Declan thought to himself as they walked slowly up the beach. *She keeps life interesting.* Life on the island had felt a lot less aimless and lonely since she'd appeared in his kitchen.

Mara seemed almost back to herself now, if still a little pale in the face.

When he saw her get sucked into the water he was sure she had dropped dead. It had been so horribly sudden. Declan didn't even remember running down to the beach. That had all been instinct. The next thing he knew, she was lying on the sand while he desperately tried to grab his inhaler. That was his exercise for this year, he promised himself.

She told him that she'd just had a "funny spell."

He told her she should see Doctor Quinn and she nodded and said she would.

It was a lie. He knew, and she knew he knew.

"Does she give you the creeps?" Mara asked him.

"Who, Quinn?"

"Yeah."

"More than anyone else on this island?"

DECLAN

She laughed. "Fair."

"So," he said after they'd been walking in silence for a while. "Before we were so rudely interrupted . . ."

"Yeah, sorry about that."

"Were you okay? After you went home?"

"Okay how?" she turned to look at Declan, curious.

"Like, he didn't say anything or do anything?"

"Like what?" she asked. Her gaze was impassive and unsettled him.

"Doesn't matter," he said, looking away, awkwardly.

They walked on a little in silence.

"So, there's something else I've been meaning to ask you," she said.

"Go ahead."

"You're sure the man you saw me with wasn't Cian?"

He thought long and hard. Memory was fallible, but not that fallible. He'd have remembered Cian. Something about the guy was off. He gave the vibe of someone who'd talk your ear off about Huey Lewis and the News while putting on a raincoat.

"Not a chance."

"So what did he look like?"

"Well, he was—" He realized that Mara was no longer walking beside him.

She'd broken into a run, sprinting like her life depended on it.

He gave chase, the muscles of his legs moaning from this fresh punishment, and found her standing outside a cottage at the foot of the cliff, her hands gripping the garden gate so tightly her knuckles were white.

"Mara . . ." he wheezed. "Please. Stop. Making. Me. Run."

She paid him no mind.

She simply stared at the white cottage with a red door and a gray slate roof. The windows painted nursery blue.

Through the small garden was a path laid with pebbles from the beach, and on either side were rows of weather-beaten ceramic figures. Declan noticed her attention was on these garden gnomes, but on closer inspection he could see they were fishermen. All identical, dressed in yellow rain-gear, each one holding a fishing rod and patiently waiting for a bite that would never come. All except the one closest to the door, which had evidently hooked a massive porcelain bass (or half of one, as only the head and upper body could be seen emerging from the soil of the garden). Mara was staring intently at it, her gaze fixated on the fish's face, wide-open mouth and staring, black eyes.

She turned to Declan and flashed him a great happy smile.

"I've been having dreams about this place," she whispered. "I think I used to live here."

Out of the corner of his eye, Declan saw shadowy movement against the white sand.

"Yeah?" he said. "Well, I think *he* lives here now." He pointed down the beach, and she followed his gaze.

A man stared back at them. He looked to be in his seventies, but he was tall and seemingly as solid as a granite pillar. His wild brown-white beard made his bald head look like an egg resting in an untidy nest, and he wore an off-white Aran sweater that looked like it had weathered centuries.

Either a farmer or a fisherman. You could tell that just by looking at him.

Forged by the land, or forged by the sea.

DECLAN

This was the man that he had seen her with. This was Santa.

Over his shoulder, Santa carried a long black metal detector, and Declan guessed that he'd been scouring the beach for coins and watches.

Mara give Declan a questioning look and he nodded.

"Yeah. The man himself."

Although, with the metal detector resting on his shoulder and skulking slowly toward them, he now reminded Declan more of Father Time carrying his scythe.

The man stopped and stared at Mara. Declan couldn't remember ever seeing eyes so piercingly blue. He seemed to have tears in his eyes, but that might just have been the breeze blowing in off the sea, seasoned with grains of sand.

For Declan, it felt uncomfortably like he was intruding on something intimate.

Mara's face furrowed back at the man. "Who are you?"

Santa smiled a little. So much sadness in such a small smile.

"'Tis you who are at me door," the man said softly. "Shouldn't I be asking that?"

"But you know me," she said. "You do, don't you?"

Again, that terrible sadness. He nodded. "Aye. You're Mara. New to the island."

Declan saw Mara's lip curl in irritation.

"I've been here two years," she said.

"You think that's long, do you?" he said with a soft chuckle.

He's probably lived here all his life. When the island came out of the sea, he was already standing on the rock, Declan thought.

"What can I do for you both?" the old man asked, as if Declan had suddenly popped into existence.

"This is hard for me to explain," Mara said. "I had . . . an accident."

"You've lost your memory," he said with a nod.

"How did you know that?" she asked.

He shrugged. "It's a small island. Not much to talk about. The weather. The Gaa. Yer one who got buried alive and lost her memory."

"I . . . I have the strangest feeling I used to live here. In this house," she said.

"That is a strange feeling. Because I've lived here my entire life. And it's not for sale."

"I'm not, that's not what I meant . . ."

He made a dismissive gesture, as if to say he'd only been joking.

"Did Mara ever visit here?" Declan asked.

"Did Mara ever visit here?" the man repeated. "She did not, Mr. . . . ?"

"Declan," he said. For some reason, it didn't feel right to expect this man to call him "Mr. Burke."

"Conn," came the reply. "A pleasure. Now, if you'll both excuse me."

He gently but firmly made a path through them and went to open the red door.

But Mara wasn't done yet.

"Conn, are there any other houses like yours on the island?"

He glanced at her over his shoulder.

"Certainly. A roof. Four walls. Nothing special about this place."

"Please. I'm trying to recover my memory. And I can't help feeling that this house . . . I feel like I'm so close to shaking something loose. Could I please come inside? Just for a few minutes?"

The old man winced.

Declan thought he looked like an alcoholic who desperately wanted to refuse the drink that had been offered him, but knew he didn't have the strength.

Conn gave a deep, heavy sigh and his hand slipped off the door.

"You can come in for a cup of tea," he said. "But please wait outside. Let me put some kind of order on the place."

They waited for a few minutes in silence and they heard something fall, and the sound of broken glass, and low cursing.

Mara cast a quizzical look at Declan.

But before he could answer, the door opened, and Conn silently waved them in.

17
Mara

Standing in Conn's sitting room, Mara knew that she had been right. The smell of the varnish on the floorboards. The way the dust hung in the sunlight. She felt like a piece of a jigsaw puzzle being slotted exactly into the place it was supposed to be. An act of completion. She had been here before. This place was familiar. It was safe.

It was, somehow, impossibly, *home*.

Conn entered from the kitchen with three mugs of tea. He stopped dead as he saw her standing there, and for a moment Mara thought he was going to drop his tray.

Then, he seemed to recover and told them to sit.

As they settled, he spoke only to Declan, which struck her as odd. She had commanded his attention outside the house, but here it seemed like he was trying his best to ignore her.

Mara began to tune out their conversation and instead took in every inch of the room, trying to jolt her tattered, threadbare memory into remembering something, anything, to explain the nagging, itching feeling of familiarity.

In that corner, there was a rocking horse. Decorated with seashells.

MARA

It was ridiculous to think of. Why would Conn, a man who had been old when Mara had been born, own a rocking horse? But she could see it in her mind's eye. More than that, she could see tiny bite marks on the horse's carved mane where some teething infant had been chewing to ease the pain. She could remember the weight of it. The smell of it. Wood sap and glue and spit-up milk . . .

"And is it any good for a drink?" Conn asked Declan, and Mara returned from her fugue.

"Honestly, only if you're desperate," Declan said, apologetically.

"Desperate. Well. Until someone opens another pub I probably am," Conn mused. "There was once a second one in Ballydonn. A man named Meagher owned it, but herself saw him off."

"You don't like the Temple?" Mara asked.

Those brilliant blue eyes settled on her.

"Oh, I like the Temple well enough," Conn says softly. "I only take issue with the priestess. Or rather, she takes issue with me."

"You mean Gráinne?" Mara asked.

Now there's someone I wouldn't want as an enemy, for all her smiles.

He nodded. "We've been having a disagreement."

"For how long?"

He laughed. "Jaysus. I'd say since she was born. She's my sister. I used to drink in the Temple, but she's been *haranguing* me recently," he said, clearly enjoying the opportunity to use the word "haranguing."

"Over what?"

"Ah, the inheritance," he said dismissively. "Property and rights. Isn't it always property and rights? When our mother passed away, she got the Temple, I got the house here, and Malachy got the shop."

"Malachy?"

The name alone was enough to send a shiver running through her.

In retrospect, it was easy to see that Conn and Gráinne were brother and sister. The blue, piercing eyes. The great height. The presence. But Malachy? What mad genes had put him in that family? He was less a branch, and a more a dark fungus growing on the family tree.

Conn seemed to read her thoughts, and find them amusing.

"Yes. He's me brother. For my sins," he said with a low chuckle.

If that's true, who did you kill? she wondered dourly.

She looked around again. Oh, to be allowed free rein in here. Wander around the rooms until more memories were shaken loose. Suddenly she had a brain wave.

"Conn, could I use your bathroom?" Mara asked.

There was a pause. He looked at her with a flash of suspicion. But what could he say?

"'Course," he rumbled, at last. "C'mere, I'll show you the way."

"Oh it's no trouble," she said brightly. "I'm sure I can find it."

"Wouldn't want you getting lost," he said, and in that moment she felt sure he knew exactly what she was trying to do.

MARA

Or maybe you're just crazy and he doesn't want some strange woman wandering about his house unescorted, the voice of reason piped up, as unwelcome as such voices always are.

He led her out of the living room and down a dark little side passage. As she turned she gave a shriek.

A stuffed seal's head screamed silently at her from the back wall of the corridor, a V of white, razor-sharp teeth visible in its lower jaw.

Below the seal's head, almost as unsettling, there was a glass case containing . . .

The second gun she's seen that day. She knew nothing about firearms. She just knew that it was very large, and very murderous looking.

"I have a license, sergeant," Conn said, seeing the expression on her face.

"That's . . . why do you have that, Conn?" she asked.

He looked at her serenely. "I'm an old man. Living alone. There's one guard on the island, and he's a complete eejit. Toilet's just through there."

Conn gestured to the door, and for a moment she worried that he was going to wait outside until she'd finished. But, as she sat on the seat, she heard him slowly shuffling down the corridor and back to the living room.

When she was done, Mara stepped back into the hallway and heard something small and hard skittering over the tiles. She looked down, and saw a tiny shard of glass glinting in the dim light.

And once she had seen one sliver, there were the others, a little trail of glass stars leading her down the corridor, toward where the seal head stared down at her in appalled outrage.

She hated that seal head. It looked like it was aware of what had happened and could not understand why this had been done to it.

They cut off my head and hung it on a wall so that they could look at it. Why? Why would they do that? What kind of animals are they?

Mara looked away and followed the trail of glass fragments into a tiny room off to the side.

It seemed to be a utility room. There was a great black safe that looked like it could withstand a collision with a high-speed tractor and come out the winner. It was flush with the wall, looming behind a decrepit, yellowing washer-and-dryer set and a wicker basket.

It was here that the trail of shards ended.

And so the question arose in Mara's mind: *Who puts broken glass in a laundry basket?*

Someone hiding something. In a hurry. With few options.

She recalled how Conn had made the two of them wait outside while he had tidied the house. The sound of breaking glass.

He was hiding something from them. Something he tried to move because he had not wanted her to see and had then broken.

Well. She had to look. Didn't she?

Inside the basket, resting on a bed of cream sheets and broken glass, was a smashed picture frame and a crumpled, torn photograph.

Carefully, gently, trying not to cut her fingers on the glass, she eased the picture out.

It was a black-and-white photo, but she couldn't be sure when it was taken.

MARA

Ireland's past decades were like families where everyone looked the same. You could tell that the twenties and thirties and the forties were related, but not how old they were, relative to each other.

As Mara looked closer, she could see it was a wedding photo, taken on the steps of the church in Ballydonn.

The groom was Conn, clean-shaven and handsome. A beautiful man, she had to admit, with a great happy grin on his face.

Standing beside him was a dark-haired, thin youth that she recognized with a shock as Malachy.

The best man, if you could believe that.

He looked almost handsome, no more than twenty years old. He still had that lascivious glint in his eye, but in a young face it looked more charmingly mischievous than predatory. More imp than ghoul.

And there was Gráinne. Well, obviously she was gorgeous. Still in her prime. Smiling at the camera like a queen whose armada had had a big day.

Then it hit Mara that she had made a mistake.

The flower girl, probably no more than fourteen, smiled at the camera with a look that was both shy and proud, innocent and somehow knowing. *This* girl, Mara realized, was Gráinne.

The older woman, she decided, must be their mother.

Finally, her attention fell to the bride, nearly hidden by her veil.

And the bride...

Oh God.

The bride.

"That's not yours," said a voice softly behind her.

She turned around and Conn, all of him, stood between her and the way out.

Seeing him in the narrow door-frame really brought home just how large he really was.

In the dim light, his eyes were lost in shadow.

He took a step toward her and she braced herself for something terrible to happen.

He is not so unlike his brother after all, she thought.

Then she felt a tug as the photograph was gently but firmly pulled from her unresisting fingers.

"I think you should leave now," he whispered.

She was, she realized, in complete agreement.

• • •

"Mara? Mara!" Declan yelled as she practically sprinted across the soft sand, trying to flee as quickly away from the house as she could. Once again, she was making him run.

When she was far enough from Conn and the cottage, she stopped, and Declan finally caught up.

"Mara, what happened?" he asked, eyes full of concern. "Did he say something, did he . . . did he fucking *do* something to you . . ."

"No!" she said. "No. He . . . he . . ."

She took a deep breath. And for a moment all she could hear was the slow, insistent crashing of the tide.

"I went . . . looking around the house."

"Ooookay, that's not good. Kinda see why he might not be happy about that . . ."

"Declan, I found something."

"Right," he said.

MARA

There was a long pause.

"You gonna tell me or we gonna play charades?" he asked.

She told him.

"Are you joking?" he asked after a while.

She shook her head.

"Do you believe me?" she asked.

He glared at her in irritation. "Do I believe that you found a photograph of yourself getting married to Conn and that you're actually, like, a hundred? No. I don't believe you. What the fuck do you expect me to say?"

Later, looking back, Mara would admit he had a point. But right now, she felt betrayed.

"So I'm crazy?" she said angrily.

"No . . ."

"Lying?"

"Wrong," he said flatly. "I don't know who you saw in that picture, but it wasn't you."

"So why did Conn take it off me and throw us out of the house?"

"After he found you rifling through his wedding photos? Yeah, there's a mystery for the ages!" he snapped.

She swung around, and whatever expression she was wearing made him raise his hands instinctively, as if he thought she was going to hit him.

She felt a flash of guilt, but not enough to kill the rage.

"I don't need your fucking sarcasm," she growled. She turned and walked away.

"Right. Pleasure as always. See you around, Mara. Try not to drown on the way home, yeah?" Declan angrily called after her as she headed back up the beach, her shoulders hunched against the cold, and her face scowling at the world.

18
Conn

Conn watched them from the curtains.

He watched their argument, silent and tiny, like two flies buzzing in a jar, before they separated and took their lonely roads home.

He cursed himself again and again.

Stupid. Stupid old man.

Letting her into the house.

What the fuck were you thinking?

He heard it in his mother's voice, as he always did when the guilt was at its harshest.

What the fuck were you thinking, you stupid fucking eejit, hah?!

The phone rang, jolting him out of his reverie, and with a weary sigh he went into the back hallway and picked it up. "Hello?" he said.

"It's me, Conn."

His brother's voice sounded distant and somehow weaker than usual.

"Malachy," he said.

He asked *Are you alright?* not with words, but with the tone.

CONN

"I'm just calling to say, I don't think I'll be up for cards on Tuesday."

"Are you sure? I could come up your way?"

"Ah no. Ah no. I'm just a bit under the weather."

We don't get sick, Malachy, Conn thought. *Not in our family. What's really wrong?*

A thought presented itself. And he clubbed it senseless and buried it again because he couldn't bear to think of it.

As if sensing his scepticism, Malachy clarified. "Honestly, I'm just not feeling right. In the head, like. You know what I mean?"

"Out of sorts?" Conn asked. "Got the hump?"

Malachy laughed. "The very expression. I'll be grand. I'll come down to you when I'm feeling more meself."

"Right so," said Conn gruffly.

"Oh, did I tell you?" Malachy continued. "Guess who came into the shop?"

"Go on."

"The Bad Penny. I had a bit of fun with her."

Conn felt his blood run cold. "What kind of fun?" he asked.

"Ah, I just spun her a few tall tales. Probably a bad idea, no?"

"Not your brightest. I'll do you one better though."

"Go on."

"She's just left."

"What? The house? Fuck. How did that happen?"

"Ah, she showed up at me door. Saying she . . . saying she remembered the place."

Malachy gave a long low moan. "Ohhhhh Jaysus. You didn't let her in?"

"I didn't know how to say no."

"No. No, Conn. N. O. It's only the first fucking word everyone learns, CHRIST."

"It gets worse. She saw the photo."

"What photo?"

"The grand day out. The one outside the church."

"The one that's supposed to be locked away in the safe? That photo?"

Conn lost his temper. "Jesus Christ, amn't I allowed to keep fucking anything? I hid it! I did, she just . . . she found it and . . ."

"Sweet merciful redeemer . . . have you called it in?"

"No. Not yet."

"You will, though, won't you?"

"Course I will."

I don't know that I will, Conn thought. *I don't know that I want the bother of it.*

"It's his fault you know. Your man."

"Morley?" Conn asked.

"He's a bad husband. She could do better."

"They're not married."

"Ah, sure, isn't that part of the problem? New ways of doing things, when the old ways worked grand?"

Did they? I wonder.

"Well. Feel better, Malachy. I'll see you soon."

"Oh you will," Malachy said quietly. "Oh you will."

Something in his voice told Conn that his worst fear had come to pass.

He knew then.

He hung up.

19
Mara

On the long, angry trudge home, she stopped to pay her respects at the grave of Mara Fitch. The hole she had clawed her way out of had been filled in, as if she had never been there.

The other graves beside hers remained.

Unmarked, unmourned, and unnamed.

She wondered if they ever would be marked, mourned, and named. Or would they simply lie, anonymous and forgotten, until their bodies melted away and the memories of these people slowly faded, as if they never existed.

She remembered those first terrified, panicked moments when she had woken up. What had she screamed?

Fuckers.

Who?

Who were they?

Who had put her in that box and buried her alive?

"It would have been a beautiful resting place, no?"

She turned and saw Cian striding toward her through the graveyard.

"What do you think?" he continued stretching his arms out over the graves, like a salesman showing off a new car. "When the time comes, the two of us, side by side, here? Or maybe we'll just get cremated? You can be the first person in history to have both done."

He gave a smile that was bared teeth and nothing else.

"Hilarious," she said.

He shrugged. "You used to have a very dark sense of humor. You say you don't know me. And I don't really think I know you anymore, Mara."

"What are you doing here?" she asked.

"What am *I* doing here? I'm chasing after my partner who's just undergone massive mental trauma and thinks it's a good idea to go running around the island with strange men that she knows absolutely nothing about."

"What men?" she asked.

"Ah give over, Mara," he said, more bored than angry. "Who else would you be seeing on this part of the island, the fucking sheep? I know you came out here to see him."

"I'm not allowed have friends?" she asked.

Cian stepped closer to her, and she fought the urge to step back onto her own grave.

"If you think Declan Burke wants to be your friend, you've lost most than just your memory."

"What are you talking about?"

"He. Wants. To. Fuck. You."

"Oh my God, you're pathetic . . ."

"He's a predator, Mara, for fuck's sake . . . He's not even allowed drink in the Temple anymore, he's notorious!"

"He was in the Temple last night!"

MARA

"Artist's bursary. Contractual obligations. Trust me. You won't see him in there again."

She slammed a mental door shut. She knew Declan. She trusted him and she did not trust the man in front of her. But even as that door closed, a few doubts managed to snake their way in. She remembered that Declan had hinted that he wasn't welcome in the Temple. And he *had* been helpful, hadn't he? He had told her how worried he was about her. He had tried to get her phone number.

No. He'd been trying to help. He was being a friend. He was just traipsing halfway across the island with her to be helpful to someone that he hardly knew . . .

She stopped. No.

She trusted Declan. And she didn't trust Cian. That was where the matter began and ended.

As if sensing that he had penetrated her defenses, if only for a moment, Cian softened his voice and whispered, "I know this is a tough time for you. But you have to let me protect you. Because you can't protect yourself. You're still vulnerable. And men like Declan are very, very good at taking advantage of women like you. I don't want you seeing him again, Mara."

He took her wrist in his hand and squeezed *just* tightly enough that she felt pain.

"For your own protection," Cian said.

• • •

The next morning, after he'd gone to work, she decided to scratch an itch.

She went through every drawer, every bookshelf, every nook and cranny, and she tried to find a single thing that she could be sure belonged to her.

She searched for proof that the house was her home, and that she and Cian had been living there for the last two years.

There was nothing.

Not so much as a bill in her name.

There was nothing to prove that this fucking sterile glass brick was anything but what she had always felt instinctively: a cage to keep her in.

She came across the photo of her mother that Cian had given her. It was tucked away in the drawer of his bedside table, extracted from the broken frame and placed flat. Her and Cian and Cian's mother . . .

No. *Her* mother.

And yet the more she looked, the more the suspicion grew. The older woman had his eyes. His light hair. That little upward fold in the upper lip.

And the more Mara looked at herself the more flaws she began to notice. She was lit differently, she was looking at a camera that was just a few degrees to her right whereas as the other two were gazing slightly to their left.

And then she saw it.

Where Mara's hand should have gone around her mother's back there was a tiny, almost imperceptible, gap between her wrist and the woman's light-blue cardigan. It was easy to miss, but impossible to ignore once seen. Apparently, the day this picture had been taken, Mara had been missing her left hand.

Fake, she thought to herself.

MARA

He used this picture to guilt me and manipulate me and it's not even my mother.

First came rage, and then fear. Finally bafflement.

Why is he going to this much trouble? What could possibly be worth it?

Sitting down at the breakfast table, Mara grabbed her journal and made a shopping list of mysteries.

Why was I buried alive?

Why is everyone lying to me? (Cian's photograph)

Who was the man that Declan saw me with in Kilty's?

Who am I?

She stopped, and bit her lip. That last one had made her feel a little lightheaded. It was true. All she had to go on regarding her own identity was the word of people she knew were liars.

Rather than dwell on that, she added another line that seemed less existential.

I will find out why I'm in Conn's wedding picture.

She looked at what she had written and then crossed it out and wrote.

I will find out why a woman who looks exactly like me is in Conn's wedding picture.

There. Much more sensible. Much more sane.

Alright then. If she was not the bride in the picture, who was it? Just some random woman who looked identical to her?

Well, maybe.

People had their doubles.

Declan had said that Mara knew Conn, but Conn claimed she had never been inside his house. But Mara *knew* she had.

So Conn was lying.

And he had gone to great lengths to keep her from seeing that photograph.

So on top of lying, he was hiding something from her.

So no. The woman in the photograph was not some random doppelgänger.

Oh. Ohhhhh.

She wrote the word *relative* and underlined it three times.

What was it Declan had said? She had a weird accent, but she sounded like she was from the island.

She wasn't some blow-in. Her family had been here for generations, the photograph was proof. Which meant . . .

Mara shuddered with the realization. She must be related to Conn. And Gráinne. And (oh dear God no) Malachy.

At least by marriage.

She shuddered.

But why the lie? Why *any* of the lies, for that matter?

Well yes, Mara, she thought grouchily. *That is why we're here.*

Why do any of this? What secret was worth going to all this trouble? What secret was worth *burying* someone . . .

She stopped mid-thought.

Mara, you're being very self-centered, aren't you? It wasn't just you they buried.

A line of three fresh graves next to a ragged hole appeared in her mind.

Who were they? Who were the others who died in the "outbreak"?

Loose threads. Time to pull them.

. . .

MARA

The weeks after their talk in the graveyard were an interbellum as Mara waited for something else to slip and expose itself.

She played the happy wife as best she could, hoping that Cian's palpable dislike and disinterest in her would do the rest. Watching her was a chore to him, she realized. He didn't want to do it any more than she wanted him to.

So she behaved. She let the days slouch by unused. She bored him every evening with "memories" that she pretended she had recovered. And she listened to all the thrilling news from the wind farm. He was strangely obsessed with the men on his crew. He knew all their names and had an encyclopedic knowledge of their friendships and enmities with each other. Every day there was a new report on whether Pavel and Dusan were still arguing over a welched bet, or how some new recruit was adjusting to life on the island. At first, Mara had mistaken Cian's enthusiasm for genuine concern for the men working under him. But the more he spoke, the more it felt like a child bragging about his toys. It was, ultimately, always, about him. How good a manager he was, the progress he was making, the kudos he was earning, how he was carrying the entire future of the island on his back like Atlas.

She let him think he had won, which was all it really took to beat him.

And he had not been un-magnanimous in victory.

He had even bought her a new mobile phone. A very basic model, with no internet access, but at least now she could make calls and receive texts if that was something she hypothetically wanted to do.

She used it as a watch. And bided her time.

20
Cian

It's worth it, Cian told himself as he stared at his naked body in the mirror. *If you ever find yourself wavering, Big Man, there's your proof.*

Not only had the wounds vanished, his skin looked as if it had never been so much as scratched. And his body?

He had always kept in good shape. Now he looked like a god.

Turning in the sunlight from the bathroom window, the mirror revealed a landscape of lean, hard muscle. His hairline, slowly but noticeably retreating since he'd turned thirty, had launched an impressive reconquest and his hair felt thick and weighty when he ran his hand through it.

He no longer felt tired. He never felt tired anymore. He hadn't been sick since he'd returned to the island and his eyes had taken on a kind of . . . sharp brightness.

Look at you, Big Man, he thought to himself. *Ready to fuck the world.*

It had been a good week, capping a great month. At the beginning of July, he'd gotten word that the expansion of the wind farm on the western coast of the island had been approved (which had been more or less a sure thing) and that he would be put in charge of it (which had not). That meant a bigger role, a bigger team, a bigger title on his résumé, and a bigger figure in his account at the end of every month. Cian would, of course, have liked to put that down to his own obvious abilities as an engineer and a leader of men, but while he was proud, he was not a proud fool.

"Put in a good word for me, did you?" he'd asked Gráinne one night as he stopped in the Temple for a celebratory drink.

"I'm sure I have not the slightest notion to what you are referring," she said coldly as she poured him his pint.

"I always knew you liked me," he said.

She fixed him with a glare. "That is a slanderous accusation," she said. "And if you repeat it again you're barred."

He laughed. She laughed, too.

"Seriously, though," she said.

He knew it was true. She hated him. They all did. The blow-in. The interloper. The Dub with the shit-eating grin. He made the whole fucking island break out in a rash.

And he didn't care. He was proud, in fact.

When they hate your guts and still give you a house and a promotion, what's that called?

It's called being indispensable.

He was good at his job. He was damn good at his job.

Everything was fucking fantastic. It was all worth it.

It was even worth sharing a house and bed with his sullen, moody, half-brain-dead darling.

She was easier now.

The situation with Declan had been neatly resolved. She seemed more . . . "happy" was the wrong word. Sedate. Pacified. She accepted his pecks on the cheek when he left for work. She chatted politely to him when he came home and before they went to bed.

She didn't go traipsing around the island with strange men.

That was all he wanted from her, and it wasn't much.

For other needs, he had Eileen. Thirty-two, divorced, and not looking for anything serious right now. On the days when he had to commute to the office in Tralee, he'd stop in on the way home. He liked her well enough. He liked the curves of her body, and the line of seven stars tattooed down her spine, and her long curly black hair that bounced on her shoulders when he was inside her.

But mostly he liked the way she spoke like an American porn star when they had sex, and hearing her moan, "Ohhh yes, Daddy," in a thick Kerry accent struck him as hilarious.

He liked that he thought her stupid and ridiculous, and that she had no idea of just how much contempt he felt for her.

Later, he knew he'd be watching himself fuck Eileen in her bedroom mirror, and he'd be awestruck at how good he looked.

Look at you, Big Man. Ready to fuck the world.

21
Mara

It was a morning that Cian had gone on one of his work pilgrimages to Tralee that Mara knew she'd have the island to herself for at least twenty four hours.

Like any small community, Inishbannock had learned the value of multi-purposing. Beside the church in Ballydonn was the Old School, a rather grim-looking Famine-era building that was, with the exception of the church itself, the largest structure on the island. It served as parish hall, cultural center, heritage museum, meeting place, and when the district judge made her thrice-yearly tour of the islands, courtroom. But, more important to Mara, it was the home of the Ballydonn Public Library.

After skimming the shelves and not finding what she needed, she reluctantly went to the front desk to ask for help.

"The local newspaper?" the librarian, a portly woman in her fifties, repeated with a sardonic air, looking down at her through owlish glasses.

"Yeah," said Mara, instantly feeling that her clever plan was not as clever as she'd thought. "I just assumed you'd keep an archive of it?"

"An archive. Of the local newspaper. That's somehow financially viable on an island with less than a thousand people in the year of Our Lord twenty—"

"So there isn't a newspaper on the island, okay, thank you," Mara said brusquely.

She looked around the library and saw a single PC in the corner, which looked like it could have told stories of the Apollo missions.

"Can I use the internet?" she asked.

"Do you mean in general or on this particular day on that particular machine?" the librarian asked.

"Not working?" Mara guessed.

The librarian simply arched an eyebrow as if she was not even going to dignify that with a response.

Trying to hide her frustration, Mara went to browse the bookshelves while she planned her next move all the while wondering how such a tiny library, in such a remote location, could still boast a complete collection of *TekWar*.

She had hoped there would be a local newspaper on the island so that she could peruse the last few issues and find, if not a complete accounting of the "outbreak," which she was more and more convinced had never happened, then at least obituaries of the three other people who'd supposedly died. Failing that, Mara had hoped to use the library's internet to find any reference to their deaths. There had to be records somewhere.

She could just come out with it and ask to see the obits, she supposed. But something told her that making her intentions known would be playing into their hands. Whoever "they" were. Better to find the information herself. If she could.

MARA

Her eyes moved over the walls, where various old black-and-white photographs displayed scenes from the island's history. There was a parade of honor for a local GAA hero after the Kerry team won the Sam Maguire. Another picture showed a view of Main Street decorated to celebrate the Eucharistic Congress of 1932.

Mara would have continued along the line of photographs, but the sequence was interrupted by a large black public phone set into the wall over a bookshelf.

On top of the bookshelf, laid open, was a stapled sheaf of paper. It looked like it had been printed very recently. The lettering was bold and sharp and the paper looked pristine and new.

It was a list of names, in alphabetical order, each one with a phone number beside it. She picked a page at random and two familiar names jumped out at her.

Rowen, Conn.

Rowen, Malachy.

She flicked back to the front and found herself.

Fitch, Mara.

And, on the next page:

Morley, Cian.

She couldn't find Declan, but he wasn't a permanent resident so that made sense.

So, this was the island's phone registry. If she wanted, she could call anyone currently living on the island . . .

Anyone *living*.

She took a deep breath.

Under the phone was a shelf of phone books. There were white phone books for residential numbers, and yellow phone books for businesses. There were some for the 066 area code (County Kerry, which included the island), and some for other counties, mostly Dublin. She noticed that most of the books were old, with the newest showing a publication date of 2019, and that they had gotten scrawnier and scrawnier with each passing year, as they had been starved by the exodus from landlines to mobile phones. And then she saw, at the end of the shelf, wedged in between the wood and the last phone book, more stapled sheaves. Some of them were yellowed and looked quite old.

Oh my God. I think I just hit pay dirt.

The current island registry, the one open under the phone, was clearly new. As if it had needed to be updated quite recently. If she could get the registry from just before the current one, and compare them, she could see what changes had been made.

She glanced up. The librarian had apparently gone on a bathroom break, or possibly decided to leave to pursue a career as an insult comic. Regardless, she was in the clear.

The old registries were undated, so she took the one at the end, hoping it was the most recent, and grabbed the current register. At a table, she went through them both line by line, underlining every discrepancy.

She found her first one quickly enough:

Connell, Martin.

And, a mere two lines later:

Do, Sara.

She noticed that Martin Connell and Sara Do, as well as both being absent from the current register, shared a landline number. Married couple, maybe? Cohabiting partners? That would make sense if they had both died in the outbreak. If they'd been living together one could have easily infected the other.

That was interesting.

The next discrepancy, however, was not interesting. That was too small a word.

Mara had begun her search assuming she would only find people missing in the current register (call it "A"), that were present in the older register ("B").

She had not expected to find that someone in A was not in B.

And she certainly had not expected that person to be her.

Fitch, Mara. Present and accounted for in the current register.

But there was no sign of her in the older one under "F."

She double-checked, but she was certain, there was simply no . . .

"Mara Fitch! Is that you?"

Gráinne had just entered the library and was calling out to her in a booming voice, more appropriate for a cattle auction than a library. Of course, the librarian was still AWOL, and so the ancient laws of the library were violated with impunity.

Mara deftly swept the two sheaves into her handbag and stood to greet Gráinne.

"Hi, Gráinne," she said, trying to sound nonchalant. "What are you doing here?"

"Oh, we just finished a Comhairle meeting."

"Comhairle?"

"Just the local island branch of the Illuminati," Gráinne deadpanned. "A few busybodies with nothing better to do than listen to two farmers argue over what field ends where. Riveting stuff. Will you stop in for a pint?"

"Ah, I really can't . . ."

"Oh, come on, I have a mortgage payment to make."

While she didn't want to go to the Temple, Mara knew that the quicker she got out of the library, the less chance of Gráinne asking what she was doing here.

"Alright then, lead on," she said.

Malachy's shop had a large CLOSED sign in the window as they passed, and Mara worried for a moment that she'd find the foul old man at his usual place at the bar. Thankfully, the Temple was empty except for Padraig, cleaning glasses behind the bar.

"Hello, Ma," he said. "Hello, M-M-Mara," he stuttered awkwardly.

She nodded a hello, and wondered if that was the first thing he had ever said to her.

"Pour us two pints of Guinness there, Padraig, I'm not on the clock yet," Gráinne said and her son dutifully complied. "*Sláinte*."

The women clinked their glasses.

"So where's Malachy?" Mara asked, trying to make it sound casual and not a demand for vital intelligence.

"Malachy?" Gráinne said, raising an eyebrow and Mara caught her giving a knowing look at Padraig, who returned it, with the exact same expression. Some things really did run in the family.

"Well now, there's a question," Gráinne said with a sigh. "He hasn't left the shop in the last few days. Shut up business. He'll want to be careful. He'll lose all his customers to yer man in Farvey."

"Oh," said Mara. "Has someone been in to check on him?"

To her surprise, she found that she was actually concerned. A very small amount, but still. Surprising.

"Ah, it's nothing to worry about," said Gráinne. "Or at least, it's nothing that worrying will fix. He's . . ." She took a deep breath and it felt like she was trying to order her words precisely. "The thing about our family, Mara . . . we know what we want. And we go and we get it. That's always been my way. My husband now, Padraig's father. He was engaged when I met him. I've told you that, haven't I, Padraig? And most women, that'd be that. But I saw him and I knew he was the man for me, and I didn't stop until he bloody well knew it, too."

Gráinne laughed and Mara did, too, out of politeness, all the while thinking, *What happened to your husband's fiancée and why do I get the feeling it involved a shovel?*

She suddenly remembered that Gráinne had lost somebody in the outbreak. Maybe it was her husband?

"But if I hadn't been able to convince him, I would have moved on," Gráinne continued. "Except, you see Malachy . . . Malachy knows what he wants. But he can't move on. And that's . . . well, it poisoned him. And it destroyed his life, truth be told. He was never the same."

"The same after what?" Mara asked.

"Ah, there was a woman," said Gráinne quietly. "Leave it at that, sure."

"You love him," Mara thought aloud.

"Of course I do," Gráinne said. "He's my brother." And her eyes narrowed as if she found the implication that she might not to be suspect.

"You remember Malachy so?" she asked. "Or have you met him since your return?"

"Oh, I met him the first day I came into Ballydonn," Mara said. "I met your other brother, too. I think I like him better if I'm honest."

She had not been expecting any particular reaction, but the chill that fell over the pub was still a surprise.

"Oh. You met Conn, did you?" Gráinne asked, taking a rather deep draft.

"Yeah," said Mara. *Tread carefully here*, she thought to herself. *This field has mines.*

"He's a bit out of your way, isn't he?" Gráinne mused. "Where did you meet him?"

"On the beach," Mara said. "I was just exploring the island. Ran into him."

This seemed to reassure Gráinne somewhat.

"Ah well. Don't tell him. But he's my favorite, too," she said with a wink. "Even if he is a cranky fucker. I hope he was polite to you?"

Mara nodded. "Hospitality itself," she said.

Why had she said that word? She could have said "pleasantness" or "friendliness" or "niceness," but she said "hospitality."

Gráinne's pupils seemed to narrow.

"Hospitality?" she repeated.

"Yeah," said Mara, sensing she had now stepped on a mine and was unsure of how to take her foot off it.

"He offered you hospitality?"

"Well . . ."

"Did he invite you into his house, Mara?" Gráinne asked.

Behind the bar, Padraig flinched. Her tone was clearly familiar to him.

MARA

"Yeah. Just for tea," Mara said.

There was a very long silence. "Hmm," Gráinne said at last. She sounded like she had drifted off, and was murmuring in her sleep. "That's not like him, now. That's not like him."

The conversation having died a quick death, Mara finished her pint and said her goodbyes. She had a busy day ahead of her, she'd wasted enough time and the two phone registries were burning a hole in her handbag.

She needed to find the man that Declan had seen her with. The man who was definitely not Cian. He'd said he had seen them together in Kilty's hostel, which meant that it was time for a visit to Farvey, Inishbannock's fabled second city.

There, just as Declan had promised, was the hostel, a medium-sized campsite, and maybe three cottages.

The campsite had perhaps eight camper vans and half as many tents, and the hostel felt barely inhabited when she stepped through the glass door.

"Oh, hello again," said a cheerful voice with a cheddar-strong Cork accent.

Mara turned to see the young woman she had run into at the entrance to the Temple on open mic night. She was wiping a bar table that looked so old and stained it would probably have been better to burn the upper layer of wood and start fresh. She was wearing a short-sleeve T-shirt and Mara could see, on her light-brown bicep, a magnificently detailed tattoo of a pale, dark-haired queen surrounded by a flock of crows. Pinned to her shirt was a small employee name tag that said, HI! I'M NATALIE!

Natalie (if the name tag was an honest source) stood up, saw Mara, and raised her hands. "I surrender."

"What?" Mara asked.

She lowered her hands sheepishly. "I just meant because last time you knocked me over . . . sorry, it was funny in my head."

"Oh," said Mara, suddenly feeling very guilty. "No, that's funny."

"Aaaand it's awkward again. Two for two. Class. Sit down, I'll be with you in a minute."

Mara nodded and sat at the bar.

Say what you would about the Temple, but it was a real Irish pub. It had an unmistakable "pubness" to it. The bar in Kilty's hostel looked like it was doing an impression of a pub, with any random furniture that could be found.

Mara was offered a beer in a plastic cup, which she refused with grace and civility and asked for a tea.

While Kilty's might not be winning any hospitality awards it had one saving virtue. It was away from Ballydonn, used only by tourists, and safe from prying local eyes. She took out the two phone registries and continued her search for missing people, and hopefully a match for her mystery man.

Going back over the sheets, she tried to find "Mara Fitch" again in the older directory. It could be that it was simply older than two years, from before she was supposedly on the island. Also, logically, Martin Connell and Sara Do could very easily have moved away in that time rather than having died in a freak outbreak . . .

She stopped.

A chill swept up her back like a winter wave.

She remembered her first meeting with Declan.

Suck it up, Dunne. You're not the only one with problems.

And there she was. In black and white.

MARA

Dunne, Mara.

And, the next line down. With the same phone number.

Dunne, Oisín.

Mara took a deep breath.

"Sorry, were you on telly or something?"

She looked up to see Natalie slumped over the bar, head balanced on both hands, gazing at her intently.

"Telly?" Mara repeated.

"I *know* I've seen you before and it's driving me mad. Are you famous? Or Insta famous?"

Mara briefly considered explaining her situation, but found she didn't have the energy and simply shook her head.

"Nah, don't think so."

"Just one of those faces, then," Natalie sighed.

I need to talk to Declan, Mara thought to herself.

She considered walking to his house, but decided against it. She might be seen on the road, and it might get back to Cian, and wouldn't *that* be a delight? She needed to meet with him somewhere innocuous, indoors, and preferably away from Ballydonn. She had an idea.

She wrote down her mobile number on a blank corner of the front page of the phone registry and tore it off.

"Hey," she said. "Is there a guy who comes in here fairly regularly? Kinda husky? Dark hair? Dublin accent? You might have seen him at the open mic night, actually."

"Oh yeah, I think I know him," Natalie replied with a nod.

"Could you give him this the next time you see him? And tell him I really, really need him to give me a call?"

"Okay?" she said, taking the number with a look that said she might not get it, but that it took all kinds to make the world go round.

22
Malachy

When the phone rang, his first thought was of the Bad Penny.

What's she done now?

He got out of bed, grumbling, and went into the kitchen to answer it.

"Malachy, where are you?" said a voice. The tone was gruff, and most would not have heard the concern in it. Malachy did.

"I'm at home, Conn," Malachy said. "Didn't I tell you I wouldn't be coming tonight?"

"Malachy," Conn rumbled. "That was *last* week."

Malachy said nothing for a moment.

"Was it . . . Jaysus, what date is it?"

He glanced at the calendar on the wall. True enough, it was a week later in the month that he had thought. He hadn't left his room in days, and they were starting to blur into each other.

"So . . ." Conn said. "You're not coming?"

Malachy felt a deep pang of regret. The truth was, he did want to spend time with his brother. He wanted to get drunk

MALACHY

and play cards and talk about meaningless, harmless shite all night long. But it wasn't time. He wasn't ready.

"I'm sorry, Conn. I . . . I'm not up to it. Not yet."

There was a long, awful pause.

Ah, he knows. He knows now. He's no fool.

"Malachy," Conn whispered. "Are you . . . not well?"

"Ah, I'm grand, sure," Malachy replied, forcing a smile on his face, which felt like the hardest thing he'd ever had to do. "Don't you be worrying."

Before his brother could answer, Malachy hung up and took a deep breath.

He wandered into the bathroom and turned on the light, which bathed him in a sickly green hue.

He looked at himself, dressed for bed in a filthy "white" vest and equally soiled striped drawstring pajama bottoms.

Christ, you're an ugly fucker, he castigated himself. *They were never able to marry you off and isn't it no wonder?*

He took a deep breath and slowly, painfully pulled the vest off and turned so that he could see his back.

What he saw forced a low moan of despair from his lips.

There it was. The hump.

A cluster of fleshy growths, between one and three inches long, had sprouted out of the hairy, mole-covered flesh of his back. Fingers. He could even see a tiny fingernail on the largest one.

Malachy Rowan, if nothing else, was not a man prone to wallowing in self-pity. He went down into the shop, to his small, understocked hardware section, and picked up a set of gardening shears from the shelf. He also took a roll of paper towels, some disinfectant, and sticky tape.

It was not the pain so much. Or the blood.

It was the realization that some of the growths had bones in them. The biggest one actually gave the shears some trouble, the bone was so thick.

He could feel the weight of them as they tumbled down his back after each one was cut, landing on the tiles with a solid, moist thud.

It was only a matter of time now.

It was, he mused as he taped five squares of kitchen roll to his back to stanch the bleeding, a textbook example of a situation that would get worse before it got better. Because it would never get better.

He swept up the severed fingers and cast them into the kitchen bin like they were table scraps.

The next time he saw Conn, he thought regretfully, it would be their last game.

23

Padraig

We didn't call a meeting for poor Daithí Griffin, Padraig mused to himself. *We'll call it for the sheep, though.*

The Comhairle, or some of them, at least, sat around the table in the basement of the Temple, waiting for Gráinne to start the meeting.

He remembered how disappointed he'd been the first time he'd come to one of these. He'd been expecting hoods and candles. Maybe some chanting. A pentagram for atmosphere, although most of the older members of the Comhairle would probably have balked at that.

Instead, it was just people that he knew, chatting in a room.

Tom Harte, who ran the petrol station, was sitting across from Padraig, with a can of Budweiser (sans coaster) on the table, telling a joke about a French footballer and a flock of geese. Every so often, he would turn and meet Padraig's eye and Padraig would look away.

He didn't even like Tom.

Tom was bad news.

Tom smelt of petrol, which meant if he got his hands on you, you smelt of petrol too for days, unless you went home and changed immediately. He wasn't nearly handsome enough to make his arrogance stomachable, and he had always just the wrong amount of stubble.

None of that meant the answer was "no."

The pool on Inishbannock was already too small to be picky, and had gotten smaller still since the "outbreak." So yes, Padraig would find himself wandering up to Harte's for petrol.

He just wished that he could telepathically send two words to Tom: *Not here*.

Tom, who was practically licking the air and hip thrusting at him, while Padraig's mother sat beside him, thankfully oblivious.

If any two words could sum up the relationship (*that fucking word*) between Padraig and Tom, that was it. *Not here*.

There never seemed to be enough space. The rooms were too small. The houses were too small. The island was too small.

Beside him, his mother stood and the room fell silent. She didn't need to bang a gavel.

Some people are the gavel.

It was a small meeting, which meant serious business was to be discussed.

The Comhairle was like a church. Who was a member? Everyone. Everyone on the island was welcome to join and participate. But, just as some parishioners came only on Christmas and Easter, and some every Sunday, and a select few every day, the Comhairle had levels.

As a general rule, the longer your family had been on the island, the deeper you were. There were exceptions of course. Sarah Do (RIP), had been born in Hội An, ten thousand kilometers from Inishbannock. And yet she had been, before her unfortunate end, right in the inner circle.

And, just like a church, it was impossible to know who truly believed what. How much was true faith, how much simply tradition and ritual.

It was probably better that way.

Padraig realized that his mother had been talking and he hadn't been paying attention.

"... Problems with the wildlife," she was saying. "Brendan lost three ewes only last week. James thinks he lost another, though we never found the carcass. I think we need to have a few patrols for the next couple of months until things settle down."

"*Will* things settle down?" Brendan Sweeney asked, with the tone of a man who was down three sheep and not at all keen to be down any more.

Gráinne gave him a look. Brendan Sweeney was a large man, but under her gaze he seemed to evaporate like a lump of butter in a hot pan.

"What I mean is . . ." he said. "It's unusual, isn't it? We don't normally see attacks this early. Especially with what happened to Daithí . . ."

Padraig winced inwardly.

Brendan, you bloody fool. We're talking about sheep, not people. The sheep are Princess Di.

Daithí was Mother Teresa.

"There's nothing unusual about these attacks," Gráinne said coldly. "They happen. They stop. It's always been that way. It's just nature taking its course."

"I just . . ." Brendan said.

"What?" Gráinne snapped.

He sighed. "It feels . . . off this time. It feels like the island is . . . it's all just off."

"It's been like this for a while now," another voice said. "It's cloudy all the time, the weather's getting worse. The fish hauls aren't as big . . ."

Gráinne raised a hand sharply and Padraig thought she was going to lose her temper.

Instead, she took a deep breath and when she spoke, it was with a quiet melancholy.

"Gentlemen," she said. "I hate to break it to you. But that's not an Inishbannock problem. That's a Planet Earth problem. And we've been blessed for most of our history. But even blessings only go so far. That's why we approved the wind farm. That's why we decided to open the campsite. That's why, God and the Minister for Rural and Community Development willing, we'll have broadband next year. We need to adapt to survive as a people. And we are. And we will."

From the back of the table, a hand was raised.

"Yes, Mr. Morley?" Gráinne asked in a tone that made every man at the table instinctively close his legs.

"Sorry, I know I'm new here," Cian said. "But this problem you're having with the sheep. I think this seems to be a bigger problem than maybe you're treating it."

"Go on," Gráinne invited.

"You have . . . *we* have a lot of people on the island now. New people. The tourists. My crew working on the wind farm. People who . . . if anything was to happen to them . . . well, we don't want have our dirty laundry aired in public, do we?"

"Indeed we do not," Gráinne agreed.

PADRAIG

"Right, so what I'm thinking is . . . we need to be a bit more aggressive?"

"What do you suggest?" Gráinne asked.

"Well . . ." Cian said, and Padraig had to admit a grudging respect for any man who could keep going under the fire of Gráinne's glare. "Why patrol when you can hunt? Why don't we just load up, go down under this island, and . . ." He mimed shooting a pistol.

A stony silence fell around the table.

Gráinne gave a laugh. Singular. Very singular.

"You're right, Mr. Morley," she said. "You are new here. Very, very new. So, let me explain two things. First. The wildlife of this island has every bit as much a right to it as we do. More, perhaps. We must always try and live in harmony with them. For their sake and for ours."

"What's the second?"

"The second is that you do not have the faintest conception what is under this island. And if you have a lick of sense, you shall keep it that way."

"I think a patrol is a great idea," Tom chimed in. "I can do tomorrow night. How 'bout it, Podge?"

He glanced over at Padraig.

Padraig wanted to tell Tom that he had said, again and again, that he hated being called "Podge." He wanted to tell them all he was leaving. That he was going to find a place far away from Inishbannock, where it didn't feel like he was spending his life begging for scraps of happiness.

Instead, he simply nodded and said "sure."

. . .

Five teams, two men each. North. South. West. East. Outskirts of Ballydonn and Farvey.

On foot. Armed with shotguns. Gráinne in the car, driving around the island, checking in.

Padraig and Tom had the north of the island. Tom waited around twenty minutes.

"Fuck!" Padraig heard him shout. "Look at the size of it!"

Padraig spun around, hand gripping his shotgun, expecting to see . . .

Well. Not that.

Tom Harte was standing in the middle of the midnight road, his pants around his ankles, his torch pointing at his pale, flaccid cock, which he jiggled playfully. But his expression was darker.

"C'mon, Podge," he said quietly. "On your knees, chop-chop."

"Fuck off, Tom," Padraig said quietly, and turned and walked away.

He heard Tom fumbling desperately with his belt and trousers, while simultaneously picking up his shotgun from where he'd dropped it on the road, and briefly hoped that he'd accidentally shoot himself in the bollocks.

"Oh what?" Tom yelled after him accusingly. "You're too good for me now?"

"Tom, there's fucking livestock on this island that's too good for you!" Padraig hissed over his shoulder. "And will you please shut the fuck up?"

"Oh what, you're scared your ma will drive up and see you enjoying a nice big . . ."

"Hello."

Both men spun around in the dark.

PADRAIG

The voice had sounded friendly. Elderly. Gentle. A grandfather talking to a small child.

Padraig could feel the hair on his skin becoming as sharp as needles.

"Hello," it came again.

"Who's there?" Padraig called out, trying desperately to keep his voice even.

"Hello."

"There . . ." Tom whispered, pointing his torch at the drystone wall.

There was a head on the wall.

A tiny old man, pale as the moon in the light of the torch, stared at them. There was nothing else of him to be seen.

"Hello," he said again. His eyes were not looking at them. He was staring straight ahead.

"Hello?" Tom answered, taking a few tentative steps toward the old man.

"Tom?" Padraig whispered.

"Hello," said the old man.

"Hello! Yes!" Tom barked angrily. "Hello, who the fuck are you?"

"Do you not recognize him, Tom?" Padraig said.

"What?" Tom said, peering intently at the wrinkled elderly features staring blankly at him.

"That's Daithí Griffin," Padraig said softly.

It was only then that Padraig noticed the two hands, aloft, in the air above Tom.

They were as large as condors, suspended on arms as long and thin as ribbon. He thought of them as "hands" but they could only be called that if one didn't have rigid notions on fingers, either regarding length or number.

"Hello . . ." the head on the wall said.

The rest happened in seconds.

The hands descended, the head vanished from the top of the wall, and a great mass seemed to bubble up to replace it. Padraig dimly saw a mouth open and Tom Harte's screaming, twisting form get wrapped firmly in those almost hands and shoved headfirst into the massive maw.

Padraig heard Tom's desperate shrieks, and then a sound like a boulder striking mud, as Tom's legs, which had been kicking furiously, shuddered and went still.

Padraig had been about to fire his shotgun, but now held off.

If Tom was dead (and he was, he was) then best to let the creature finish its meal. He knew from long, bitter experience that a disappearance was easier to deal with than a corpse. Or half of one.

Grabbing Tom's gun, Padraig kept both barrels trained on it as the fallen torch half lit the creature. He could make out Daithí Griffin's head, growing out of a plateau of flesh, like a boil, the eyes rolled back.

He waited. He waited for the last crunch of bone, and then the silence.

In the distance, he heard a distant roar.

It was his mother coming to check on the patrol. The harsh headlights bathed the road and suddenly he could see it. Every awful inch of it.

And in that moment he felt a hatred that he'd never even known was possible.

Padraig fired and the creature made a sound like an entire choir screaming in pain.

PADRAIG

He saw the great hands fold back and settle on its back, like the wings of a wasp, and then it skittered through the undergrowth, as weightless as a nightmare.

They were almost impossible to kill, but they did not like pain.

The Range Rover pulled to a stop and the door flew open.

"It got Tom!" he yelled. "This way!"

"Padraig!" he heard his mother call after him. "Padraig, wait!"

• • •

You weren't supposed to chase them.

They were to be driven off, with fire or gunshot. But never hunted. Never pursued.

It wasn't that it had killed Tom. He hadn't loved Tom. He hadn't even liked him. He, in fact, had hated Tom as a prisoner in a cell might hate a painting of the outside world. Tom had been a miserable, pale imitation of everything he wanted and could not have.

And the island couldn't let him have even that.

So Padraig raced through the darkness, searching for any trace of the thing that had stolen Daithí Griffin's face and eaten Tom Harte alive.

If he could not kill the island, he would kill the creature.

And then, suddenly, the earth gave way beneath him and he felt his legs dangling over nothingness.

Panicked, his hands touched what felt like brick and he pulled himself up.

He lay on the ground, gasping for air. He heard the trump of boots on the ground and white light fell on his face.

Gráinne, looking *so* old, was staring down at him with an expression of pure shock.

How could you do that to me?

"Padraig!" she said. "What are you like, love?"

"I . . . I . . . Mam, it killed Tom. I saw it. I just. I couldn't . . . I . . . I . . . I can't do this anymore . . ."

"Ah, love," she said in a hoarse whisper.

She offered him her hand and pulled him up.

She embraced him.

"I know it's hard, *a mhic*," she said. "Don't think for a second I don't."

He let his mother hold him for a few minutes. Taking her torch, he cast it around.

They were standing near the ruins of a tiny cottage, two walls left barely standing, held up by ivy.

Padraig had been here before. He knew all the secret places on the island. Anywhere that you could hide away, or hide someone away. Living or dead. He knew them all.

But it was not a place he would have come willingly. He knew its history.

He turned to look at his mother, and could see in her face that she knew it, too, and wished nothing more than to be gone from this place.

Padraig glanced down at where he had tripped and staggered back, his arm reaching out to guard Gráinne.

"Fuck . . ." he breathed.

He had nearly dropped down a well. Or, rather, the remains of a well. A stone semi-circle still stood upright, but the rest of the well had caved in, leaving a massive black pit in the earth.

PADRAIG

"Well," said Gráinne somberly. "We know where it came up from, at least. We can seal that up. Safer for everyone. Come on."

She turned, and headed back in the direction of the car.

He followed her.

She asked him if he thought that Tom Harte had seemed depressed the last few weeks.

He sighed, and nodded.

24
Declan

After his row with Mara on the beach, Declan had gone home and retreated into himself for weeks.

He tried to write but was too angry and nothing came. Anger turned to frustration, which turned to apathy, which turned to depression, which stayed and stayed and stayed, layer upon layer. Day after day.

His sleep cycle warped, and then broke, and then flipped, and he found himself sleeping through the day and lying awake at night, his mind shining, anxious and ragged as exposed wire.

One night, as he lay in bed, he heard what he thought must have been a fox crying, an awful, eerily human scream of agony.

And then, a sound that he had only heard in movies. A sound that, even living in the inner city in Dublin, he had never heard and that he certainly never expected to hear on this, the last, most remote settlement in the Republic.

A gunshot.

The report rang out through the silent Inishbannock night.

DECLAN

Wearily, unsteadily, he got out of bed and shambled toward the window.

Far in the distance, a car had stopped in the middle of the road, its high beams on. There was someone standing on the road, and Declan thought he could see this figure holding a shotgun. A second person emerged from the car, and the first vaulted over the dry-stone wall into the field beyond. The driver pursued the shooter, running with impressive speed while shining a torch ahead of them.

By the light of the torch he saw what they were chasing.

You're dreaming, he told himself. *That's all it is. You finally tired yourself out and got some sleep.*

So Declan felt nothing as he watched the thing clench and writhe toward a ruin in the middle of the field, its flesh pale as chicken fat, a multitude of mouths grimacing and gnashing over its body like open sores. Because he knew it was a dream, that it had to be a dream.

If I was awake. If I was awake and saw that thing?
I would scream and scream until my lungs gave out.

25
Mara

It was a couple of days after talking with Natalie that she finally received a single-word text from a number she didn't recognize:

> Yeah?

It could only be Declan.
Great, he's still pissed off. How fun.
She decided to be the bigger woman and not get drawn into an argument.

> Hey. So I realize you're probably sick of me and my weird bullshit but in case you're not I have a lot more info now and I really need someone I can talk to who won't think I'm crazy. Can I buy you a coffee in Kilty's?

There was a long pause before her phone flashed again.

MARA

> Mara, if you actually think your weird bullshit can top my weird bullshit? You're on . . .

• • •

Natalie flashed her a salacious grin as she walked into the bar that evening.

"He's waitin' for you," she said with a wink, nodding at Declan sitting in the corner.

She was so very clearly happy at having played matchmaker that Mara didn't have the heart to disabuse her.

Sliding onto the stool next to Declan, she gave him a once-over. He looked pale, and a bit hollow around the eyes, like he hadn't been sleeping.

"So I've been trying to find out more about the guy you saw me here with."

Declan looked pained.

"Yeah," he murmured. "About him . . ."

But she was already rifling through her bag and taking out the two phone registries she'd stolen from the library. Softly, Mara explained how she'd used them to learn more about who had died in the outbreak.

"And you think this Mara Dunne . . ."

"Well, you said that's what Quinn called me, right?"

"I mean, I think so? It was a while ago now . . ."

"Declan . . ."

He nodded, firmly. As if deciding to stop second-guessing himself. "She did. She definitely did."

"There's no Mara Fitch in this first directory," she told him. "Only Mara Dunne. Who shared a phone number with Oisín Dunne."

"So you think . . ."

"I know. I know it's crazy . . ."

"Oh, I think I've got you beat for crazy," he said with a deep breath.

"Go on," she said.

He's scared, she thought. *Something has spooked him.*

"Few nights ago," he murmured. "I saw something from my window. There were these two . . . farmers, I think? And they were shooting at something."

"What was it?" she asked.

"Mara," he said quietly. "If I knew how to describe it, I wouldn't have said 'something.'"

"An animal?"

He shook his head. "I thought I must have dreamed it. But when I went down to the road the next day, I found a shell casing."

"Weeks ago, I found a shotgun stashed under a hedge. On another part of the island. They must have been shooting over there, too," Mara said.

"What the fuck is going on?"

"The old woman who showed me the gun, Bridie. I just thought she was daft, but she said they're eating the sheep."

"They?"

"Whatever they are. She called them the Fomor . . ."

There was an excited squeal from behind the bar and Declan and Mara both almost jumped out of their skin.

"Sorry," said Natalie. "Didn't mean to eavesdrop. Were you talking about the Fomor?"

Mara and Declan shared a stunned look.

"You . . . know about the Fomor?" Mara asked.

"Course!" she replied. "I fucking LOVE Irish mythology, look . . ."

She turned to show the tattoo that Mara had seen before. "That's my Morrigan. I've also got one on my back, here . . . No, I can't show you that," she said after a second's regretful reflection. "But yeah, I love all of that. The Tuatha Dé Danann. The Fomor. Ask me anything."

"Okay," said Mara, not about to look a gift horse in the mouth. "What are they?"

"Oh," Natalie replied, as she apparently had been expecting something a bit more specific. "Okay, well. The Fomorians. Or Fomors. Or Fomori. They're basically the villains of the Mythological Cycle. They're monsters who come from the sea and make war on the different peoples living in Ireland. They bring disease, eat children . . ."

"What do they look like?" Declan interrupted. "I mean . . . what are they supposed to look like?"

"Ah, so," she said, with air of an expert about to expound on a favorite topic. "So the Gaels were really obsessed with this idea of physical, sort of, wholeness? Like, they wouldn't let you be king if you were missing an arm or an eye. And the Fomorians are kind of the ultimate expression of that fear. Like they all have, like, one arm or three arms or no head or two. Basically the human body, just gone . . . wrong."

"Right," Declan whispered, suddenly looking very pale. "Right. Thanks."

There was an awkward silence.

"Right. Well," said Natalie, clearly sensing that the conversation had reached a natural end. "I will . . . okay. Bye."

She went back to the bar.

Mara and Declan stared at each other. She had a sudden urge to take his hand. It felt like she was slipping into madness, and he was the only other person who could see it happening.

There was a long silence.

"I think I owe you an apology," he said at last.

"Why?" she asked.

"I left you on the beach because of what you said about finding that picture . . ."

"No, look, I'm sorry. I shouldn't have expected you to believe me."

"Mara, I do believe you," he said. "After what I saw . . . I think it *was* you in that picture."

More madness. She tried to put the brakes on. "I've been thinking about that. I think the person who I saw in that picture might have been a relative of mine. I mean, obviously it couldn't have been me."

"Yeah. That's what I used to think," Declan said in a hushed voice.

"What do you mean?"

"After I saw them shooting at that . . . whatever it was. I decided to go to the library. See if there was any books about . . . I dunno. And I saw those old photographs they have in the library. You know them?"

"Yeah?"

"Did you look at them?" Declan asked Mara.

"Not closely."

"Well, I did," he said. "And I found this."

He took out his phone and showed her a photo he had taken of one of the pictures. She recognized it as the parade to celebrate Kerry's victory in the All-Ireland. It looked like the entire island was crammed onto Main Street.

"When would you say that picture you found in Conn's house was from?" he asked.

She sighed. "I dunno. I couldn't tell. Twenties? Thirties? It all looks the same."

"Well, this is from 1980. And look who's there . . ."

He zoomed in with finger and thumb and there, grainy but still recognizable, was Conn Rowen. He looked to be in his fifties or thereabouts. Hale and hearty, with an impressive brown beard, but already clearly starting to go bald.

"And look who he's with . . ." Declan continued.

There she was.

Mara Fitch.

Mara Dunne?

Mara Rowen?

She was standing beside Conn, her arm entwined with his. A couple, clearly.

And between the old black-and-white picture she had found in Conn's laundry basket, to the picture before her now, to the image she had seen in the mirror this morning, there was not an inch of difference.

It was the same woman.

It was her.

"So," Declan whispered quietly. "Did I win?"

"Win what?"

"Does my weird bullshit beat your weird bullshit?"

She realized that if he was the kind of man who could make jokes at a time like this, then he was someone she wanted in her life.

"Well, technically," she said with an affronted air. "This is ALL my weird bullshit. Don't you go appropriating my weird bullshit."

"Sorry," he said with a laugh.

"This has been my weird bullshit since I woke up in that damn coffin."

She had said that, perhaps, a little too loudly.

There was the crash of a mug splintering on the ground and their heads snapped around to see Natalie leaning against the bar for support, a trembling finger pointed at Mara.

"I *knew* I recognized ya!" she said, her Cork accent coming out as stark as paint under the stress. "You fucking DIED!"

26
Mara

"Big question first," Natalie said as she nervously tapped the bar with long black-and-pink fingernails.

"Go ahead," said Mara.

"Uhhhhh, like. You know. God. Heaven. Hell? How fucked am I?"

"I . . . sorry, I don't remember," said Mara apologetically.

"Don't remember as in 'just endless black nothingness' or . . ."

"As in, 'I don't remember anything.' But I don't remember anything from before I woke up in the coffin, and I'm pretty sure that stuff happened so . . . who knows? Besides. I don't think I was actually, properly dead. I mean. I can't have been, right?"

"Right. Right," Natalie said, clearly not knowing whether to be worried or relieved.

"So, you know me?" Mara said. "You remember me?"

"Yeah. I saw you come in here once with your . . ." She glanced awkwardly between the two. "Your . . . guy . . . friend?"

"Yeah," said Mara. "We're still trying to figure that out."

"You don't know who he was?"

"We're like Socrates over here," said Declan.

Mara and Natalie exchanged a curious glance.

"Greek?" Natalie chanced.

"All we know is that we know nothing," Declan clarified.

"Right so," said Natalie after a few seconds.

"But it was definitely *me*, you saw?" Mara pushed.

"Yeah. I remember because you both looked really nervous, like? It was my first day on the island actually. You sat in the corner and you whispered to each other. And you pretty much ignored me."

"Sorry," said Mara.

"'S'alright," said Natalie.

"Did you listen to us talking? Like you did just now?" Mara asked.

Natalie looked a little embarrassed. "Not really. I think you were talking about moving? Yeah. You were saying that you wanted to leave the island. And he was all, 'We will, we will, but not yet.' He was trying to keep you calm and then . . . you'd obviously had enough because you stormed out."

"And then what happened?" Mara asked.

Natalie shrugged. "He paid and left. Gave a good tip. Sorry, it really wasn't as dramatic as I'm making it sound. You didn't flip a table or anything."

Mara frowned. "Then why did you even remember me?"

Natalie blushed. "Don't judge me, okay? So. That same week. My first week on the island. This really cute Danish couple, think Ryan Gosling and Kate Moss—but Danish— they were staying in the campsite and they came into the bar and it was their last day on the island. So we get chatting and they . . . asked me if I wanted to go down to the beach with them and have a few drinks. And I did. We went down to the beach. Had a few drinks. And stuff happened."

"This was your first week?" Declan asked.

"Yeah," said Natalie with a smile. "Good start to the summer. Anyway. So, I woke up on the beach and I start walking home. This is like . . . five in the morning, yeah? But I went the wrong way because . . ."

"You were pissed?" Declan suggested.

"I was *slightly chemically confused*," Natalie said grandly. "And I ended up walking into Ballydonn instead of back to the hostel. And there were people there. Outside the church."

"Did you recognize them?" Mara asked.

Natalie shook her head.

"What were they doing?"

"They were making a shrine," she said. "They were laying flowers. And lighting candles. And putting out photographs. And then they prayed. I didn't want to interrupt, so I just stayed beside the pump watching them. And then they finished and walked away. Some of them there were even in tears, I think. Like, you could tell something awful had happened. After they went, I walked up to see what had happened and I saw you."

"Me?"

"Your picture."

"Yeah," Declan nodded. "I saw it, too. The morning they announced the quarantine."

"And there was the guy. The guy you were with was also dead," Natalie said. "And I was, y'know, shocked. I was like, 'Fuck, I SAW her. Just a few days ago. She was alive.' And I just burst into tears. Because, y'know . . ."

Natalie stopped. Mara was looking at Declan with an unsettlingly intense look.

"Declan," Mara said quietly. "You saw that picture of the man, too?"

"Yeah," he whispered, not meeting her gaze. "I did."

"Why didn't you tell me?" she said, coldly furious.

Declan looked miserable. "I . . . the night you showed up in my house, I didn't want to tell you because . . . you seemed like you'd been through enough. And I couldn't be sure. And you had a knife."

"I mean," Natalie chipped in. "As a neutral party, that sounds like a good excuse to me."

Mara did not agree. "That was *weeks* ago, Declan, all this time you never mentioned . . ."

"I thought I was wrong!" he blustered. "When I heard Cian was still alive, and he was your boyfriend, I just assumed that he was the bloke I'd seen you with here, and that I'd made a mistake. And then when I saw Cian . . . I've been trying to figure out how to tell you since that night on the pier . . ." He trailed off miserably.

At that moment, Natalie decided to be a hero. "*Anyway*," she said, trying to move them past the current awkwardness. "I found my way back to the hostel, and the next morning everything went nuts. There was a guard wearing a mask, who came down telling everyone there was a quarantine, and not to leave or go anywhere. I thought I was going to die! I was like, 'Oh shit, that's what killed those people, and I went into the village, and now I've probably got this thing' . . . you know?"

Mara heard Declan give a deep sigh.

MARA

"Then, suddenly it's over!" Natalie spread her hands past her ears. "And we're all supposed to go back to normal, and I'm like . . . no one's reported this! I've managed to get on the internet a few times and no one's even mentioned it. I don't think anyone on the mainland even knows that there was an outbreak on the island. And I've tried asking people in the village and no one will tell me anything. At first I just thought it was because I'm, y'know . . ."

There was an awkward beat.

"You mean . . ." Mara said quietly.

"From Cork, yeah," Natalie said. "Everyone hates people from Cork. Especially in Kerry. Big hurling rivalry."

"That's true," said Declan, nodding solemnly.

"But now I think . . . I dunno. Something's sketch. This whole island is sketch. It's a sketchy island. So wait, you're not actually dead?"

"I am not actually dead," Mara confirmed.

"So does that mean those other people are still . . . alive?"

Mara shook her head. "I don't know. Somehow I don't think so."

"Oh," said Natalie. "I'm really sorry."

Mara shrugged. "I don't even know who they were. Who that man was—Oisín? That's part of the problem." A thought occurred to her. "Natalie, just so I can be sure, this wasn't the guy you saw me with?" Mara asked, bringing up a picture of Cian on her phone.

"Hello . . ." Natalie murmured softly. "No, not him. Would remember."

"That's her boyfriend," Declan supplied, helpfully.

"Oh," said Natalie and her eyes narrowed slightly.

"What?" Mara asked.

"How long have you been together?"

"Two years. Allegedly."

"Allegedly? Oh. Right. Your brain."

"My brain, yeah."

"Okay," said Natalie. But Mara could sense a . . . what was it now? A little judgment in Natalie's tone.

Oh. Oh fuck.

You both looked really nervous.

You were talking about leaving the island.

He was all, "We will, we will, but not yet."

Suddenly, like a Rorschach test that had looked like a butterfly and now morphed into a skull, the events of the past few weeks took on a new shape.

Everyone lying to you.

This memory of a vanished man.

The feelings of resentment and guilt she always felt around Cian.

His possessiveness.

His jealousy.

What if . . . what if he had a good reason?

What if you gave him a good reason, Mara?

What if you were having an affair?

She dismissed the thought. No, that didn't explain it. It didn't explain why she'd been buried alive.

It didn't explain the photos or her name being listed as "Dunne" in the older phone register.

It didn't explain *anything*.

She zoned back into the conversation. Declan was complaining that the shrine had been cleared away, otherwise they could go into the village and Mara could see the face of the man that both he and Natalie had seen her with.

MARA

"He's in the graveyard," Mara said dully. "When I . . . got out. There were three other graves beside mine. No markings. No gravestones. But I'm pretty sure that's where the people who died are buried."

"Well, have you been back there since?" Natalie asked. "I mean, they have to have put up some gravestones by now, right? You can't just bury people and pretend they never existed. Someone's going to ask questions eventually?"

"We could go and check?" Declan suggested.

"C'mon," said Natalie. "Field trip to the graveyard. I'll drive."

27
Mara

"I thought visitors weren't allowed to drive cars on the island?" Declan said quietly after Natalie had raised the shutters on the tiny garage behind the hostel.

"I mean, technically it's not a car?" Mara pointed out.

"It" was a tiny 1980s Suzuki Carry van that had been painted to look like the A-Team van in a way that reminded Mara of a scrawny schoolboy wearing a leather jacket to look tough.

The years had not been kind to it, and the sea air less so. Mara suspected it had not been washed in the last decade, purely because the thick skin of grime, mud, and pulped insect life was all that was holding the vehicle together. Cleaning this van would be like an eighty-nine-year-old chain-smoker quitting cigarettes. Too late now, and the shock could well be fatal.

"It's Pajo's," Natalie told Declan. "He gets me to do supply runs from the village in this thing."

"Who's Pajo?" Mara asked.

"Pajo Kilty. My boss. I've seen him literally once since coming here. He's the worst boss and the best boss. All aboard."

MARA

Mara sat in the passenger seat while Declan squatted behind them in the cabin. She reached for the passenger seat belt only to find that there wasn't one, nor was there any sign that there ever had been. Declan leaned over to watch with increasing anxiety as Natalie slowly and methodically ran through a start-up procedure.

"Okay, ignition. Indicate. Hand brake, and away we go . . ."

The van shuddered and the engine whined into agonized life.

"I think it's in pain," Mara said. "I feel guilty riding in this thing."

"Uh, Natalie, you *do* have a license, yeah?" Declan asked as Natalie successfully coaxed the van out onto the road and narrowly missed powderizing a garden gnome.

"Nah, don't worry. We're not on the mainland. You don't need one out here," Natalie said.

Mara, no legal expert, was nonetheless pretty certain that was not the case.

. . .

We should have waited until tomorrow, Mara thought. *I wasn't ready to come back here at night.*

Natalie had turned on her phone flashlight and the sound of the three of them tramping through the bracken and brambles of the graveyard dispelled a little of the feeling of dread but, Mara realized, she would much rather not be here.

"I can't believe we're doing this," Natalie said, her voice breathy with excitement. "It's like we're *asking* to be murdered."

"Yeah. Great," Declan muttered.

Mara stopped. There was the lamppost. There was the tree. There was the grave of Mara Fitch.

"Here," she said, pointing to the ground.

Natalie shone her light on the ground and blades of grass shimmered like the hairs rising on the back of an enraged cat.

"You sure?" Declan asked. "That doesn't look like a grave."

"They re-sodded it," Mara whispered. "They covered it up. Literally."

Natalie stood up straight, her lips pursed and her brow scrunched. "Hang on. You woke up in a coffin?"

"I did," Mara said, in a tone that said the topic under discussion was the one topic she did not want to be thinking of right now.

"And how did you get out? Exactly?"

"I . . . I just punched until the lid broke. What?"

Natalie was looking at her in astonishment. "So you just Bruce Lee'd your way out?" She turned to Declan. "*You* don't think that's weird?"

"What?" Declan said.

"She must be a hundred pounds wet! You don't think it's weird that a woman her size was able to punch her way out of a solid-wood coffin that was buried six feet under?"

"Well . . . yeah," said Declan. "But I can't *say* that, what year do you think this is?"

"It was raining," Mara explained. "The soil over the coffin was just muddy water. I cracked the lid and the weight of the water broke it and I just . . . swam."

Natalie raised a sceptical eyebrow but said nothing.

"And now the grave's been filled in and covered up. Did they change anything else?" asked Declan.

MARA

"Yeah" said Mara. "Those are new."

Two headstones, one a black marble book with gold lettering, the other a simple white oval, now stood over the graves beside where Mara's had been.

She walked slowly down the lip of the burial plots, reading the stones as she went.

The first:

> MARTIN CONNELL (35) AND SARA DO (31)
> TOGETHER IN LIFE, TOGETHER IN DEATH,
> TOGETHER FOREVER

And the second:

> OISÍN DUNNE
>
> BELOVED HUSBAND, BROTHER, AND SON
> AR DHEIS DÉ GO RAIBH A ANAM

And on this one a ceramic photograph had been lovingly affixed.

A man. Tall. Pale. Brown hair. Green eyes. Big nose with a broken bridge. Slightly crooked front teeth. Smiling.

In that moment, Mara knew that she had taken the picture. The eyes in that photograph had gazed upon her, and the love that filled them was all for her. She reached out and brushed cold stone, and that was when the strength in her legs gave out and she was on her knees. Wailing.

Natalie almost leapt back at the sound. Declan put his hand to his mouth and looked away.

Mara wailed, not just in grief, but in fear.

She was digging deep into the mire of her memories and finding bones and grinning skulls. She didn't know what they meant, but they terrified her.

She could see a headless corpse, lying on kitchen tiles, splayed like a frog.

And Mara remembered rage. The feeling of her fingernails slipping into flesh as soft as butter.

And the perfect, lovely sensation of bone cracking and splintering between her teeth.

28
Mara

There was a car that she did not recognize in the driveway, a dark-blue Range Rover, parked close to Cian's silver Volvo, the two vehicles forming a blockade in front of her own door.

Natalie had tried to convince her to come back to the hostel, or at least let her and Declan come with, but Mara had told them there was no point. Cian was still on the mainland. Or so she had thought.

Well, let tonight be the night then.

And let him bring whatever reinforcements he wanted.

She walked through the front door and heard the sound of a conversation abruptly ending.

She took a deep breath.

Whatever comes next, you have lived through worse. Be strong.

She stepped into the living room.

She was not surprised to see Cian lounging in his favorite armchair, a faint hickey (that she knew she had not given him) just visible above the fold of his collar.

Nor, really, was she surprised to see Gráinne sitting across from him on the sofa.

Gráinne had her hair down, her long silver locks hanging loose. And she was wearing a man's jacket. Even the look she fixed on Mara was somehow more masculine. Less refined. Less controlled.

She stood as Mara came through the door, and Mara had a brief moment of panicked suspicion that Gráinne was going to try to hit her.

Instead, Gráinne stopped and appraised her with a look of mild disgust.

"Well," she said, looking at Mara but clearly not speaking to her. "I think you two have a lot to discuss. Good night, Cian."

"Good night, Gráinne," Cian replied.

Mara said nothing until the front door had closed.

"Where were you?" he asked.

His tone was as flat and cold as a steak knife.

"Taking a walk around the island," she said, her tone matching his.

"Who with?" he asked.

"Where were you?" she asked. "I thought you weren't supposed to be back until tomorrow?"

"Counting on that, were you?" he snapped. "Jesus. Tell me it wasn't that fat prick. And tell me at least it wasn't in our bed?"

She gestured to her collarbone. "You got a little something there, love," she said sweetly. "I hear toothpaste works wonders."

"Don't change the subject..."

"Cian. Cian, Cian, Cian," she said, realizing that she was enjoying this. The building anger. The anticipation. She was going to relish this fight, she knew it. "I know you've been lying to me."

MARA

She knew she'd hit. There was only silence. He was off-balance now. She'd changed the dance and he was trying to figure out the new rhythm.

"I'm not really Mara Fitch," she said.

His face was pale, his eyes were darting. She could practically hear the little wheels in his brain clicking.

Oh, you're fucking scared now, aren't you?

She reached into her handbag and pulled out the two phone registries.

"I went to the library," she told him. "And look what I found. Here's the most up-to-date list of people on the island. And there's you and me. And here's one from just before the 'outbreak.' And there's you, Cian. But I'm not living with you. I'm living with Oisín Dunne. And I'm married to him. What the fuck did you *do* to him?! And why did you lie about . . ."

She stopped.

Cian was laughing. Face buried in his hands. Sides shaking. He threw his head back and shouted, "Oh Jesus!" He stood up, turning his back to her. "Of course! Of course you'd find a way to be the victim! How could I ever have doubted you? Fucking tragic!"

He was laughing still, but she could hear the anger in it, like shards of glass hidden in candy floss.

"Okay," he said, spreading his arms like a magician about to do a trick. "You want the truth? Fine. Yes, Mara. We have been lying to you. All of us. The whole fucking island. Well, everyone who knows you at least. And you know why? You know what our big evil master plan is? We're trying to stop you *destroying your life. Again.*

"I know you were in the library. I know you stole the registries. Gráinne told me. And I knew, I just *knew* you were going to do this."

"Do what?" Mara asked.

"'Oh, I'm actually Mara Dunne,' 'Oh, I'm supposed to be with Oisín, he's the real man of my dreams, not Cian, who's put up with *every shitty thing I've ever done to him and is still too stupid to fucking walk!*'"

He picked up a coffee mug that Gráinne had left on the sofa arm and flung it at the wall where it shattered.

"I *am* Mara Dunne!" Mara yelled. "I visited Oisín's grave! I remember his face!"

"OF COURSE YOU DO, YOU SAT ON IT ENOUGH TIMES!" he roared.

There was a long, angry, heaving silence.

"Let's get some things straight," Cian said, breathing hard, picking up the older phone registry. "You're not on here," he said. "Because the house is in my name. I moved here first when we were still building. You followed me over and we didn't bother updating the register because we never use the landline anyway, because we're not fucking cave people. Yeah? Okay. Mara Dunne is not you. Her name was Mara Alice Dunne and everyone called her 'Alice.' She hated the name 'Mara' because she thought it was an old woman's name. Still with me? Two women on the same island with the same name. I know, what a coincidence. Wow."

Mara suddenly realized what he had said and felt a lump of ice forming in her stomach.

"Was?" she asked dully.

"Yeah, Mara," Cian said slowly. "Picked up on the past tense there, did you? See, Alice wasn't exactly what you'd call 'well adjusted.' She suffered from schizophrenia, anxiety, manic depression, paranoia, all the colors of the batshit rainbow. Awful for her, not so good for her husband, either. Poor Oisín. Gráinne's son."

Mara reeled. Whatever else Cian was saying, that part rang very true.

Yes. Just look at Padraig. Of course they're brothers. Is that why Gráinne was here tonight?

"And Oisín, I mean, he's trying to be a good man, he's trying to look after his wife. But he's cracking. He's lonely. He's miserable. He's vulnerable and oh, look. Who's this? Beautiful Mara Fitch who's just arrived on the island and doesn't know anybody. Who's just looking for a *friend*. Because that's how it always starts."

He gave her a look. Disgust, with a little pity for seasoning.

"But this isn't Dublin, Mara. You can't fuck a married man out here and not expect everyone to know. You can't expect his family not to find out. You can't expect his *wife* not to find out."

Mara had stopped breathing. She felt the weightless panic of a nightmare that keeps getting worse.

"So what do you think poor Alice did when she found out her husband had found another Mara? What does a paranoid schizophrenic do when she finds out she's been betrayed by the only human being she trusts?"

"You're lying . . ."

"She takes some petrol, she douses every room in the house they built together, and then she has one last smoke."

Mara folded herself into a chair. She had seen the house. The burnt remains. She had known that someone had died there. She had felt it.

Every piece was falling into place and the picture they revealed was horrifying.

"And I actually believed you, Mara. When you told me how sorry you were. How you never meant it to get so bad. That you were just lonely, and depressed, and that you'd never meant to hurt anyone. You told me you'd broken it off. I really thought we'd hit rock bottom and the only way was up."

Cian was staring out the window, his shoulders slumped, his voice trembling and yet numb, like he was delivering a eulogy and trying to get the words out without breaking into tears.

"And then I get a call from Gráinne telling me that you're dead. And that they'd found you. In bed. With him."

Mara felt a shudder of self-loathing rippling over her.

He turned and it almost looked like his eyes were glowing with rage and sadness.

"So when it turned out that you were still alive? And that you couldn't remember anything about your life before the outbreak? Yeah, we lied to you, Mara. Because we thought if you ever learned what a fucking monster you really are, and how much carnage you have caused to everyone who ever got close to you, that might, y'know, *upset* you." He spat the words like a cobra spitting venom. "Might make your recovery *a little harder*. We tried to help you. *I* tried to help you. And you tore my fucking heart out. Again."

And on those words he turned, walked up the stairs. She heard the bedroom door slam like a gunshot.

29
Declan

> So did he kill her or what?

Declan sat up in bed and stared blearily at Natalie's text, trying to form the words to reply.

> No. But she says she can't be around us anymore

> You don't really believe it do you?

It had been four days since their trip to the graveyard. It had really felt like they were onto something. Mara's reaction to Oisín's grave had been so visceral, he had truly believed that she was his wife and that the Big Lie was about to come crashing down.

And then . . .

Well. It had come crashing down. But sometimes you really are better off not knowing.

Did he believe it? Did he believe that Mara had been sleeping with a married man who had a vulnerable wife, and that Mara had driven her to suicide?

That even after all that, she had still pursued him?

He wanted to say Mara could never do something like that but . . . how could he? He didn't even know *this* Mara that well, not really. And as for who she was before she'd been buried? That might as well be a completely different woman.

He stared at Natalie's plaintive question on the screen and, poet that he was, answered with a shrug emoji.

There was no response. It really was amazing how some people could send different kinds of silence by text. This was an angry, sullen silence. A silence that let you know you were being judged.

> You have to admit it makes a lot of sense
> You thought they were having an affair too.
> We both did

Natalie replied instantly.

> I didn't know Mara then

He wanted to text, *You don't know her now*, but her next message arrived before he had a chance.

> Does she believe it? What Cian told her?

Declan sighed wearily.

> Yeah. I think she does. At least, she definitely feels guilty about spending so much time with me. She said she can see why Cian wasn't too happy about that. Given her "history"

DECLAN

> Oh fuck off

> Anyway. She doesn't want to see me anymore

There was another silence, but this one was sad and sympathetic.

> I'm sorry

He tried to think of something less cliché than "it is what it is." Natalie's typing began again.

> But . . .
> I think it's super sus. I mean, OK, if he doesn't want her hanging around with you I can KINDA understand that. Sorry. But not letting her see me just seems like he's isolating her. I mean it's not like I'm going to fuck her.

He was going to write something about enjoying a nice Danish or two, but his guardian angel tapped him on the shoulder and warned him this would not be a wise path to take.

> Sure you wouldn't

> I think someone's projecting

• • •

Declan decided to take a leisurely morning walk down to Farvey for, he told himself, no reason in particular.

His phone buzzed in his pocket and he was surprised how happy he was to see it was Natalie.

> Why does no one on the mainland know about the outbreak?

Declan thought. An excellent question.

> The islanders hushed it up?

> Why?

> Tourism?
> Trying to keep it secret like the shark in Jaws?

There was another pause.
At last a text arrived, wrapped in shame.

> I've never seen Jaws

• • •

"*How* have you not seen *Jaws*?" Declan asked Natalie as she made him a terrible coffee on Pajo Kilty's terrible coffee machine.

"It's one movie I haven't seen, why does everyone get like this when I tell them?" she asked as she passed him the cup. "There's your milk."

He took a sip and an awful thought hit him.

"Natalie," he said in a hushed voice. "Tell me you've seen *Star Wars*."

DECLAN

She glared at him and pointed to the door. "Okay, if you're going to be insulting you can just leave."

"Sorry," he said with a grin.

She looked around furtively and then leaned in. "You know. We could still go digging around ourselves?"

He smiled sadly. "We'd have to make it quick."

"Why?"

"They're kicking me off the island."

They had appeared yesterday morning at his door like the Gestapo in an old war movie. Gráinne had given him a soft smile, while her eyes looked like she was imagining skinning him with a potato peeler. Padraig stood by her side, the silent muscle.

She had, very apologetically, informed him that the Comhairle had recently had a budget meeting and discovered, to their immense embarrassment, that they did not have enough money to continue funding his residency on the island. She had graciously given him a week to clear out and said that she hoped he would come back to Inishbannock at some point in the distant future.

She had put a slight shine on the word "distant."

Declan had not said anything all through this because, quite frankly, the woman terrified him. But as they turned and walked back up the driveway he called after her.

"Is this about Mara?"

She had stopped and looked at him with studied curiosity. "Mara Fitch?" Gráinne had asked.

"Is there another Mara?" he had replied, and where had he gotten the courage to do that?

She took a step toward him then and Declan noted that Padraig did not move. Whatever was going to happen, the man obviously felt his mother was in no danger.

"No, Mr. Burke," Gráinne had said. "There isn't. Not anymore. There was my daughter-in-law, Mara Alice. Well. I thought of her more as my daughter, if I'm honest. And then some stranger came into our lives. And killed her. So you can understand, Mr. Burke, if we would rather you left, and not open up any more old wounds? Safe home."

• • •

"WHAT," was Natalie's stunned response.
"Yup."
"BASTARDS."
"Yup."
"Can you fight it?"
"Forget it, Jake. It's Inishbannock."
She looked at him awkwardly, clearly aware she wasn't getting the reference, but not willing to admit that to him.

Oh, Natalie. All this time you've wasted having sex with beautiful strangers on beaches and you could have been watching movies.

"I don't think so," he said with a weary shrug.
"So that's it?"
"That's it."
"Okay, want to come with me to the mainland?" she asked brightly.
"Why?"
"Well, if we've only got until the end of the week to solve this thing, we're probably going to need proper internet access, right?"
He smiled.

• • •

DECLAN

Every two weeks, a large ferry would come to the island, bringing supplies and visitors. It was even large enough to carry a car or two, if needed. Outside of those fortnightly visits, the only tether between Inishbannock and the mainland was Stiofán's tiny boat, which ran between Inishbannock and Dingle at noon, two o'clock, and six o'clock every day. For the princely sum of twenty-five euros, you could sit on the splintery bench at the bow, feel the wild Atlantic buck and try to shake you and the boat off like an unbroken stallion, and sense the boatman's eyes burning two smoldering holes in the back of your scalp.

Declan could not recall sleeping with Stiofán's mother, setting fire to his house, and shooting his dog, but assumed he must have done so. Nothing else could justify the sheer, palpable loathing he had felt from the ferryman the day Stiofán had first brought him to the island.

Indeed, part of the reason why Declan hadn't visited the mainland during his entire stay on Inishbannock was the certain knowledge that if he fell into the sea on the crossing over, Stiofán would not move a finger to save him.

When they arrived on the jetty, Declan was somehow relieved to see that Stiofán was every bit as surly and aggressive with Natalie. Nothing personal, then.

"So what's the plan when we get over there?" Natalie asked, trying to pitch her voice loudly enough to be heard over the roar of the engine and ocean, while still quiet enough not to be spied on by Stiofán.

"Remember that picture I showed you?"

"The woman who looks like Mara in the seventies or whenever?"

"Yeah. That's where we start."

• • •

"Ah, civilization," Natalie said, stretching her legs as she disembarked onto the wharf.

Declan nodded. It was strange how your perspective could change. When he'd arrived from Dublin, Dingle had seemed like a quaint little hamlet. But after weeks on Inishbannock, it felt like a bustling metropolis. There were people. Dozens of people. Out on the main road, he could see a *traffic jam* for God's sake.

"I'll be back to pick yiz up at half six," Stiofán grumbled. "Don't miss the boat. Or do. I don't give a shite."

• • •

"Ohhh my God, internet, I've missed you so much," Natalie said, scrolling through her social media feed in the Old Forge internet café. "I'm already getting angry and anxious. I feel like me again," she added, taking a bite from her scone.

"Okay, when you're done can you find anywhere with marriage records for County Kerry?"

"Here we go," she said after a few minutes browsing. "Should have all the church records from 1900 onward on here."

"We're looking for a marriage license for Conn Rowen."

"Got him. Oh."

He looked up at her. "What is it?"

"There's two. Looks like he was married twice."

Declan studied the screen.

"Nah. Look, this one's from 1929. He's old, he's not that old. This is the one we want. 1978."

DECLAN

She clicked it, bringing up a PDF of a marriage license, a rectangular grid populated with a combination of typed lettering and sloppy handwriting.

"Marriage solemnized at the Roman Catholic Church of Saint Brendan's, Ballydonn," Declan read aloud. "Date married: 4 April 1978. Conn Rowen. Age. Full? What's that mean?"

"It just means he's over twenty-one. Like, he's 'fully of age.' Doesn't need anyone's permission to get married," said Natalie.

"How'd you know that?" he asked, impressed.

"I was helping my nan last year. Family genealogy thing. Hang on. Hang the fuck on, look there."

Declan looked where she was pointing. It was the bride's name.

"Mary . . . Fitch."

He dug out his phone and pulled up the secondhand photograph he had taken from the Ballydonn library.

There she was. Mary Fitch. Her arms interlocked with that of her much older husband. A smile on her face as she watched the parade that, even in this grainy copy of a grainy photograph, could not mask the sadness in her eyes.

"Mother?" Natalie asked quietly. "Aunt?"

Declan breathed deeply. "I think we're past that now, don't you?" he said at last. "Pull up that other one."

"The one from 1929?"

"Yeah."

"But it can't be him, it can't be . . . fuck. It's totally him. Look. Same church. Same address. Same priest."

"So Conn Rowen was married twice. Once in 1929 to . . ." His eyes scanned the document. "Máire Carroll?"

"Máire, Mary, Mara. Bit of a theme going, no?"

"No but look, it's a different woman. His parents are the same but hers are different. Look, Máire Carroll's mother's name is Kathleen but Mary Fitch's mother is named Emma. It's a different woman."

"Yeah. I think you're supposed to think that," Natalie whispered. "I think that's the point."

Declan let out a long breath. "Mara said she found a photo in Conn's house. One that he'd obviously tried to hide from her. It was an old black-and-white picture of Conn's wedding day. And she said that the bride looked exactly like her."

Natalie's eyes widened.

"So . . . you think that was . . ." She tapped the screen. "This wedding? 1929?"

"Yeah, I think so," Declan said.

"Ah here," said Natalie. "We're going proper *X-Files* now, you know that? What should we do?"

"I think we need to see that photo for ourselves," he said.

"Breaking into an old man's house? Sure why not?"

"If it makes you feel any better, this old man will probably snap us over his knee if he catches us."

"Actually doesn't," she said quietly. "And there's something else."

"What?"

"If this is Mara," she said, tapping the picture on his phone. "And it was Mara in the other photo. That's weird. That's magic. Pure and simple. She's just not aging. But what about him?"

"Conn?"

"Yeah. He gets married in 1929. And he has to be at least twenty-one, right?"

DECLAN

"Age full."

"Age full. And this picture was taken in, you said, 1980?"

"Yeah."

"Declan," she said. "Does that man look seventy-two to you? Considering that's the absolute *minimum* he could be?"

Declan furrowed his brow. "I dunno. I mean . . . regular exercise. Clean living? Sea air? Maybe?"

"Okay," Natalie said, patiently. "Let me rephrase that. You've met this guy, right?"

"Yeah."

"Did he look like he could be over a hundred and ten?"

"No fucking chance."

"All right then. So, we're filing that under 'X' too, yeah?"

· · ·

I don't want to go back, Declan thought as Inishbannock loomed vast against the sky on the choppy gray-and-white-marbled sea.

There was a pall on the island, he now realized. His visit to Dingle had shown him that. It wasn't just the depression or the isolation that had become his near-constant companions since coming to Inishbannock. Or rather, he was starting to realize that the depression wasn't coming from him.

The island felt sick. It felt like a pale morning after drinking too much, shuffling through the house in dull pain, feeling untethered and ghostlike.

He glanced over at Natalie, who was hugging herself against the cold and watching the island with an unquiet expression.

"Home sweet home," she muttered.

"Thanks for talking me into this," he said.

She frowned. "You serious?"

"Yeah," he said. "I'm glad you're here."

She smiled and nodded in agreement.

And then suddenly her eyes popped wide. She pointed a finger and almost jumped for joy.

He followed her gaze and he was just in time to see a pair of large black flippers vanish beneath the current.

Then he saw a black doglike head emerge, and another and another . . .

He was amazed, not just at the sheer number of seals, but their size.

"Oh my God, Declan, look!" Natalie said excitedly. The sea around the boat was now black with bodies. There must have been hundreds of the creatures.

Suddenly, Natalie shrieked and almost went over the side of the boat as something massive collided with the hull.

She staggered back. Declan caught her.

"It's okay!" he said and gave a relieved laugh. "One of them must have . . . FUCK . . ."

Another blow and this time Declan swore he heard wood cracking.

From the stern of the boat, Stiofán shut off the engine and fired off a machine-gun volley of furious profanity. "SIT THE FUCK DOWN YOU PAIR OF FUCK-SHITE EEJITS. GET THE FUCK DOWN."

They dropped to their knees and braced themselves against the frame of the boat as the tiny craft rocked with blow after blow.

It felt like the seals were throwing themselves at the boat. Cracking their heads against it just to break it open.

You're going to die, Declan solemnly told himself as he screamed in panic. *You're going to drown. Water will fill your lungs and you won't be able to breathe. The death you always feared the most and it's going to happen to you. Right now.*

And then, as suddenly as it had started, the assault ended.

The shoal of seals passed them by, evidently bored of their game.

Natalie and Declan looked up at Stiofán, whose red beard seemed even more vibrant now that his face was as white as bone. He lit a cigarette with a trembling hand and took a deep, gasping drag.

"I didn't know they did that," Declan called to him.

"What? Try to kill you?" Stiofán answered. "Well. Now you know."

30
Mara

"Mara," said Doctor Quinn quietly. "Do you know why you're here?"

Mara came back from wherever she'd been drifting off to and looked at the doctor with weary, bloodshot eyes.

She suppressed an urge to laugh. It was funny. In a grim, unfunny way.

In the days after Cian's revelation, she had started journaling again, trying to put her thoughts down on paper and seeing if they were any less insane.

One morning, after trying and failing to think of anything to write down, she had carelessly tossed the journal back in the drawer.

When she went to get it the next morning, however, the journal was in the middle of the drawer. Perfectly aligned. Perfectly centered. As if it had been taken out and placed carefully back by someone who liked everything just so.

After that, of course, it all seemed too easy to trace back.

Cian had given her the picture of her mother after she had complained to her journal that there were no family photos in the house.

MARA

He had found her on the north side of the island after she had written that she was going to talk to Declan.

When her quarantine had ended, Quinn had been absolutely adamant that she keep writing in her journal.

Well. Now she knew why.

And so, partly out of boredom. Partly out of curiosity. Partly out of spite she had taken out the journal one morning and written: *I am a monster. I should just end it all.*

And, just like magic, Doctor Quinn had made a house call.

So yes, Doctor. I do know why you're here.

She realized that Quinn was waiting for her to answer.

"Because Cian is very, very, very, very worried about me," she said in a voice that not so much dripped sarcasm as swam in it.

"Yes," Quinn said seriously. "He is."

She shifted uneasily in her seat.

"Mara, I know you must resent me."

"For what?"

"For not being totally honest with you about . . . everything. Everything that was going on with you and Cian, and Oisín, and . . . but I only did that because I genuinely believed the shock would be too much for you. That the shock of learning . . ."

"That I'd killed someone?" Mara interrupted.

"You didn't," said Doctor Quinn firmly. "I'm not going to say I approve of the decisions you made. But Mara Alice made her choices, too. And she was not a well woman. Now, I'm going to prescribe you some antidepressants . . ."

"Why?"

"Because you're clearly depressed."

"I'm not depressed."

"I think I know . . ."

"I know you think you know. But I actually know."

"I am going to give Cian a prescription and he can pick it up for you from the mainland. And in a week or two we'll see if you're doing any better. Or whether you need something stronger."

31
Doctor Helen Quinn

After her visit to Mara, Doctor Quinn returned home and made a phone call.

"How is the patient?" asked the voice on the other end.

Quinn sighed deeply.

"I think we're in a downward spiral. Either she's becoming suicidally depressed . . ."

"Or?"

"Or she knows that Cian's been reading her journal."

"Either way."

"Either way. It might be time for radical measures."

"You always say that."

"Uh-huh. When was the last time?"

"The time you were absolutely right and we should have listened to you. Point taken. If we were to do that. What do you think is the issue?"

Quinn didn't need to think.

"Cian. She's not happy with him."

"Would you be?"

Quinn laughed bitterly.

"Looks aren't everything, I suppose."

"No. He's no good for her."

"So when?"

"Not yet, Helen. I've got too many irons in the fire at the moment."

"Why? What's going on?"

There was a weary sigh at the other end of the line.

"The next few days are going to be . . ."

"Difficult?"

"Horrific. Things are going to get very bad before they get better."

"You've been saying that for a long time. I'm still waiting for the part where things get better."

"We've got a tiger by the tail, Helen. If we're not being eaten alive, it's a good day. Can we meet this Friday?"

"Sure, let me just get my calendar," Quinn said and rooted around in her handbag.

"Bitch!" she exclaimed.

"Excuse me?"

"I . . . I think she stole my wallet," Quinn said, dumbfounded.

32
Mara

Just leave. Just leave. Just leave.

She'd had a moment of clarity during Doctor Quinn's visit. She would have to stay here, in this house she hated, with a man she loathed, and learn to smile or she would be drugged. Either she took the drugs or they would be put in her food.

And then, like a shining light of inspiration: *Just leave.*

That was how she found herself half running down the road to the pier just outside of Ballydonn with Doctor Quinn's wallet in her pocket.

She didn't know where she was going or how far she could go, she just knew she had to get off Inishbannock.

Stiofán was sitting, not in his boat, but on an iron bollard, looking anxiously out at the sea as he waited for passengers for his last trip of the day.

She bent over, trying desperately to catch her breath. As soon as he saw her he sprang to his feet.

"What do you want?" he asked her, cagily.

She looked at him. Suddenly, she realized how foolish she was being.

There's no way. There's no way they'll just let you leave.

"I want to go," she told him. "I want to get off the island."

"Yeah?" he said, uncertainly.

"But you're not going to let me, are you?" she asked him, her anger rising. "Let me guess. The sea's too rough. The engine's not working. There's a big scary . . . kraken . . . waiting to eat me alive if I even *think* about leaving this fucking island. Well? What is it?"

She advanced toward him and, despite his great height, he took a step back.

"What is it?" he repeated. "What's what?"

"Are you going to get me off this island? Yes or no?"

"I dunno! Depends!" he yelped.

"On what?!" she barked.

"On whether or not you have twenty-five quid."

"Oh," she said, the righteous wind suddenly taken out of her sails.

She rooted around in Doctor Quinn's wallet, which, like any sensible island dweller's, had plenty of hard cash.

"Here," she said, passing him two tens and a five.

"Right then," he said. "Welcome aboard."

He stepped aside and gestured with his hand like a coachman directing her to enter her carriage.

This . . . This is really happening. I'll get to the mainland. And once I hit solid ground I won't stop running . . .

The tiny boat appeared to shrink before her gaze. It seemed to flicker on the water, unreal and translucent. She tried to step onto it and her leg suddenly went numb.

No. No. I have to leave. I have to.

She summoned every ounce of strength she had and, through sheer force of will, made her foot touch the rim of the boat.

And then came the punishment.

She felt the same awful sensation of sickness, fever and stomach cramp, from that day when she had been swept into the sea.

Her legs gave out and she fell roughly onto the concrete jetty.

No. No!

She tried to crawl, moving arms that felt broken in every bone, begging her body to pull herself into the boat.

She managed to touch it. Once.

And then her vision blackened and she was lying flat on the concrete.

As Mara shuddered and gasped and wished with all her heart that she could just *die* to end the pain, Stiofán walked around her body like a vulture circling a carcass.

"Alright. We're going now. Don't you want to go? Are you sure? You said you wanted to go, but I don't think you do. Tell you what. I'm going to the pub. I'm going to spend this. And you come back when you're ready, yeah? Sound."

Dimly, she heard his boots crunching on the rough gravel as he slowly walked away up the jetty.

It was almost twenty minutes before she even had the strength to lift her head.

33
Natalie

"Alright, I'm not trying to be sexist or anything..."

"Oh, I'm sure you'll do great."

"But this *absolutely* is a lad's kitchen."

"See, you're just nervous because you promised the greatest omelettes I ever tasted and now you're just laying the groundwork..."

"No!"

"...of blaming my kitchen for your failure."

"When I *said* that..."

"Yeah?"

"I assumed you would have more ingredients than, y'know, eggs."

"You don't make omelettes with eggs? You're blowing my mind."

"Eggs are the beginning of omelettes, my young apprentice, not the end."

"Honestly, they smell great."

"Yeah, well, you know what they say, sea air and a brush with death is the best sauce."

NATALIE

Natalie blew a loose strand of hair out of her face and flipped one omelette on to a waiting plate and laid it in front of Declan.

"Put that inside you, now," she said, pushing her Cork accent to the maximum setting.

Declan did not answer as he was already well on his way to discharging his orders.

Natalie plated her own omelette and looked around Decan's kitchen. like a nomad seeking water in the wilderness.

"Seriously, do you not even have ketchup?"

"I did," he said, in a muffled voice.

"What happened?"

"Some mad woman broke into his kitchen in the middle of the night and ate everything. And he was such a champ about it."

Natalie looked up in shock. Mara stood in the doorway that led to Declan's garden. Pale and shaken, but with a tough, hardy smile on her face. Like a wolf that had survived a long winter.

"So. How's everything been with . . ." Mara began.

Natalie cut her off by wrapping her wiry arms around her. And then Declan's pillowy embrace swallowed both of them. They said nothing, just stood in Declan's kitchen and let the hug do its work.

"Hey," said Natalie after a few moments. "Are you hungry?"

"No," said Mara with a deep sigh. "I am five seconds away from eating that chair."

"Sit on it instead and I'll make you an omelette."

"They are," said Declan with a solemn air of noblesse oblige, "the greatest omelettes I have ever tasted."

They ate in silence for a while.

"Can I say something?" Mara said after she had gratefully devoured the last bite.

They both nodded.

"You are both . . . I can't even put into words how grateful I am. To both of you. I honestly don't know how I would have survived . . . all this. If I didn't have the two of you. If I didn't have you both saying, 'Yeah, you're not crazy. This is really fucked up.' If I had to do this on my own?" She exhaled deeply. "I owe you both. Forever. Always."

Natalie took her hand.

"And that's why I'm really scared to ask you to do this. And I will absolutely understand if you tell me you can't. That it's a step too far."

"Oh shit . . ." said Natalie, but her stomach took an excited turn.

"I need to break into Conn Rowen's cottage," Mara said. "I was hoping . . . you both would be willing to help."

There was a long silence. At last, Declan gave a solemn sigh.

"Well, Mara. I mean. That's a really big ask. But, we're your friends. So I suppose I can put aside my deep misgivings for the sake of our friend . . ."

"Fuck off, Declan." Natalie laughed. "Look at you, trying to milk it. Mara, we had the same idea. We were going to break into Conn's cottage tonight."

Mara looked at them in shock and then burst out laughing. "Sorry. The two scumbags from the big cities, I should have expected housebreaking was plan A. You!" she turned on Declan in mock fury. "Trying to guilt trip me, you bollocks!"

"Sorry." Declan laughed.

NATALIE

"Wait a minute," Mara said, turning to Natalie. "Why were you so scared? What did you think I was going to ask?"

"Oh," said Natalie dismissively. "Honestly, I was scared you were going to suggest a threesome. And, like, I wasn't a hard no or anything. It's just, Declan and I would have had to sidebar to set down some ground rules."

There was an awkward pause.

"What ground rules?" Declan asked.

"Well . . . doesn't matter now. C'mon, let's plan a crime."

"I mean, just academically?"

"You'll never know," she cooed. And gave him a wink.

34
Conn

The cottage was a magic cottage, both too big and too small. It was too big because it was empty, as only the home of a widower could be.

Cavernous. Maze-like. An empty cathedral. A dead city.

He mused that it was as much for that reason as any other that he had invited her in.

You have an empty house, what else would you do but try and fill it with someone?

He knew it had been foolish. He, perhaps, would even go so far as to admit that it had been fatally stupid.

But the older he got the more he realized he was no longer in control of his actions. He was a machine, driven by routine and need over which he had no say.

After all, if he really had control over his own actions, he would have thrown himself into the sea a long time ago.

In fact, a few days ago, he had come close.

Padraig, his nephew, had come down to the cottage, out of the blue, and offered to take him fishing.

As Padraig had rowed them out, Conn had mused that Padraig would have made a good fisherman. He was clearly at home with boats. He wondered if Padraig resented working in the Temple, or if he was just happy to have his place in life set out for him.

They had talked and Conn had perhaps not been as guarded as he should have been.

Ah well, it was only Padraig. Padraig was harmless.

He barely even remembered what they talked about. All the time he'd been looking into the water and wondering if he fell whether he could just will himself to stop swimming or whether the instinct to survive would be too great.

He didn't, of course. He was not that cruel. Padraig had lost enough.

He had simply asked his nephew to bring him home.

He hadn't felt like fishing.

And Conn believed the house was too small because he was afraid to leave. Malachy's fear, that their mother had been watching them from the tree on the night of Mara's return, had nestled in Conn's mind and put down little black roots. So he stayed inside as much as possible. Walking around the maze he had built for himself.

And when he did go out, braving the darkness to walk to what passed for a pub in Kilty's hostel, he could not bring himself to look at the trees, for fear he would catch a glimpse of his mother staring back at him with blind fish eyes.

When he heard rustling in the bushes, he imagined her crouched and naked, eating songbirds in her filthy fingers.

He could hear his mother keening on the wind and could see her hiding in the folds of the curtains. She was so to the forefront of his mind that, one night, when he opened the door and saw Gráinne standing outside holding a bottle of thirty-year-old whiskey, he had actually screamed and taken a step back.

"Jesus, Conn!" Gráinne barked, holding the bottle tight after almost dropping it. "I'm not that bad, surely?"

Conn could have debated the point. Indeed, he felt he had more than enough evidence to sway judge, jury, and public opinion, but he was too relieved to say anything.

In a moment of weakness, he gestured for his sister to come in.

She gave him a smile and passed him the bottle.

He looked at it dumbly and picked at the red satin ribbon she'd tied around the neck.

"What's this?" he muttered. "A bribe, is it?"

Her smile faded, in her eyes at least. "It's your present, you eejit. Don't tell me you forgot your own birthday?"

He set the bottle down. "I don't keep track anymore. Do you?"

"Of course I do," she said. "It's important to mark how far we've come."

"Only if you've got somewhere to go," he said sadly.

The silence that followed was uncomfortable, so he directed his gaze back to the bottle.

"Jaysus. That must have cost you a fair penny. Will you join me for a drink, Gráinne?"

"I'd love to," she said.

The whiskey went down easily. Too easily. He could feel things melting within him. Grudges. Barriers. Possibly stomach lining. He took a deep breath to remind himself where he was.

"How do you do it, Gráinne?" he asked softly.

"How do you mean, Conn?"

"Look at you. You're still going. You're still strong as ever. Remembering birthdays. And look at me. And look

CONN

at Malachy. Chewed-up old husks, the pair of us. How do you keep living? How do you keep telling yourself that it matters?"

"It does matter," she said, without a hint of hesitation. "I have O— I have Padraig. And the Temple. And I have my brothers. And the island. And every soul on it. It all matters, Conn. It's life. If it doesn't matter, what does?"

"Aye. Aye, there's the question."

"Have you seen Malachy?"

He shrugged. "He's your neighbor, not mine."

"He hasn't come down to see you?"

"Sick. He says."

"Sick?"

"In his head. He says."

She reached out and rapped her knuckles on the wooden table.

He did the same.

"I suppose you've heard?" he asked. "Herself came to visit me."

"Oh?"

"I let her in. I know I shouldn't have. It just . . . seeing her. I couldn't . . . I had to . . ."

"Conn." His sister reached out and took both his hands in hers. "I would never judge you. Not for that. We've all suffered. But sometimes I think it's you who've suffered more than any of us. And if I ever made you feel that . . . that didn't matter to me. If I ever made you feel that. I'm sorry. I'm truly sorry."

The whiskey was doing its work and he could feel tears in his eyes.

"Why are you crying, Conn?" she whispered.

"Because," he replied. "I want to believe that. I want to believe that you're here with this whiskey because it's my birthday, and I'm your brother, and you love me, and you want to make sure I'm alright, but I fucking *know* that the next words to come out of your mouth are going to be about what I have in that safe back there. And I know you're going to tell me that there's no point in me having it. And that it's too dangerous. And that it'd be better off with you.

"And you know what? You're absolutely right. But it's mine. You got the Temple. Malachy got the shop. I got the house. And the cloak. It's all I have to remember her. And I am so tired of fighting tooth and nail for the tiny little bit that's mine."

Gráinne pulled her hands away. She studied his face, and Conn wondered if she was analyzing the lines that had formed over the years, thinking about how much life had aged him, wishing he would stop with all the fuss and just go down easy. But Conn learned long ago he couldn't often predict what his sister thought of him. This time was no different.

At last she stood.

"Conn," she said. "I promise you, I will never mention it to you again. I'm going to go now. Will you embrace me?"

He stood and embraced his sister and when that was done, she left without another word.

Conn considered simply staying and drinking as much of the whiskey as he could before passing out, but it seemed a crime. The whiskey was too good to waste on a depressed session alone in an empty house. If he put the whiskey away, he could imagine there was a happy occasion in his future where he would get to use it.

CONN

There was plenty of cheap booze in Kilty's to get drunk on.

He strode down the moonlit road, hands in his pockets, shoulders hunched, and eyes downcast, trying not to meet the gaze of the trees. He could feel that he was being watched, but he always felt like that and paid it no mind.

His boot crunched something small and hard. At first Conn thought it was simply a pebble, but something in the texture or the sound it made when he ground it against the road gave him pause. As he walked on, he realized he was walking on a bed of them, whatever they were. He took out his torch and shone it at the ground. For a moment he thought there must have been a brief freak hailstorm. A field of tiny white shapes shone bright against the darkness of the road, like stars in the night sky.

With a trembling hand, Conn reached out and took one between his thumb and forefinger and held it up to the light.

It was tiny, perfect, and pristine. As white and spotless as an infant's soul.

A child's tooth.

He turned the light back to the road. There must have been thousands of them. Enough for a hundred mouths or more. He dropped the tooth and glanced around in near panic.

Something had shed the teeth. And, in all likelihood, had grown more.

Something out here, slinking between tree and hedge, between road and wall.

Time to head off home.

He heard something stirring in the darkness and swung around, his heart trying to claw its way out of his throat and make a break for it.

"Is that you, Conn?" came a weary voice.

His torch found Malachy's face, creased with pain and a wan smile. He looked as old as sin.

"Malachy," Conn choked out. "What are you doing out here?"

"I thought I'd drop in for a game," said Malachy. "Where you off to?"

"I was heading over to Farvey," Conn said. "For a drink."

"Ah now. Drinking with the tourists? Have you no shame, man?"

Conn glanced down at the road. "You're right," he said. "Come back to the house. Gráinne dropped off a nice bottle of whiskey. We'll have that instead."

"Gráinne was down, was she?" Malachy asked, taking a position beside his brother as they walked on.

Conn winced inwardly as he heard teeth crunching under Malachy's tread. He wondered if his brother noticed them. Whether he had or not, he knew Malachy would say nothing. Such things were not discussed on the island.

"She was," Conn replied.

"And you both survived?"

"Oh, we were on our best behavior. The two of us."

"So what, the whiskey was a peace offering?"

"A birthday present, she says."

"Is it your birthday?"

"Apparently."

"Many happy returns of the day."

"Well. They'll be 'many,' at least."

. . .

CONN

They dealt the cards as usual and quickly lapsed into intense silence.

Conn lost the first few hands and was soon sitting bare chested while Malachy had yet to lose a single item of clothing.

Conn realized that, for the first time in a very long time, Malachy was playing to win.

Or at least, not to lose. He's trying to drag the game out as long as he can.

It was then that he knew for certain. He had suspected, of course. Ever since Malachy had called and said that he would be missing their usual game.

The visual proof came when Conn won his first hand, laying down a flush against Malachy's two pair of aces and eights.

Malachy gave a sad smile and removed his shirt.

Underneath his vest, on the left shoulder, Conn could see the fingers.

He said nothing, and dealt them both a new hand.

"Conn," Malachy said at last.

Conn grunted in response.

"Do you remember what I made you promise? After we lost Mam?"

Conn nodded.

"I think it's time."

"Don't be jumping the gun. There's things we can try."

"Oh, I know. I know. But you see, I've tried them all already. I've been cutting meself for weeks now. Trimming meself like a hedge!" He gave a laugh. "I know it's a lot to ask."

"'A lot to ask,' he says . . ."

"But you promised . . ."

"Play the game, Malachy," Conn said shortly, laying down his hand.

"Ah, Conn, can't you see I've already lost?"

Without even consulting Conn's hand, his brother stood and pulled off his vest to show the thing that now grew over his heart.

Conn looked away.

Ah well. Ah well. That was it, then.

"I've heard," said Malachy. "That if you do it here. Like, where me neck meets me head, I won't even feel it."

. . .

He wanted to do it sober, but Malachy wanted to do it drunk.

So they went into the safe room and Conn laid old yellow newspapers on the floor. Then, Malachy knelt down, with his back to his brother, and his hands folded in his lap.

He let the barrel hang in the air, just a few inches off the nape of his brother's neck.

The air around him felt simultaneously hot and cold. Like death. At once burning and freezing.

"Should I . . . do you want me to say a prayer? Or something?" Conn asked.

Malachy gave a hollow laugh. "Ah, I think we're a bit past that now."

"What should I say then?"

"Say what you feel."

"This is Malachy Rowen. He was an awful bollocks."

Malachy laughed but the tears were flowing freely.

"But he was my brother. And I loved him."

Malachy nodded. "I love you too, C–"

CONN

The word was torn from Malachy's mouth as the bullet passed through his neck, hit his lower jaw and pulled it from the skull. With a report so loud that Conn felt hammers hitting his brain, the head of his brother vanished into a jagged mélange of red and brown shapes and the body hit the ground like a sack of potatoes, chest down.

Whatever happened next his mind decided was not worth keeping.

He came to, washing his hands in the sink. He caught sight of himself in the mirror and was filled with such a rage that he broke the glass with his bare hands and then proceeded to kick the sink until it broke from the wall.

It was because of this—this sudden outburst of violence—that he did not hear the sound of something heavy breaking down his front door.

By the time he heard them coming, it was too late.

35
Mara

"There he goes," Natalie had whispered as they crouched behind the drystone wall, barely daring to breathe.

Mara carefully tipped her head up and saw Conn, a hunched figure vanishing down the road to Farvey.

Herself, Declan, and Natalie had taken a longer route, crossing the fields to avoid meeting anyone on the way.

"Should we go?" Declan asked, his voice high and scratchy with nerves.

"Stall the ball," Natalie said. "Let's just make sure he didn't forget something..."

They waited another few agonizing minutes. The road remained empty.

"Right," said Natalie. "I've worked that shift before. He won't leave Kilty's until the bar closes. That gives us around four hours."

"Are you sure?" Declan asked.

"No? Sorry, you wanted a safe burglary where nothing could possibly go wrong?"

"So he *doesn't* always stay until the bar closes?"

"Yeah, Declan, he's one of those organized alcoholics who always sticks to a rigid schedule."

Mara could sense a row about to break out and raised her hands. "Okay, okay. Declan, you're right. I want you to stay outside and keep watch. Text us if you see Conn coming back."

Declan protested, but not too much.

• • •

It was very embarrassing, Mara mused, to begin a burglary and realize that you hadn't factored in that the front door might be locked.

"Back door's locked, too," said Natalie, rounding the corner of the house. "That's mad. No one on the island locks their doors. Where does he think he's living, Brooklyn? I just hope he doesn't have an alarm." She began rooting around in Conn's garden.

"Natalie?" said Mara. "What are you doing there, love?"

"What's it look like?" Natalie said, lifting a rock the size of a horse's head. "I'm going in through the window."

"Stop. If he comes back and sees the window broken he'll know . . ."

"You know what, Mara? I'm starting to think you don't want to break into this house . . . what?"

Mara had raised a hand to silence her as she studied the line of ceramic fishermen. Her eyes went to the last one, with the great porcelain bass. She knelt down and lifted it. A mass exodus of wood lice scattered as the base of the fish cleared the ground. There, wrapped in a sheet of plastic, was a rusted door key.

Natalie stared at Mara in shock. "Okay. How did you know that was going to be there?" she asked.

Mara shook her head. "I think I remembered it."

She turned the key in the door and quietly pushed it open. The smell of whiskey hung in the air as they entered Conn's living room.

"What are we looking for?" Natalie asked her.

Mara shrugged helplessly. "I don't know," she admitted.

"We're really bad at this," Natalie said at last, frowning.

Mara could only agree. "I suppose, pictures of me and Conn. Anything that might prove that I used to live here."

"Okay, you check in here. I'll search the rest of the house," Natalie whispered as she crept down the hallway.

Mara shone her phone around the darkened room and almost passed out as she heard an earsplitting screech.

"JESUS WHAT?!" she yelled.

"Sorry!" Natalie called. "Fucking seal head. Scared the shite out of me."

"Oh yeah. Real looker, isn't he?"

"Why would you do that? Why would *anyone* do that?"

"Different times."

Her heart still racing, Mara sat down on the sofa. She realized that there was something on the cushion and pulled it out. It was an old Aran sweater.

She had seen Conn wearing this very sweater on the beach and, she now remembered, he had been wearing it in the picture of the two of them watching the parade on Main Street. A sweater like this wasn't something you wore for a few years and then cast away. They were made to last lifetimes.

She could smell him on it. Not in a bad way. Not even remotely a bad way. There was something about his scent that

MARA

made her feel calm. Without even thinking about it she lifted the sweater to her face and breathed in deeply.

The earthy scent seemed to unlock gate after gate of her memories as a sense of familiarity flooded her mind. She remembered sitting here on this very couch, with his great oaken arms wrapped around her, watching the turf burning in the fire. She could almost feel his whiskery lips on her brow.

And she remembered the feeling of love. Warm and solid as brick.

She had lain here in his arms and felt truly, wholly loved.

"Mara? Mara what is it?"

Natalie was shaking her shoulder.

"I . . . I . . ." she stammered and felt the tears running freely down her cheeks.

She was trying to form the words to tell Natalie what had happened when she suddenly realized that her phone was buzzing in her hand like an angry hornet.

She lifted it and saw, on the screen, a whole chain of messages from Declan.

> HE'S BACK
> HE'S NOT ALONE
> GET OUT!
> TOO LATE!
> THEY'RE COMING UP THE PATH!
> HIDE!

Mara and Natalie both looked into each other's eyes as they heard muffled voices coming toward the front door.

Natalie grabbed Mara by the hand and dragged her into the kitchen.

They planted themselves on either side of the doorway.

The second someone entered this room they'd be discovered. But if they were incredibly lucky, Conn would go straight to bed and they could sneak out undetected while he slept. Except Declan had said he wasn't alone . . .

Mara glanced over at Natalie, who looked scared enough to scream.

She raised a finger to her lips and Natalie nodded and bravely tried to smile.

The front door opened.

36
Natalie

You've fucking done it again.

As she heard the two men moving around in the next room, Natalie pressed her body against the kitchen wall, trying to keep as quiet as possible. And all the while her mind was screaming at her. *You've fucking done it again.*

You had to prove to everyone how brave you were. How mad you were. How cool you were. How few fucks you give. And now people you care about are going to get hurt (and one of them is you). Just like it always happens. But this is going to be worse. Much worse. Jail if you're lucky. A shallow grave if you're not. Well fucking done.

She looked over at Mara, who seemed to have melted into the shadows.

She was utterly calm, and completely still. Like a leopard, waiting for the right moment to spring.

Natalie remembered something Declan had asked her after they'd come back from the mainland.

"Does Mara scare you?"

She had thought he'd been joking. When she realized he was serious she had replied, *"I thought you liked her?"*

"I do!" he had answered. "*I didn't ask if you liked her. I asked if she scared you.*"

Now, she understood what he'd meant. Mara felt . . . off. Some unnamed primal sense was telling Natalie that the person next to her was no such thing. She was in the reptile house, watching some ancient lidless creature lurking in brackish water, whose ancestors had bid farewell to hers long ago.

And then Mara turned to look at Natalie, giving her a smile while raising a finger to her lips. She was back. Mara. Her friend.

Nothing wrong here.

They listened as the men talked and Natalie heard the clinking of glass, the sound of liquid being poured, the shuffling of cards. The conversation was low and Natalie soon gave up trying to hear what they were saying.

Then, she heard chair legs screeching on tiles as the two men got to their feet. She had to fight every instinct not to scream as she heard footsteps coming toward the kitchen. A lightheaded relief flooded her body when they turned and headed down the hallway instead.

She glanced over at Mara, trying to catch her attention. *Now. Now. We have to run for it now. We'll never get a better chance.*

But Mara did not move an inch. Not even a hair of an inch.

When the shot came, Natalie actually did scream, a tiny, anguished yelp, and clamped her hands over her mouth. *Oh fuck, oh fuck, oh fuck, he's got a gun.*

She heard someone treading heavily into the hallway, another door opening, and then the sound of running water.

NATALIE

She felt a buzzing in her pocket and, like in a dream, took out her phone to see a message from Declan.

> SOMEONE ELSE
> LOOK OUT

She heard the front door shatter like an eggshell and what sounded like two large bodies entering the living room. There was a flurry of footsteps coming up the hallway in answer.

Yelling, screaming.

Two gunshots and the kitchen window shattered.

Silence followed, as thick as the crust of the Earth.

Then, slow, languid footsteps on wet tile.

She could hear breathing, heavy and strained.

A shadow fell on the kitchen floor, a man holding something long in his hand.

Whoever he was, he was literally inches away from them. If Natalie so much as moved her little finger past the lip of the doorway, he would see her. If he took one step forward, she was dead.

But he didn't.

Seemingly satisfied, he turned and stalked down the hallway.

She could hear low muttering coming from the living room, and she thought she heard the word "amen" in Irish. "Ah-men," not "ay-men."

The prayer was cut off by a shout from the back room. "FUCK! COME HERE!"

And this time Natalie saw Mara flinch. That had shaken her. She seemed to have taken everything else in stride but that voice, apparently, was enough to spook her.

Heavy feet, tramping past the kitchen door and up the hallway. They stopped, and there was a low moan, as if someone was witnessing something past their ability to endure.

"Get the tools. Quick. We need to get out of here," came the first voice, remarkably calm under the circumstances. Dublin accent, Natalie was pretty sure.

For what felt like hours, she and Mara listened to the sound of an acetylene torch cutting through metal. Finally, two sets of footsteps, walking in unison, carrying something big and heavy between them.

The same voice, cold, cruel, and mocking, called out, "See ya, Conn!"

And then, silence.

Natalie realized that she had stopped breathing some time ago and took a massive breath.

"Oh Jesus . . ." Mara had decoupled from the wall and was standing in the doorway, looking in horror at the living room.

Conn lay on the floor, burst and spilt. He had taken a shot square in the chest and had fallen with his own shotgun still in his hand.

The two women stood in numb horror, staring at the dead old man.

"Why . . ." Mara whispered, and Natalie could hear that she was on the verge of tears. "Why would they—" She stopped.

They had both heard it.

Whining, down the hallway, like a pale, ill serpent. The sound of a baby crying.

An unwell baby. Hungry and weak.

They looked at each other, appalled. How could there be a baby here? They turned from the body and ran down

NATALIE

the hallway, turning left at the stuffed seal head and then halting.

The body, and perhaps a third of the head of Malachy Rowen, lay half naked on the concrete floor of the safe room. In death, he made Conn look pristine and dignified.

This one was too much. Natalie turned and got sick while Mara simply stared. The vista of violence was so garish and awful that it took Natalie a full two minutes to even notice the safe. Or rather, what was left of it.

What had been done to Malachy's head had been repeated on the safe door. Still locked, the safe boasted a huge jagged hole and something had clearly been extracted as it was completely empty.

So whatever was in that safe was worth killing Conn for, Natalie mused.

The sound of the baby's cry came once again.

"You heard that, right?" Mara asked.

Natalie nodded.

"Okay, you take that side, I'll search over here."

Swallowing her revulsion, Natalie stepped around the body and began searching among a stack of cardboard boxes filled with cleaning and garden supplies.

Has it stopped? She shuddered and hoped that she would not come across a tiny corpse.

"Nothing over here . . ." Mara called.

She was interrupted by another thin, plaintive cry.

And this time, unfortunately, there was no mistaking where the sound was coming from.

Natalie saw the movement out of the corner of her eye. *No. No, no, no, this can't be happening. Let me wake up now.*

The arms twitched and spasmed like the legs of a fly that had rolled upside down and was now righting itself. They found purchase on the concrete floor and raised the torso, as if the body was doing a push-up.

The naked semi-headless body of Malachy Rowen, a hinge of jaw and flesh still hanging from the neck, raised itself from the blood-slick floor. Natalie, or the part of Natalie that was not in a mad panic, dully realized that there were fingers growing out of the shoulders. She hadn't noticed them before, as she had not let herself look too closely at the corpse.

Now, she could not look away.

Now, the thing had her total and rapt attention.

For there, on the chest of Malachy Rowan, just over where his heart had once beat, a face looked out. A tiny baby's face, with blue eyes that looked out on the world with horror and bewilderment. And she felt such pity for it, even as every atom of her being recoiled in utter abhorrence.

The face opened its mouth and there came the cry again, thin and weak and also full of rage at a world that had allowed it to come into being in this form.

It took its first crawling steps toward them and that was enough.

Natalie did not need to tell Mara that they could not stay here any longer, that they could not go *near* this thing. She glanced up and saw a tiny window where the wall met the ceiling. Wordlessly, they worked in frantic harmony to make a ladder out of a stool and a few of the full cardboard boxes.

She looked over her shoulder and saw that the thing, still crying, still bleeding, was staggering toward them, arms outstretched. The mouth seemed to be chewing itself to pieces.

NATALIE

Bits of bloody gum dribbled down its chin as tiny, needle-like piranha teeth grew from the flesh of the maw.

Natalie wasn't even thinking, her arms and legs were moving by themselves. She clambered up the boxes and began hammering desperately at the tiny windowpane. But the thick glass held firm, until Mara climbed after her and smashed clean through it with her bare fist.

Even in the white-hot terror of the moment, with the *thing* lurching toward her, its bloody finger grasping for her back, Natalie took a second to gaze at Mara in sheer wonder.

How is she so strong?

Mara vanished through the hole in the window, and for a heart-stopping moment, Natalie thought she'd been left behind to die. But then Mara's arm, slick with blood from where she'd gashed her knuckles, came through the gap, grabbed Natalie by the shoulders and yanked her to safety, just as she felt something grip weakly at her heel.

The next thing she knew, she was standing in Conn Rowen's garden and Mara's bloodied hands were roughly shaking her. "Natalie! NATALIE!"

• • •

She could hear someone screaming wildly and it took her far too long to realize that it was her.

Which was odd, because she felt perfectly calm.

Her body was trembling and she was screaming.

But inside, she felt nothing.

The thing she had seen in the safe room had burned the fear out of her.

She just stared wide-eyed at Mara, unable to move, incapable of even processing what she was screaming. Mara grabbed her by the hand and tried to drag her away from the house.

Dully, Natalie realized she had fallen silent, but she could still hear screaming.

Both women looked up to see Declan running down the hill toward the house, sprinting madly.

Natalie finally could hear what he was screaming.

It was the very last thing she wanted to hear.

"IT'S COMING! IT'S COMING! GET BACK IN THE FUCKING HOUSE!"

37

Declan

The thirty-five minutes or so that Declan had spent crouched behind the wall overlooking Conn Rowen's cottage were the worst of his life, and it wasn't even close.

He had knelt in the dirt, ashamed at his own cowardice as he watched Mara and Natalie break in.

He had been so focused on the cottage that by the time he noticed the Rowen brothers coming back up the road it was too late.

You've killed them, he screamed at himself as he desperately texted a warning to Mara.

You've fucking killed them both.

He had watched the two older men enter the house and waited desperately for some sign of commotion. When it never came, he felt a tiny mote of relief and guessed that Mara and Natalie had received his warning just in time.

For agonizing minutes, he debated whether to risk texting Mara to see if they were still alive, but decided that the risk of exposing them was too great.

And then, the bottom fell out of his stomach as he heard a single gunshot.

Fuck . . .

That was it. Someone was dead. Mara or Natalie. And he had no doubt a second shot would follow any moment . . .

In the distance, he heard the sound of an engine tearing down the narrow country road. Cars were so rare on the island that it actually took him a second to understand the noise.

He watched in stunned shock as a dark-blue Range Rover skidded to a stop outside Conn's cottage and two large men wearing dark clothes and balaclavas, and carrying shotguns, burst out of the vehicle.

Declan almost threw his hands up in the air in sheer bafflement. *What. WHAT?!*

He had just enough time to fire off a frantic warning to Natalie and Mara (if either was even still alive) when one of the men produced a small police battering ram and smashed Conn's front door practically off its hinges. Both men ran into the house and Declan listened in rapt horror as another two shots rang out in the still night air. One of the men then reemerged, grabbed a tool bag from the back seat of the car, and vanished back into the house.

He was frozen in fear. Completely paralyzed.

Beads of cold sweat ran down his forehead.

He waited in numb silence until he saw the men emerge, carrying a large black wooden crate between them. The man carrying the rear seemed to be taking most of the weight. The front man held the crate with one hand while the other clasped what looked like a bottle of whiskey.

Within moments the crate, the tools, the guns, the bottle of whiskey, and the men were in the car, speeding south.

Still, Declan could not move.

DECLAN

What kept him crouched behind the wall was not fear for his own life. It was the dread of what he would find splayed and bloodied on the floor of the cottage.

But, at last, he took a deep breath and stood.

He'd been staring at the house for so long that its square shape had burned itself into his vision. Turning away, he leaned on the wall, just to give his eyes a break, and looked out to the darkness.

In the field was a tree, black and dead.

And in the branches something moved.

Declan's eyes told him what was, but he couldn't believe them, so he shifted closer.

What he saw made the rest of the day's terrors look paltry in comparison.

There was a woman, or rather, half a woman. The top half of her body was naked. Long wisps of filthy silver hair grew from her head and trailed all the way down to her waist, where her body ceased the pretense of humanity. The lower half of her body was a massive fleshy phallus, thick and prehensile and the color of spoiled milk. He could see dark veins pulsing under the translucent flesh. She was coiled around the tree like a serpent and fixed him with eyes that spoke of a furious terror. She seemed mad with fear, her lips trembling and her tongue dancing in her skull, making a wet tapping noise as it hit the roof of her mouth.

The hands had too many fingers, and the fingers too much nail.

She stared at him and shrieked three times, as the phallus began to unwind from the tree as if prepared to strike.

Declan did not see any of this.

Declan was already running.

He ran like an animal. His only thought, if you could even call it a thought, and not a mad panicked impulse, was to get inside the cottage and barricade the door against the woman, the nightmare, the *thing* that he heard screaming behind him.

That's when he saw Natalie and Mara, pale, shaken, and bloodied, but very much alive, pulling themselves out from a tiny window. He felt a brief, white-hot burst of joy in the midst of almost total terror as he tore toward the house.

He yelled at them to get back inside and couldn't understand why they weren't listening. Out of time, he tried to simply push them toward the front door, but Mara was like iron.

He heard Natalie shriek madly, "OHFUCKFUCK FUCKWHATTHEFUCKWHATTHEFUCKISTHAT FUCKINGTHING?!"

It was on them now, raised up on its tail, seven, eight feet tall, towering.

The light from the open front door revealed it in all its awfulness. The wrinkles on its flesh seemed to writhe between light and shadow.

It stared at them, with glassy white eyes.

No, it stared at Mara. And the expression on its pale, ancient, venomous, features . . .

Well.

The word "hate" seemed too small.

This was old hate. Inhuman and great and strange.

Deep hate. Hate beyond what a mere human soul could muster.

It stood there, frozen. It was as if the hatred it felt for Mara was so strong it was temporarily paralyzed.

But any second the moment would break . . .

DECLAN

And then, Declan heard a baby crying.

It was not that the thing that staggered out of Conn Rowen's front door was worse than the nightmare that had chased him down the hill.

But it was too much.

The sight of Malachy Rowen's semi-headless corpse, with an infant's face gurgling in agony in his chest, lurching toward them made him feel like his heart might explode and that he would drop dead.

The eyes of the witch flitted from Mara to the bloody abomination. Declan felt Mara's hand gripping his like warm iron and her voice came strong and calm. "When I say run . . . go left."

The serpent, the woman, the *thing* lunched forward and Mara screamed, "Run!"

He did. They all did.

He did not have to worry about exhaustion. The sounds that were coming from behind gave him the energy to run past all limits of endurance. He could see Natalie ahead of him, racing back up the path to the road, her hair whipping back and forth.

The baby cry had abruptly cut off and now there was only the sound of flesh leaving flesh and bones splintering.

It was only when they reached the top of the hill that Declan dared look back.

He saw the serpent in the light of the open doorway devouring the twice-dead body of Malachy Rowen, and he could hear the hissing, leathery sound of skin being flayed from bone and muscle.

The old woman's head snapped around mid-chew and the monster shrieked before whipping itself over the garden wall with a speed that should not have been possible for something that big.

"Declan? Where's Mara . . . ?" Natalie wheezed, bent over as she tried to catch her breath.

"I . . . I thought she was behind me . . ." he replied numbly.

They both looked down and saw that the creature was pursuing a figure up the path, toward the cliff. In the darkness, silhouetted against the clouded moon, Declan could just make out a tiny figure running along the lip of the drop-off.

"Oh God," he whispered. "It's her. It's after Mara."

38
Mara

There had not been a plan other than to lead the creature away from Declan and Natalie.

They had gone one way, so she had gone the other.

Mara had known, simply from the way that the old hag's eyes had fixed on her, that she was its only concern. Where she ran, the thing would follow.

Well, she had gotten exactly what she wanted.

Mara could hear the thing shrieking and hissing behind her as she ran along the edge of the cliff.

She could feel the last ounce of adrenaline siphoning away and knew that any second now she would not be able to run anymore. She was still bleeding from her hand and the near constant terror of the last hour was taking a heavy toll.

Soon she would pass out and either topple over the edge of the cliff or be torn apart by . . .

The cliff . . .

The ocean, black as oil, shimmered below her.

Don't even think about it.

Maybe . . . maybe I'd survive and swim to shore . . .

It's too far down. You'll kill yourself.

Maybe dead down there.

Definitely dead up here.

And then, suddenly, the decision was made for her. Her foot struck a rock and she went tumbling, her exhausted legs giving out under her.

As she stumbled off the cliff, she felt six-inch fingernails scraping her calf like tree branches.

The last thing Mara saw before her body smashed against the rocks was the old woman's face, contorted in utter hate, glaring down at her.

I know that face, Mara thought to herself. *She was at the wedding.*

And then she broke on the rocks and rolled limply into the cold black sea.

Somehow, still alive, somehow.

She drifted in a cold womb, unable even to move. Encased in water, the same terrible sick feeling returned.

I wasn't sick. I was never sick. It's the sea. I just want to swim away but it rejects me.

Dimly, she could see dark shapes circling her in the water.

She felt sharp teeth prickling her skin and then she was pulled back to the shore. The seals retreated to the ocean, leaving Mara on the beach.

From a great distance, Mara heard Declan swear as he shone his phone on her drenched carcass. She could feel herself lying on the wet sand—wet from both the salt water and her own blood, heavy trails of it running down her back. Still stunned, her legs twisted at obscene angles.

Mara blinked open her eyes and gazed at her friends, still in a haze of pain. But she was starting to feel better already.

MARA

"Hey..." she said, smiling at them. "We all good? Everyone okay?"

They said nothing. Mara noticed they were looking at her chest. She put a hand over her right breast and her fingers slipped into a massive gash. As she felt the size and depth of the wound, she had a moment of blind panic.

I'm going to die. I can't survive a wound like this. No one could. How am I even still breathing?

And then she felt the walls of flesh closing and actually had to yank her fingers out to stop them from being trapped in her chest cavity.

Natalie and Declan both shone their phones on her body. Everywhere the light touched, her skin was knitting and healing with magical speed, leaving only flawless, whole flesh behind. The wounds shriveled and shrank like slugs in salt.

Mara could feel broken bones knitting and re-forging within her. Wet, bloodied, and totally whole.

When she got to her feet, both Declan and Natalie took a step back in terror. She looked at them both, and saw her own shock and fear reflected in their eyes.

You've been asking yourself the wrong question, she told herself. *Ever since you woke up in the coffin, you've been asking, "Who are you?"*

The question is not who.

The question is what.

39
Declan

The worm woman had vanished back to whatever cave it had slithered out of.

That did not make the journey back to Declan's house any less tense.

The night had been such an endless chain of terrors that it did not seem possible that they had earned even the slightest reprieve. Something terrible, they felt, would happen again before they reached safety.

Three times, a bird stirring in the bushes, or some other innocent sound, sparked a panic, and they ran down the pitch-black road, certain that they were being chased by the worm woman.

When they reached Declan's cottage, Mara needed sleep. After she'd gone upstairs to the spare bedroom, Declan made Natalie a cup of tea.

She looked at him wordlessly, a single eyebrow raised.

He poured the tea down the sink and found some vodka.

They drank in silence.

"Was that real?" she said at last.

He nodded.

DECLAN

"All of it?"

He nodded again.

She buried her face in her hands and took a deep breath.

"When I first met you both together in Kilty's, you were talking about Fomor. That creature was what you were talking about, weren't you?"

Declan shook his head. "No. We were talking about something I saw. Something else."

"Oh fuck, there's more of them?" she asked.

"Yeah. Yeah, looks that way."

"What did you see?"

"I can't describe it," Declan said. "But it wasn't that thing that chased us tonight."

"How can you be sure?"

"Because what I saw was bigger. A lot bigger."

"Declan, I'm starting to think we need to get off this island. Away from all this weird shit."

"What about Mara?" he asked.

"How do you mean?"

"She's got nowhere to go," he said. "How's she supposed to escape the weird shit?"

"Declan," Natalie said quietly. "I think we both know she's part of the weird shit."

40

Mara, Mary, Máire, and Mara Alice

She's on a beach, walking along a beautiful white strand, beneath a stony gray sky. The sea, as ever, is black as oil.

There is a woman looking out at the ocean, longingly.

Mara goes to her.

They stand side by side, listening to the waves. She doesn't know how long they rest together. Time has run off and left them to their own devices.

"You're burned," Mara notes.

There are weals and blisters running up and down the woman's arms. Her face. Her neck. Her hair has been charred black.

Odd that she did not notice it before, but the woman does not seem to mind. She seems beyond pain now.

"I am burned," she replies. "But we are all drowned. Come with me."

They walk down the beach, which does not end. There are mounds in the sand, each one around the length of a bed.

"So many," Mara mutters.

"There will be more," the burned woman tells her. "After you."

Something different now.

They find two more women standing beside two open graves in the sand.

MARA, MARY, MÁIRE, AND MARA ALICE

They could be sisters. They could be twins.

One is wearing the ancient dress of an Irish peasant woman. The other's clothes are recent enough to merely look unfashionable.

"Who are you?" asks one.

"Cé sibhse?" asks the other.

"I'm Mara."

"Mary," says one twin.

"Is mise Máire," says the other.

"Mara Alice," says the burned woman with a lipless smile. "Curiouser and curiouser."

They all continue together in a companionable silence.

"If you are Mara Alice," says Mara.

"I am Mara Alice."

"Is it true then, that I killed you and stole your husband?"

The burned woman laughs.

"Jesus, Mary, and Joseph," says one of the twins. "That is nothing to be laughing about."

"Ní chúis sin a bheith ag gáire," the other agrees.

"Did you never hear it said," the burned woman asks somberly, "that when we sin, we sin against ourselves? It is truer for us than most."

They come to the end of the beach and stand at the last grave.

Overlooking the grave is a house, a tiny rough cottage, with a large well beside it.

She knows that house, it has floors that smell of misery, and walls that feel like rage.

And the well.

She knows what it is to climb down that well, to scream in darkness. Total and utter.

She knows that well. She knows it well.

They stand around the last grave in solemn contemplation.

"Who is buried here?" Mara asks.

"The first of us," Mara Alice says quietly. "The uncloaked woman. The first to be drowned in the burial tide."

Máire begins to sing, and the words seem to peel Mara's soul, exposing something wet and raw to cold air.

"Tá mé 'mo shuí, ó d'éirigh an ghealach aréir . . ."

Mary sings with her, their voices joining in perfect harmony. And then Mara hears more voices. And more. A choir. A great wall of sorrow and pain, arranged as music and lyric.

The song seems to rise from the very earth.

"How long has this been going on?" Mara asks.

The burned woman stretches an arm back up the beach, the wind catching flakes of blackened skin and casting them out over the sea like rose petals.

Mara follows her gaze back along the line of graves.

"And when will it end?" she asks.

The burned woman takes her by the hand and pulls her onto the grave.

"We shouldn't . . ." Mara begins.

"We must," Mara Alice replies. "We've mourned too long. It is time to wake the dead. You're close, Mara. I was closer. But, well, you see what happened to me. You have to be faster. You have to be better. You have to be fiercer. You have to remember. You have to burn."

And suddenly she is kissing her and Mara is burning. She feels fire enveloping her. All she can taste is ash, all she can smell is black smoke and charring flesh.

The burnt woman pulls away and shrieks, "Find the heart!"

And beneath her feet, something ancient and strong and so, so very angry breaks the soil and she is falling forever . . .

41
Mara

Mara landed on the floorboards of Declan's spare room, headfirst.

She blinked in pain, both from the blow and the sunlight streaming in through the window.

Hurried footsteps found her, and Declan and Natalie appeared in the doorway, identical looks of concern on their faces.

"Heeeeey," Mara mumbled groggily. "Everyone sleep well?"

They both nodded.

"Good. Because we've got a busy day ahead of us."

. . .

"So, are you going to tell us what we're looking for?" Declan asked Mara as the A-Team van trundled toward the western side of the island.

"I had a dream," Mara told him, her eyes never leaving the road.

"Okay?" Declan said.

"You know Mara Alice? Oisín's wife? She was in it."

"Mara, you know dreams aren't real, yeah?" Natalie said. "Fuck off, sheep!" She slapped the horn to warn the ovine in question to not even think of walking onto the road, and the van gave a croak like a sick toad.

"My memories are starting to come back," Mara said. "And she told me . . ."

"Mara Alice?"

"Yeah. She told me to 'find the heart.'"

"What's that supposed to mean?" Declan asked. "The heart of the island?"

"Home," said Natalie. "Duh. Home is where the heart is?"

"So . . . she wants you to go home?"

"Not my home. Her home."

"And you know where that is?"

"Yeah," said Mara. "I know where that is."

· · ·

The house, or rather, the remains of the house still stood, barely.

Mara cautiously stepped over the yellow tape that had cordoned off the charred ruin and looked around nervously.

"What is this place?" Declan asked.

"This was home," Mara said softly. "I lived here with Oisín. We were married. And do you know what? I think I was happy here."

"I know I'm a little late to the party," Natalie said. "But didn't you say you also lived in Conn's house?"

"I did. And I lived here with Oisín."

MARA

"You? Not Mara Alice?" Natalie said, brow furrowed. "So . . . we're saying she never existed?"

"No, she existed," said Mara with a sad smile. "She was me. They were all me. Mara Alice Dunne. Mary Rowen. Máire Rowen."

She watched as they digested that in silence.

"I don't know what I am," Mara told them. "All I know is, I don't age."

"You don't . . ." Declan's words dried up. He cleared his throat and started again. "You've never, like, felt the urge to drink our blood or anything?"

"Yours? No," she said. "Kidding," she added, after seeing the look on his face. "Do you believe me?"

They both nodded.

"After last night?" Natalie said. "Consider me convinced."

"Me too," Declan said.

Mara breathed out deeply.

She didn't say anything. She didn't need to. They knew.

"Okay, what exactly are we saying is going on here?" Natalie asked. "Like, alright, you were married to Conn Rowen in the twenties, yeah? As Máire Rowen née Carroll? So what happens to her? Why does Máire Carroll become Mary Fitch?"

"Conn gets older," Declan said. "She doesn't. And Máire starts wondering why."

"So then what happens?" Natalie asked with an ominous note.

"They bury her," Mara whispered. "They bury her. Me. And I wake up. And I don't remember anything. That's what they do. That's the cycle."

She remembered sitting in Declan's living room as Doctor Quinn fed her fact after fact, slowly stitching a new past for her.

"And then they come up with a new name. A new life. A new husband. It's all happened before."

"But Máire and Mary were both married to Conn," Declan noted.

"And then Mara Alice was married to his nephew. Jesus. Do you think they just pass her around the family?" Natalie asked.

Mara glanced at her in utter horror.

"Sorry," Natalie mumbled. "Sorry, I shouldn't have said that."

"If it's true, you should say it," Mara said. "Not saying anything is worse."

"How long has this been going on?" Natalie asked her.

In her mind's eye she saw the line of graves stretching down the beach to the horizon.

"Too long," Mara said. "And I'm ending it now."

"What I want to know is why?" Declan asked. "Why are they doing this to you? What's the point, what's the point of *any* of this?!"

Mara wasn't listening.

She had dropped to her knees and was crawling over the wooden floor. The boards were blackened and warped from a great heat. Mara worked her fingers into the cracks on either side of one board and pulled. The wood snapped. She flipped the blackened wood over to the pale, unburnt side.

There, stark and lurid, thin fingers of rusty black ran over the surface.

"That's . . . a lot of blood," Natalie said.

MARA

Mara dropped the board and shot to her feet. She could hear a voice in her mind, a memory as sharp and solid as an ice pick pushed into her brain: *"Oisín, I KNOW. I KNOW EVERYTHING."* The voice was bristling with rage and implacable hatred, barely human.

The voice was hers.

She remembered smoke clouding her eyes, the crackle of flames, heat running over her skin in waves.

She remembered standing in the middle of a burning house, grappling with someone.

No. Killing someone.

She could feel her fingers pressing into soft flesh, her lips pulled back in a savage grin.

The figure, a man, she thought, was pinned to the wall and trying to prize her fingers from his throat.

Begging. Begging to live. Trying to reach the part of her that was still human.

He failed. Her fingers pierced skin.

Now the memory began to break down, as if her mind was struggling to capture the intensity of what happened next.

Blood in the mouth.

Smoke.

Flesh tearing like freshly made bread.

And hatred. Pure hatred, black as tar.

I'll kill them all. Everyone walking on this island dies tonight.

Natalie tried to put a hand on her shoulder, but Mara shook her off. She staggered, her legs turning to water, a furious, agonized scream shuddering from her throat.

"What is it?" Declan asked.

She took a deep breath and nodded to herself. "I . . . I think this is where Oisín died," she told them.

"What happened?" Natalie asked. "Did he die in the fire or . . ."

Mara cut her off.

"Natalie. Can you get your hands on a few shovels?"

"Sure," Natalie said. "Who are we burying?"

"No one," Mara said. "Quite the opposite."

42
Oisín

It was amazing, Oisín mused, how even on an island as small as Inishbannock you could avoid the same person for years. It helped, of course, if the person you were steering clear of also didn't want to see you.

He had not seen his oldest uncle since before the wedding, almost eleven years ago now.

It wasn't fair. Oisín hadn't asked to be chosen. He hadn't asked for any of this. And if there was a single man still living on the island who should understand that, it was Conn Rowen.

He was banking a lot on Conn's understanding tonight.

In fact, he thought glumly as he picked up the phone and dialed for the cliffside cottage, he might well be taking his life into his hands with a single call.

"Hello," came a gruff voice at the end.

"Hi, Uncle Conn. It's Oisín."

There was a long silence.

"What do you want?" Conn asked at last.

"I was wondering if you wanted to come up to the house tonight for a game of cards?"

"What? Cards?"

He had not expected that mixture of incredulity and shock.

"Or whatever. I was just talking to Uncle Malachy and he said that you and he like to play cards."

"Did he?"

"And I thought it might be a good way to, I dunno. Get back in touch."

"What kind of . . . card game . . . did Malachy tell you we play?"

"He didn't. He just said you play cards sometimes. We don't have to. We can play something else, I think I have a box of chessmen around somewhere."

"I don't think so, Oisín."

He heard a sound as if Conn was about to hang up and blurted out, "She won't be here! She's going down singing in the Temple tonight."

There was a long pause.

"Conn, please. I need to talk. And you're the only one I can talk to. Please."

There was a longer pause.

"I don't play cards sober. Make sure you have some good whiskey in."

"I will," *said Oisín with a relieved laugh.* "See you tonight."

• • •

"Singing, is it? She likes to sing?"

"Yeah," *Oisín said, dealing out the cards for the next hand.* "She loves to sing."

Oisín took out his phone and played his ringtone. It was a recording of his wife singing. The voice was utterly mesmerizing and the old man listened as if in a trance. Oisín put the phone away and the spell broke.

"And you're not down there to see her?" Conn asked.

Oisín shook his head.

"I'm giving her some space. We've hit a rough patch."

Conn's eyes narrowed suspiciously, like a man who was intimately acquainted with rough patches and took them very seriously.

"Did yours sing?" Oisín asked.

Conn took a sip of his drink. "Máire was a great one for the singing. Mary . . . no, I don't remember Mary singing. But then, she was never as happy as Máire."

"I don't think Mara Alice is very happy, either," said Oisín.

A silence fell on the room. The kind of silence that usually follows, "So I got the results."

Conn said nothing, and studied his cards like they were holy texts.

"Conn, after Máire was gone, Mary stayed with you? You got a second chance?"

His uncle grunted.

"How did you manage that?"

"What the feck do you mean? Manage what?"

"It's not normal, is it? When she's brought back? It's usually a different man."

"It is."

"But not with you. You got two bites of the apple."

"The next in line was your uncle Malachy. It was decided that he was not a suitable husband for her. That he wouldn't be able to keep her content for fifty days, let alone fifty years. We were married for fifty years, Oisín. Do you know how many men on this island were able to last that long?"

Oisín shook his head.

Conn tapped his chest proudly. "Me. Mise mé féin. So it was decided that when Máire went away, and Mary arrived, that I would be her husband once more. Instead of Malachy."

"Who decided that, Uncle Conn?" Oisín asked quietly.

Conn took another sip of his whiskey. "I did," he said. "I told the Comhairle that if they tried to pair my wife with Malachy, I'd burn the whole fucking island to the ground. I told them I'd give her the cloak."

In the distance, Oisín could hear the faraway baying of a sheepdog.

"Malachy doesn't know that," Conn said. "He can't."

Oisín nodded.

"So. I see where your head is at," Conn said. "You think Mara Alice is not long for this world? And you want to know how you can convince the Comhairle to keep you on the payroll instead of passing her to Padraig?"

Oisín gave a grim smile. "Actually, I think there's been talk on the Comhairle of trying a woman next time."

"What?"

"Next Mara might be a lesbian, like."

"Why would they do that?"

"Arrah, gotta keep up with the times."

"True enough. Who knows, might work better. What'll Padraig have to say about that?"

"What did Malachy say?"

"Ah."

They continued to play in silence.

"So why did you do it?" Oisín asked.

"Why?" Conn stared at him.

"You were married to her for fifty years. And another fifteen with Mary. You risked your life every day for sixty-five years."

"Sure, look in the mirror and tell me why. You're what, forty now? Don't look a day over twenty-five."

OISÍN

"That's all it was? That was the only reason?"

"Fuck off. What are you doing, Oisín? What are you trying to dig out of me?"

"You loved her. Didn't you? Like, I mean, you properly loved her?"

Conn said nothing. He simply stared at Oisín with cold fury in his ancient eyes. "I know what it is," he said at last. "And I am not that big a fool."

"I know what she is, too," Oisín whispered. "And I am that big a fool."

"What is this?" Conn demanded. "Why did you invite me here, boy?"

"You threatened to give her the cloak. If they wouldn't let you be her husband again. Would you have done it?"

"Of course not!" Conn said.

"No?"

"Do you have any idea what would have happened? The fucking carnage? This whole island has had a tiger by the tail for four hundred fucking years and you want to just let go? What do you think the tiger's going to do? Heh? Let bygones be bygones?"

"She's not an animal."

"She's worse. She's almost a person."

"You don't believe that. I know you feel how I feel. Even now. I know that's why you haven't been near us ever since I became her husband. You're not afraid. You still love her."

Conn sprang to his feet and drew back his hand. Oisín braced for a blow that never came.

Instead, Conn lowered his palm, threw on his coat, and made for the door.

"Did you never want to set her free?!" Oisín called after him.

Conn stopped dead at the door. "Every day," he whispered.

"How many people have we lost?" Oisín pleaded. "Aren't you sick of checking yourself every day to see if you're turning? Aren't you sick of lying? I mean, she's not even bringing the fish and the weather like she used to. The whole island's sick. You can feel it, can't you? What are we even getting out of it?"

"We get to live," Conn said gruffly.

"Conn. That's not enough. Not anymore. I don't know what kind of life you're living, but when I think about staying here as long as you have . . . no thanks."

"What are you asking me, boy?" Conn repeated softly.

Oisín finally said it. "Give me the cloak. Please. Let me end this."

Conn stood as still as a dead tree. He said nothing. But Oisín, to his amazement, saw a tiny, barely perceptible nod.

"Let me talk to her," Oisín said. "And if she's willing . . . I'll bring her down to the cottage."

Another nod, and Conn was gone.

Oisín heaved a sigh of relief and hoped that he hadn't made a terrible mistake. In his mind he rehearsed everything that he would say to her.

I'm sorry that I lied to you.

I'm sorry that I did this to you.

I'm sorry that I was a part of this.

He wondered if it would be enough.

He heard a key grinding in the lock of the front door and footsteps coming toward the kitchen.

He turned to look at her.

And in that moment he knew it was already too late.

The anger that he had always sensed in his wife, the restless unquiet of a caged animal, had risen and transformed her. Her face was feral, her mouth wider, her ears flattened back like an alley cat's. Worst of all, her eyes burned with an awful, inhuman fury.

OISÍN

She stood in the center of the kitchen, and her head tilted curiously, as if she was seeing Oisín for the first time and didn't know quite what to make of him.

"Alice," he whispered desperately. "I'm sorry . . ."

"Sorry?" *she repeated, like a bird mimicking the sound of a word without understanding its meaning.*

Oisín refused to look away. He'd accept her anger in whatever form it took.

"I'm so sorry," he whispered gently.

"I know," she said.

Suddenly, her body seemed to blur.

He was pinned to the wall. And what felt like iron nails pierced the skin of his neck, and all he could see were teeth.

"I know," *she repeated.* "Oisín, I know. I KNOW EVERYTHING."

43
Declan

Declan watched in numb horror as, one by one, Mara unearthed the three coffins, leaving the lids naked and exposed. She placed her hands on the coffin of Oisín Dunne.

"Mara, wait," Declan called.

"What?" she answered, without turning around.

"It's just . . . what if it's dangerous? We don't actually know for certain there wasn't an outbreak . . ."

He turned his head away and reflexively placed a hand over his mouth as Mara tore open the coffin lid with a savage snarl.

"Yeah," she said. "We do."

As Mara stared down at Oisín's body, Declan felt he could see all the life drain out of her. Her shoulders slumped, her hands hung limply by her sides. She staggered to her feet and opened the next coffin. And then the third.

She turned to look at them. There were tears in her eyes, but her voice was steady. "Thank you both for everything you've done. But you need to get away from me. Don't come looking. Don't even talk about me. Go home. Live your lives. Forget the island. Forget everything."

DECLAN

She began to walk toward the graveyard wall. Declan tried to stop her but she easily pushed past him.

"Wait! Where are you going? We can't just leave them like this!"

"It doesn't matter," she replied. "None of it matters."

"Where are you going?"

"Home."

"You can't walk home alone!" he called after her. "We've seen what's on this island, Mara. This place is full of monsters!"

Mara turned and gave him a sad smile. "And I'm the worst one."

He would have gone after her, had he not heard Natalie scream. Spinning around, he saw her leaning over the three coffins, crying and trembling. He ran to her side, looking inside them for the first time. He was immediately and violently sick.

It was not that they were dead bodies.

It was not that they were rotted and decayed.

It was not that they had been charred and burned.

It was that they were not bodies at all.

They were simply parts.

They were people who had been smashed.

And torn.

And broken.

Until they were not people anymore.

44
Cian

He would always be grateful to her.

For many reasons. The good times had been good.

Later, when he looked back on those first few months on the island, full of wonder and discovery, he would admit to himself that it was because of her that they had been the best times.

She was the first face he had seen when he arrived on the island, and her smile had made him feel welcome, that he was not making the biggest mistake of his life.

She was waiting for him on the tiny jetty, wrapped in a coat that did not quite hide a trim figure, and her dark-brown hair flew in the wind like a war banner.

She grinned as he stepped uneasily off the boat and ambled toward him, hand outstretched.

"Doctor Quinn?" he asked, almost yelling to be heard over the rough sea and shaking her hand gratefully.

"Helen, please. Cian Morley? Fáilte go dtí Inishbannock."

"Thank you."

"How was the boat over?" Helen asked.

"Um . . ." He leaned in a little to be heard without shouting and before realizing the gesture could be misconstrued.

CIAN

Helen, he noted, did not lean back. In fact, her eyes flashed with interest.

He filed that away. She was older than him, maybe by as much as twenty years. But if she was up for it, perhaps . . .

"I think I must have offended the boatman," he confided to her.

"Oh no," she said breezily. "He's like that with everyone. Isn't that right, Stiofán?"

"What?" the boatman barked from where he was tying the boat to the jetty.

"I said you're a hateful bollocks."

"Fuck off, cunt," he replied, as if she'd asked about the weather.

"Come on," she said to Cian with a cheeky wink. "I'm taking you home."

They drove over the island and he got a chance to see the cliffs and sea in all its rough, bleak beauty.

She pulled to a stop outside a construction site where the bare skeleton of a new build stood.

"So there's your house," she said dryly. "Around a hundred thousand over budget and half a year over schedule. But it'll be lovely when it's finally done. Well, get out. You brought a tent, right?"

He looked at her in stunned shock. She held a blank expression for a few seconds before breaking into a delightfully evil cackle.

"Oh I had ya!" she crowed. "Relax, you're staying with me until it's finished."

He burst out laughing as she pulled back onto the road.

"So, question for you?" he said.

"Shoot."

"I thought people weren't allowed to have cars on the island?"

"I'm a doctor. I'm not people."

"Ah, makes sense."

"A few residents are allowed to have cars if it's deemed vital to their work."

"Deemed by who?"

"The Comhairle. Think of it as a county council but with less democracy and more meetings."

"So how do I get a car?"

"You join the Comhairle. And you demonstrate that your work requires the use of a car. Or you get a bike. Or you get in good with someone who already has a car."

He smiled. "Doesn't the only doctor on the island have better things to do than ferrying tourists around?"

Helen looked at him quite seriously. "One, you're not a tourist. The wind farm is going to do amazing things for this place. And as long as you're here, you're part of our community. We look after our own. And two, no one on this fecking island ever gets sick and I am bored out of my mind half the time."

He smiled. "Yeah, so I've heard."

She looked at him a little suspiciously. "What have you heard?"

"Just . . . the island. They say people on Inishbannock live very long lives. That they don't get sick. Isn't that the legend?"

She shrugged. "Sea air. Lot of fresh fish."

"That's all?"

"How do you mean? It's not Tír na nÓg if that's what you're thinking."

"I dunno. I guess I've just been thinking about death a lot recently."

She nodded. "Who did you lose?"

He looked out the window. The mainland was visible on the horizon over the sea, a reminder that he had not gone far enough.

"My mam. Last year. Alzheimer's."

"Ah, Cian, I'm sorry," she said softly. "That's awful."

He dipped his chin in acknowledgment then changed the subject: "So I'm going to be living with you?"

"You are. You'll have the spare bedroom. Not nearly as fancy as your place is going to be, but it's comfortable."

"You're going to have to put up with me for months."

"I am. Poor me."

"How did you get stuck with that?"

"Everyone on the Comhairle drew lots."

"You drew the short straw?"

She snorted. "I rigged it. I saw your picture."

He laughed and actually blushed a little. She smiled.

"Sorry. Fair warning. The women on this island have spent their lives around beardy old fishermen. They'll eat you alive if you're not careful."

"Promises, promises," he replied.

• • •

He did end up using the spare room, but only to store his clothes.

Helen was a wonderful lover. She could be dirty, or sweet, or tender, and had an uncanny knack for knowing the right mode for his moods. And she was funny, too. Their afterglow-warmed chats in the tossed sheets were regularly interrupted with gales of raucous laughter. But sometimes the unwanted thought crept in to his mind that his relationship with this older, nurturing woman was his way of dealing with . . .

And then he would push it away. It felt good. It made him happy. It made her happy.

No need to bring Freud into this.

If he felt guilty at all, it was in knowing that Helen was falling in love with him. That was regrettable. He liked her a great deal and he didn't want to hurt her. Ultimately, she was a means to an end.

When he finally struck, it was when she was at her most vulnerable.

• • •

"Not yet, not yet, not yet, I am SO CLOSE . . ."

"Helen . . ."

"OH FFFFFFFFFFUCK YES . . ."

"Helen. How old are you really?"

Her body suddenly stiffened and he yelped as she pulled away so quickly she almost took an inch off him.

He sat up. She had retreated to the end of the bed. Her hair, wild and disheveled, covered half her face, and one eye looked out at him, hurt and accusing. A hand came up across her breasts and the other modestly covered her lap.

"What?" she mumbled. "Why would you ask me that? Why would you ask me that now?!"

She looked down at her naked body, as if trying to find the wrinkle or sag that had sold her out to the enemy.

"I found your medical license," he said. "Your first one. And I did some maths."

"I . . . I'm not that old . . ." she mumbled defensively.

He lifted a hand to reassure her.

"I don't care," he said. "It won't change how I feel about you. Or how beautiful I think you are. I just want to know the truth. How old are you, Helen?"

After a moment, she whispered a number. He didn't catch it, but the first two syllables were "seven," which told him enough.

CIAN

He nodded.

"Why don't you come back to bed? And tell me all about it."

• • •

"I shouldn't have told you any of this," she whispered nervously against his chest. "If the others find out . . ."

"I promise," he said as he stroked her hair. "I won't tell a soul. Who'd believe me anyway?"

"You believed me," she murmured curiously to herself.

He didn't tell her why he believed it. It was not that it was believable. It was that he desperately needed it to be true. Watching his mother fading away, not just her body, but her mind. Watching her very soul slowly decaying before his eyes, day after agonizing day . . .

For even a chance at escaping that, Cian would put his faith in anything.

• • •

He played it very carefully. Once he had been accepted into the Comhairle with Helen's enthusiastic support and his house finished, he began slowly and carefully dismantling their relationship.

It was not a sudden breakup. He could not risk anyone suspecting what he was up to, and he did not want to make an enemy of Helen. And, truth be told, he didn't want to hurt her more than he had to. Fortunately, Helen had not wanted to attract any gossip so they had kept their relationship secret.

At last, he regretfully told her that he felt their romance had run its course, but that he hoped they could still be friends.

She had accepted with grace and dignity, and a smile that almost masked the fact that her heart was breaking at being alone again.

They had hugged and she had even offered to drive him home.

In his new house, he showered and changed into his best clothes for a night out. Styled his hair. Put on some cologne. Prepared for war.

He would have to be clever about it.

But he always was, you had to give him that.

He couldn't simply drop the whole truth on her. He'd let her ask the questions. Do the talking. Reveal her insecurities. Her unhappiness. Her confusion. Her doubt.

He'd build her carefully, painstakingly, secretly.

Like a bomb.

And then, one night, he would set her off.

• • •

He walked down the pier on the way to the Temple, his heart in his throat.

He stopped outside the alleyway to steel his nerves.

A gasp and a moan drew his attention.

Far down at the end of the alleyway, just beside the side entrance to the Temple, he could see the shadowy figure of a bearded man, his back against the wall and his hands folded behind his head, cushioning his skull as it pressed rhythmically against the pebble-dash.

Another figure knelt before the bearded man, mostly invisible in the shadows, though he could make out a white sweater with a black-and-red-check pattern as the shoulders bobbed rhythmically up and down.

Realizing that he was intruding, Cian walked on.

It seemed like the whole island had come out for the open mic night, with the exception of the good doctor. He was vain enough to

CIAN

think that she was still nursing a broken heart, but even when they'd been together she'd never been much for a night out in the Temple. He got the impression that Helen didn't really like anyone else on Inishbannock. Or maybe it was simply that she'd been here too long, and had gotten bored with them. Maybe that's why she had fallen for Cian so hard, simply because he was new.

He took a quick survey of the crowded bar. Malachy Rowen laughing at something his sister, Gráinne, had said while passing him his pint. Even Stiofán the boatman, enemy to all mankind, was sitting in the corner chatting with Derbhle, the librarian, and apparently, amazingly, both were drawing some enjoyment from the experience.

"Hi, Cian!" a cheerful voice piped up behind him.

He turned and saw a Vietnamese woman of around thirty-five waving to him with a rum and Coke in one hand.

He smiled. "Hi, Sara."

Sara Do and her husband, Martin Connell, ran the local bakery, and he'd been introduced to them both when he'd joined the Comhairle. Martin had struck him as a massive dried shite in a beard trying to pass as human, but he'd taken a shine to Sara. He'd gotten the sense that island life was driving her slowly mad with boredom. He could relate.

"I'm glad you came," she said brightly.

"Why is that?"

"Because we gotta get you a girlfriend."

"Oh?"

"Yeah. Handsome single guy like you. You're a liability. With all these married women around, we gotta get you taken off the board before any drama happens. So, let me tell you who here is available, I know everybody . . ."

Ordinarily, Cian wouldn't have been averse to Sara playing matchmaker, but he had someone squarely in his sights tonight. He tried to change the subject.

"Is Martin not with you?"

Her brow furrowed a little as if suddenly remembering that her husband existed.

"He's here. Somewhere. He said he was going to the bar to wet his whistle and then he just disappeared . . ."

Cian looked up. Martin Connell had just entered the room from the toilets, followed by Padraig Dunne. He didn't normally pay attention to what people were wearing, but he couldn't help noticing that Padraig was sporting a white sweater with a black-and-red-check pattern.

"What's so funny?" Sara asked.

"Nothing," he said, trying to stifle a laugh. "Forget it."

Well, Cian reasoned. Martin had been getting his whistle wet. Points for honesty.

The man in question ambled over to join them and put his arm around his wife, pecking her chastely on the cheek.

Cian said hi to him and made the universal gesture for "I'm going to make you think I'm going for a pint before sitting with you whereas in actuality you will never see me again tonight, you utter bore of a man" before pushing his way through to the bar.

"Your usual, Mr. Morley?" Gráinne asked.

"Please," he said with a grin. "Great crowd tonight."

"Oh yes, you've never been down for open mic before, have you?"

"I'm expecting great things."

She fixed him with quite a serious look. "Inishbannock will exceed your expectations. Trust me."

She tilted her head to the figure who was taking the stage. A hush fell on the crowd and Cian felt not only anticipation but tension. It *felt like he was back in Dublin Zoo, watching a tiger pacing back and forth, inches away, behind thick glass. Not in danger, but very close to it.*

She was beautiful. Long brown hair and great, sad eyes. When she took the mic, she didn't even introduce herself.

They knew who she was.

She began to sing, and while he recognized the song, he didn't recognize what it did to him.

"Tá mé 'mo shuí, ó d'éirigh an ghealach aréir."

Her voice seemed to send a chill over his skin. He felt tiny hairs rising on the back of his neck. If he hadn't believed what Helen had told him about her before, he believed it now.

Not human.

When the song ended, there was a moment of hushed awe, and then a triumphant roar.

She gave a modest little half bow, replaced the mic in the stand, and stepped off the stage. Cian studied her as she made her way to the bathroom. He waited outside the door until he heard her re-emerge and then bumped into her.

It felt like banging his shoulder into a tree. He saw her face pop with shock and concern as he reeled back against the wall.

"Oh my God, I am so sorry!" she said.

"Ow, fuck, who do you play for, Leinster or Munster?" he asked with a grin, massaging his shoulder.

"I'm going to assume you're talking about rugby?" she said uncertainly.

"I was," he said. "I saw you sing by the way. You were absolutely stunning."

She blushed.

"Well, thank you. Mr. . . ."

"Cian Morley," he said. "New to the parish."

"Oh, right. The guy. The Dublin guy. The wind farm."
"What it says on my business cards. And you are?"
"Mara Dunne. Everyone calls me Alice."

• • •

Cian awoke in his armchair, where he'd been sleeping off a combination of thirty-year-old whiskey and a comedown from the previous night's terror and adrenaline. Night had fallen, and the world outside the window was black.

Irritably, he scratched his side. The bite had healed up flawlessly, but in the last few days the area had become tender and itchy. He'd started to notice strange pink blotches on the skin. Probably just a summer rash.

His phone kept buzzing and he picked it up without checking the caller ID.

"Mara," he slurred. "Where the fuck are you?"

"Oh Christ," came a voice on the other end. "She's not with you?"

He almost didn't recognize her voice, she sounded so terrified. He could picture her whispering into her phone while hiding under the bed.

"Helen?" he said.

"Cian, I need you."

"What's wrong?"

"Where's Mara?"

"She hasn't been home all day. I don't know where she is."

"Fuck!"

"What is it?"

"I just heard a window being broken downstairs. Cian, I think she's here."

CIAN

"Calm down. I'll be right over."

"Cian, what if she knows?!"

He didn't answer. If she was right, what could he possibly have told her that would calm her down? He just searched frantically for his car keys and ran for the door.

45
Doctor Helen Quinn

After Cian hung up, Helen experienced a sudden, white-hot panic. But then, just as quickly as it arrived, it faded.

She realized that she didn't care.

She had been on the island too long.

Draped in a cold composure, she dressed. She brushed her hair and put on her favorite brooch, a gift from her mother, and went down to meet the monster in the kitchen.

Her old cast-iron teapot was steaming on the hob.

Mara sat at the kitchen table with a cup of tea in front of her. If she hadn't been caked in mud up to her elbows, with the kitchen chilled from the breeze of the newly smashed window, the scene would have appeared to be a perfectly ordinary midnight chat.

"You remembered where the tea was?" Helen asked politely.

Mara smiled.

"Sit down, Doctor," she said.

Helen did.

Mara gave a chuckle.

"Is something funny?" Helen asked.

"I was just thinking, you probably know exactly what I'm going to say. We've probably had this conversation . . . how many times?"

Helen swallowed nervously. "I don't know what you mean?"

Mara raised a finger. "Now, before we go any further. Let me ask you a question. Did I love Oisín?"

Helen nodded. "Yes. You did."

"Right. But see, here's the thing. I've just seen what I did to him."

Helen's eyes trailed down to the mud caked on Mara's arms. "Oh God," she whispered.

"That was a violent outbreak, wasn't it? So here's my question, Helen. If I loved Oisín and I did that to him? What do you think I'll do to you?"

"Mara . . ."

"So. We are done with lies, yes?"

Helen nodded desperately.

"Say it," Mara whispered.

"We're done with lies," Helen answered, her voice catching in her throat.

"Good. That's very good. Because I have so many questions for you, Helen. I scarcely know where to start. What am I?"

"I don't know."

"Helen . . ."

"I don't! If there's a word for what you are, I don't know it."

"The first time we met you fed me a load of bullshit. About my parents, my past. Was any of that true?"

"No," said Helen.

"So who am I? What's . . . what's my real name?"

"What?"

"Who am I?! Am I Mara, Máire, Mara Alice, Mary . . . ?"

Helen actually laughed. "You think I know?! The only ones who know that are out there in the dark eating sheep."

"What do you mean?"

Helen gave a grim smile. "You don't actually know anything, do you? You're just trying to scare me."

Mara stood and flipped the solid-oak table with a flick of her wrist. It smashed into the wall with a crash so loud Helen felt it in her bones. Instinctively, she jumped back, knocked into the fridge, and fell to the floor.

"Maybe," said Mara. "Do you feel scared?"

Helen nodded.

"Oh," Mara said, kneeling down until they were face-to-face. "This isn't scary. Do you know what's scary? Waking up in a coffin."

"That wasn't supposed to happen!"

"Oh! Now we're getting to it. Please, Helen. Explain to me what was *supposed* to happen."

"Every time . . . you're re-set. We bury you. After three days and three nights the body is exhumed. Your memory is always gone. We . . . help you create a new version of yourself."

"You wipe my memory?"

"Yes."

"How?"

Helen tried to avoid her gaze. Mara took a hold of her chin and forced her to meet her eyes.

"We drown you," she whispered.

Mara looked at her in disbelief.

"You drown me?"

"Yes."

"How . . . how many times? How many times have you done this to me?"

"I was born here seventy-seven years ago," Helen said. "You were already here, looking just like you do now. And they'd been doing it for centuries."

Mara staggered back and buried her face in her hands. Helen could hear Mara mumbling to herself, something that sounded like "nonononono."

Finally she threw her head back and screamed. "WHY! Why did you DO this to me?!"

"We have to . . ." Helen said.

"You're a doctor!" Mara screamed. "You're supposed to HELP people!"

"I AM!" Helen yelled, anger finally overtaking fear. "I'M PROTECTING THEM FROM YOU! Every time you recover your memories someone dies! You're a MONSTER, Mara, and every so often you get out of your cage and the blood flows in rivers!"

"Then why keep me in the cage? Just let me go!"

"Because then *everyone* dies . . ."

Suddenly, the kitchen was flooded in harsh white light.

Both women's heads swiveled. Mara's turned to the window. Helen's twisted to the knife rack on the kitchen counter. She drew a carver, and lunged.

46
Mara

Mara felt the knife enter her chest, just under her right breast.

So fast as to be painless.

There was a moment where Helen's eyes were locked with hers.

It was an instant so intense, so intimate, that for a moment she almost forgot who she was. Was she Mara, staring at Helen in shock? Or was she Helen, looking at the woman she had stabbed, whose blood was trickling across the kitchen tiles?

And then the connection broke, and Helen pulled the knife back, and stabbed her again and again.

Mara wanted to move, to defend herself, to throw the snarling wild-eyed woman off her.

But all her strength was gone. It was like she was watching a film, a passive observer.

A terrible thought hit her: *What if she kills me?*

A worse one followed: *What if she can't?*

The knife slit her again, and she felt something that had to be important burst under the blade like an overripe orange.

MARA

What if this never ends? What if she just keeps stabbing me forever?

So it was almost a relief when her vision began fading.

Helen was now a blurry nightmare of hair and terrified eyes and spit-flecked teeth, slowly melting into blackness.

And then, dimly, she saw a figure emerge from the shadows behind the doctor, something big and weighty in its hand.

47
Cian

Cian still had his old key.

He unlocked the front door and ran into the kitchen and found them in a fight to the death, his former lover straddling his current one in a lake of blood, trying desperately to kill her with a carving knife as the wounds healed over and over.

She never even saw him.

She likely didn't even feel it when he took the old iron kettle and hit her on the back of the head so hard her skull caved in.

48
Mara

"I'm sorry," Cian mumbled. "I'm sorry I couldn't tell you the truth."

He grabbed her, embraced her, blood and all, and sobbed that he was so glad that she was alright.

Mara was overwhelmed, nothing made sense. She stared at the body on the floor.

The back of Helen's head was a black mass of blood-caked hair, and she was lying as stiffly and unnaturally as a plastic doll. No point even checking. She was dead.

Cian had killed Helen.

Cian had killed Helen to save *her*.

Already, the flesh of Mara's body was knitting itself back together, but she had no doubt that if he had not intervened, the doctor would have ended her life.

And then came the guilt.

Helen had only attacked because she feared her life was in danger. Mara had broken into her home in the dead of night, she had threatened her.

"I . . . it's . . . I wasn't really going to hurt her, I-I-I was just trying to scare her, I just wanted to know the truth and then she . . ." Mara began to stammer a confession.

"It's okay, it's okay," Cian soothed her, stroking her hair and kissing her forehead.

"But we need to go. We need to get out of here now."

Back in the Volvo, Mara sat, numb and wet, covered in her own blood for the second time in less than twelve hours. Out of the corner of her eye, she watched as Cian calmly drove them home.

"Now that Helen's gone, they're going to come after us. Do you know what they're going to do?" he asked her.

"They're going to drown me," she intoned quietly. "And bury me. And dig me up. And then this will all start again."

He nodded, almost proudly. "You've been doing some detective work."

"You knew about this? The whole time?"

"Yes," he said.

She was so angry she literally couldn't form the words.

"Before you . . . do anything," he said. "Let me explain. I've been trying to save you ever since I found out what they've been doing to you."

"Really?"

"You don't believe me?"

"No. Not at all. Not even a little. I think you're a liar and every word that comes out of your mouth . . ." Mara felt her hackles raise, but swiftly recalled Helen's caved-in skull and pulled herself back from the edge.

"Okay. I get the point. And you're right, I lied to you. Can I tell you why?"

She fumed in silence.

MARA

"Mara, I'm not the first guy who wanted to help you. Do you know now what happened to Oisín?"

She focused on the road ahead.

"You have . . . a temper. You're not always in control. And when you lose control . . . well, I think you've figured that out by now. And every time I wanted to tell you the truth, I remembered that you killed your last husband."

"Well, we have murder in common, don't we?"

He kept his gaze on the wheel, but his jaw pulsed. "I killed her to save your life," he said, all wounded pride.

"I wasn't talking about the doctor. You killed Conn Rowen, didn't you?"

His head whipped around in shock just as they pulled into the driveway. Cian turned off the engine.

She tensed. Whatever came next, she would not be taken unawares.

"How do you know that?" he asked at last.

"Doesn't matter," she said. "I know it."

I knew it was you when I heard the killer's voice and had a sudden urge to rip his throat out with my teeth, she thought to herself.

"Then it doesn't matter if we did it, does it?" he asked.

"Who's 'we'?"

"You gotta let me have some secrets, darling."

"I think there have been enough secrets," Mara growled.

"A friend. Someone who's on our side. When we're safe off the island I'll tell you who."

. . .

Once inside, Mara was directed by Cian to strip and put her bloodied, muddied clothes in a bin liner, which he then took away, promising to dispose of them. He told her to pack a bag, a few changes of clothes, phone, charger.

She showered for what felt like three hours and changed into clean clothes. While she was upstairs she could hear him talking on the phone in hushed, desperate tones.

She still didn't trust him, but then she remembered Helen Quinn's lifeless body sprawled on the kitchen floor.

He had done that. He had done that to save her.

That had to count for something.

And what other choice did she have?

Either Cian was her only way off the island, or there was no way off the island.

She took out her phone and wrote a quick text to Natalie and Declan:

> I'm getting out. Will call you when it's safe.
> Thanks for everything.
> Love you both.

"Your clothes are taken care of," Cian said as she came downstairs. "But we don't have a lot of time. Sooner or later they're going to find out that Helen's . . . they're going to find Helen."

"Who are they?" she asked.

"You know some of them," Cian said with a shrug. "Just normal people. There's only a few of them that keep all the secrets, most folk on the island have no idea what's going on. Helen was running the whole thing. And when they find her? Nowhere on the island is safe. They'll come after you. And drown you again. And this will all have been for nothing. Especially if they've found Conn's body, too."

MARA

"Why did you kill him?"

He grimaced. "Wasn't the plan. He was supposed to be out drinking last night. I was just trying to rob his safe."

"Why? What was in the safe? What was worth that?"

Cian gave a strange smile. "Here's a question. Why haven't you just left? You were obviously miserable here. With me. Why didn't you just get on a boat and leave?"

"I . . . I tried. I couldn't."

He nodded. "You're bound to the island. That thing that Conn kept in his safe? That's what's keeping you here. You can't leave without it."

Every time I went into the sea. Every time my feet left the island, I felt like I was dying. A burial tide.

It was unbelievable, but she knew it was true nonetheless.

"What is it?" Mara asked.

"Honestly?" he said with an embarrassed smile. "I never asked. And I never opened the box. Guess we'll find out tonight."

"And are you going to tell me where we're going?" she asked him as they pulled out of the driveway.

"Ballydonn," he said. "The Temple."

Her shoulders tensed. "Isn't that the most dangerous place we could be?"

Cian shook his head. "The most dangerous place we could be is home. We're isolated out here. They could surround the house and trap us like rats. We go to Ballydonn and head to the Temple. Lots of witnesses. They won't be able to touch us."

"So what, we wait in the Temple, have a drink . . ."

"I'm driving, but you go ahead."

"For how long?"

"We need two things. The box we took from Conn's cottage and a boat. My friend is going to bring us both."

She started to put two and two together. Cian was an outsider with not many friends on the island, but he still had a large group of people under his control.

"Your friend is one of the engineers on the wind farm. And he's going to bring us one of the boats you use to inspect the offshore windmills."

He gave a smile. "That's certainly one plausible theory."

She watched the island go past the window and wondered if she'd ever miss it.

Such a strange, dead place.

They drove up Main Street and Cian parked opposite the church. The second the engine shut off, Mara felt a surge of paranoia.

"C'mon, let's get off the street," Cian said in a hushed voice.

As they moved down the silent road, Mara kept imagining that the echo of their footsteps was the sound of someone following them. She almost broke into a run as she heard the sound of music and laughter coming from the Temple. But as soon as they entered, she felt the heat, and music, and noise of the packed pub and felt a little safer.

Cian was right. Safety in numbers.

The same three-man band, the one that had been playing the night she and Declan had gone for a walk on the pier, was up on the stage playing "The Reel of Bogie" and the atmosphere buzzed with energy. Cian found them a small free table in the center of the pub, and she sat down, trying to look like she was out for a fun night and hadn't been nearly stabbed to death by a woman who was now lying on her kitchen floor with a smashed skull.

"What happens now?" she whispered to him.

"We wait," he said. "We sit, we relax, we stay in view of all these nice people, and we pass the time until my friend texts us."

Cian took out his phone and laid it on the table. The screen remained black.

To distract herself, Mara took a survey of the bar. She noticed Malachy's usual stool was empty, despite the packed pub. With a pang, she realized that it would probably take a long time for anyone to figure out that Malachy was missing. As far as Gráinne knew, Malachy had withdrawn into a depression and wasn't speaking with anyone. She had despised Malachy, from the moment she had met him and sensed that poisonous cocktail of hate and anger and lecherous desire wafting off him like tobacco fumes and cold sweat.

And yet, when she thought of him, staggering toward her with an infant abomination yowling at her from his chest . . .

When she thought of how he had ended, and how his body would never be found and buried, how he would never be properly mourned . . .

When she thought of how the awful, inexplicable, inhuman malevolence of Inishbannock had warped and tortured and ultimately devoured him . . .

She shed a tear for the old man.

One.

And promised herself that she would escape this island forever.

There was a smash of glass and a raucous cheer from the crowd.

Mara glanced around and saw Padraig all agog at her, with his mouth hanging open. Suddenly, the spell broke, and he was on his knees, picking up bits of broken glass and mumbling apologies to the people around him.

A shadow passed over Mara's vision.

"Hello there, lovebirds. You know, I don't think I've seen the two of you in here together since . . . well, since our recent troubles."

Gráinne was standing over them, a pint in each hand. "On the house," she said, placing the pints down in front of them.

"Not for me, thanks, Gráinne," said Cian with a smile. "I'm driving now, remember?"

"Oh, of course. And congratulations on joining the vehicular elite," Gráinne said. "Well then, do you mind if I join you?"

"Not at all," Cian said. "I was just about to make a call."

He got up, grabbing his phone, and before Mara could protest, Gráinne had taken his seat.

"*Sláinte*," she said, raising her glass and Mara wordlessly clinked it.

"It's good to see you two getting on," Gráinne noted. "It's none of my business of course. But I've been sensing that there was a bit of tension between the two of you."

Mara drank, even though the last thing she wanted was anything going into her nauseous stomach.

Setting foot in the Temple was a terrible mistake.

Why had she let Cian talk her into coming here?

Gráinne was Conn's sister.

She was Oisín's mother.

MARA

There was no way she was ignorant of what had been going on.

"It's awful when a couple fights. It has a way of rippling out and affecting the whole family. The whole community. Do you know what I mean by that, Mara?"

Mara nodded. "Yeah."

"Oh!" Gráinne exclaimed. "I've just realized. I owe you something."

Mara felt her blood run cold.

"A story! Didn't I say I'd tell you one?"

"Get up there, Gráinne!" someone called from the crowd.

When did everyone start looking at me? Mara wondered.

Where's Cian?

But she already knew. She already knew.

She watched as Gráinne stepped onto the stage and took the mic.

49

Gráinne

"*Dia daoibh, a chairde.* I have a story for you all. It's an old one. One I think you all know. But doesn't it get better as time goes on?"

The bar had fallen completely silent, now.

"A long time ago, and a very good time it was . . ." Gráinne began. "There was a man named Donn, a fisherman. And would you believe he lived on this very island? Now, Inishbannock was known in those days as Inis Bocht. The poor island. And indeed, it earned the name. For there was barely enough sun in the sky to warm a man, or enough trees on the island to shelter him, or enough good soil to bury him. And the people of the island, what few there were, they had to fish to survive or else eat the seaweed that washed up on the shore.

"And Donn was no more fortunate than any other man who lived in those times, and he was always hungry.

"Well one day, he was walking along the beach and he sees a seal come out of the sea. And at first, he was all for to kill it and eat it. But then, doesn't he see the seal take off its skin, and underneath there is a beautiful woman, as naked as a newborn babe.

"She left the seal skin on the beach and wandered off, to do whatever it is that magical naked women do to entertain themselves. And Donn, being a cunning and a clever man, took the cloak and put it in a box, and dropped it down the well beside his cottage. And then he ran back and found the naked woman weeping on the beach.

"'What is it that troubles you?' he asked her, as if he did not know, the scoundrel.

"'Please help me, sir,' she said. 'For I have lost something very dear to me, and without it I cannot leave.'

"He helped her search—for in truth he knew that she could search for a hundred years and never find it. And when she could not find the cloak, he took her home and, with some cajoling, made her his wife."

Mara felt numb. A low, cruel chuckle rippled through the crowd like a snake swimming through dark waters.

"They had many children. And they were happy. And a strange thing happened. The waters around the island became full of fish. The soil became rich and good, and the people of the island began to grow crops. And no storms ever troubled them. And no one ever became sick. Oh, they would grow old. But slowly. And they were never troubled with illness. And in time, the island became known not as Inis Bocht, but Inis an Beannacht. The island of the blessing. And the people of the island soon realized that it was because of Donn's wife that their good fortune had come. For even though Donn grew old and gray, and their children grew and had children of their own, she never aged.

"And then, at last, came a day when Donn took to his bed and said to his wife, 'Fetch the priest. I will die soon, and I have something I must confess.'

"'What is it that you must confess?' she asked him.

"'It was I who stole your cloak,' he told her. 'It was I who kept you here all these years.'

"'And where did you put it?' she asked him.

"And he told her where he had hidden it.

"'Now will you fetch the priest?' he asked her. 'For I must confess my sins before I die.'

"'There is no priest who can save you now,' she told him. 'I shall see to that.'

"And she cursed him. She cursed him and all his issue, so that when the time came for them to die, they would instead become like the Fomor of old and live on the island forever in torment. And no sooner had she said the words than Donn turned into a hideous beast and vanished out the door. The woman climbed into the well but she could not find the cloak.

"For the people of the island had learned where Donn had hidden it and had stowed the cloak away amongst themselves. For they knew that if Donn's wife ever left, they would be back in misery and want. She went wailing through the village, begging them to return the cloak to her, cursing and howling, and oh the sound was terrible indeed. And they shut every door and window against her.

"And so she issued her final curse.

"'If ever I do escape this wretched place, I swear to you now, there shall not be a sinner left alive on Inishbannock, so terrible will be my wrath!'

"And with that, she ran to the cliff and threw herself into the sea.

"Well, the islanders thought that the matter was settled.

"But the next morning they found her body washed up on the beach. Cold and blue and dead as could be. They gave her burial, but not in hallowed ground.

"They buried her at the crossroads in a shallow grave, as she was a suicide.

"But three days later, the landlord of the public house, a man named Ruán, was walking past the crossroads and he was singing a song to himself. And who does he see, rising out of the very ground, but Donn's wife who they had thought dead.

"He took her back to his home. And would you believe, it was the very house that we are standing in now.

"'Where am I?' she asked him.

"'Do you not remember?' Ruán said.

"'Who am I?' she asked.

"'Do you not remember that?' he asked her.

"'I remember nothing,' she told him. 'I was asleep, I think. And I heard your song. And it roused me.'

"'Well then,' he said. 'My name is Ruán. And you are my wife. And your name is . . .'"

Gráinne stopped. And furrowed her brow.

Mara stared up at her, her eyes glinting like knives.

"Do you know? I can't remember. I don't think it matters." She looked down at Mara with a cold, pitiless smile. "Do you?"

50
Mara

It was something she had wondered ever since she had learned she was not normal.

How strong am I?

Not strong enough, as it turned out.

Dozens of hands grabbed her arms and legs and neck, and hoisted her into the air with a leering, raucous cheer.

Mara screamed until she was gagged with a thick piece of rope that pricked her tongue with its rough fibers. She struggled mightily but, with no purchase on the ground, she couldn't break free. She was forced to her knees and held in place as her ankles and wrists were tied together.

One of them slapped her face. She never saw who it was. Someone just saw an opportunity to hurt her, and took it.

Then there was a cheer as three men carried something great and heavy and black into the room and set it down on the floor with a loud bang.

She stared at it, numb with terror.

It was a great cast-iron pot.

MARA

It immediately reminded her of the bath in Helen's house, the one that had given her a panic attack when she had tried to bathe in it.

Ah. All the pieces coming together.

Gráinne detached the water tap from behind the bar and Mara watched as she began to fill the pot to the brim.

She knew it was idiotic, but part of her was still hoping that Cian would burst in and somehow save her.

No. No, this was the plan all along. And you knew. You were just too desperate to believe it.

"Alright," Gráinne said, shutting off the water. "That'll do. Bring her forward."

Desperation gave her new strength. Mara strained with everything she had against the ropes as she was lifted and dragged toward the drowning bowl. She almost wrenched free of their grip and for her trouble had her head violently knocked against the rim. Water splashed against her face and she saw stars.

She could see nothing now. Her vision was blurring with tears.

She felt a hand gently caressing her hair and a soft voice in her ear.

"You know, Mara," Gráinne whispered. "You have been part of our family for so long. I always loved you. And I always hated that we had to do this to you. I always felt so sorry for you. But then you killed my son. And now? Now, I'm just glad I get to do this again."

She felt Gráinne's fingers gripping her hair until her scalp was on fire and her head was shoved into the water. Her mouth already gagged, she felt the water rising up her nostrils like burning petrol.

She couldn't even scream. She wanted to scream so badly.

She felt a moment of blessed relief as Gráinne pulled her out of the water.

"They say it's a painless death," she heard her hiss in her ear. "Shower of fucking liars, aren't they?"

Mara was pushed down again and she knew this would be the last time.

There was nothing but darkness. And fear. And pain.

Her lungs were burning. She felt like they must surely scorch a hole in her chest, white-hot.

You have to burn, Mara Alice had told her.

She was burning now.

Please let me die, she begged.

Just let me . . .

51
Mara Alice

We're just talking, she thought. You're allowed talk to men who aren't your husband.

But she knew this wasn't just a talk.

The silence had the wrong feel to it.

As she walked down the quay with this man she had just met, she reminded herself that nothing was going to happen.

You're just angry at Oisín. And a little bit drunk. And lonely. And there's a gorgeous guy who's new to the island and is clearly very interested in you.

When she put it like that, it made it seem more likely that something was going to happen, not less.

"What's wrong?" Cian asked her.

"How do you mean?" she replied.

"You look guilty. Like I just caught you smoking behind the bike shed."

"How dare you," she said with false outrage.

"Ah, I should have known. You were a good girl."

She shrugged. "I dunno. Maybe. Maybe I was a complete terror. I've no way of knowing."

"How do you mean?" he asked.

Alice gave an embarrassed smile. "Years ago, there was a big storm on the island. I was caught in it and, something, a tree branch or whatever, smacked me right in the head. My husband found me in a field, completely unconscious. He thought I was dead. He brought me home and I woke up, but I'd lost my memory. Everything. So I have no idea if I ever smoked cigarettes behind the bike sheds or not."

She'd told the story a few times, normally to tourists when she'd had occasion to visit Farvey. Their reactions usually ranged from sympathy to amazement. No one had ever reacted the way the blond man from Dublin did now.

He fixed her with a bored, pitying gaze. "You know that's bullshit, right?"

"What?" she replied.

He sighed wearily. "That's not how amnesia works. At all. Unless you're a soap opera character or a cartoon caveman."

"Well . . ." she said. "It happened to me."

"Did it?" he asked her.

She didn't know what to say to that.

"Alright, here's a question. This storm. That gave you amnesia. How long ago was this?"

"Eleven years," she said.

"And has there been a storm on the island since then?" Cian prompted.

She didn't answer.

"That's a bit weird, isn't it? Right on the Atlantic? Nothing in over ten years? Hang on, so how old were you when it happened?"

"Twenty-eight?"

"Meaning you're, what, almost forty now? Fuck. What's your secret?" He raised an eyebrow.

"I . . . I . . . don't know what you're . . ."

Behind them, they heard the back door of the Temple open and Cian pushed her close against the wall. He raised a finger to shush her.

They listened as footsteps moved unsteadily away from them, down the quay, to the tune of a drunken, slurred rendition of "Baby Got Back" in a Kerry accent.

When silence returned, he let her go.

"Sorry," he whispered. "They can't see me talking to you."

"Who are you?" she demanded. "Why are you asking me all these questions—"

"You mean the ones you've been asking yourself?" He cut her off. "Look, we can't talk here, it's too dangerous."

Cian turned and hurried away, back up the quay.

"I'm in the new build on the north side of the island," he said over his shoulder. "Come find me if you want to know the truth."

. . .

"Oisín, I KNOW. I KNOW EVERYTHING."

Her husband gazed down at her from where she had him pinned to the wall.

"Alice . . ." he wheezed, struggling desperately to loosen her choke hold. ". . . Please . . ."

"You lied to me."

"Yes . . ."

"For ELEVEN YEARS."

"Yes . . ."

"Why shouldn't I . . ."

"Because I love you."

It shouldn't have worked. It was a cheap trick. She knew she should tear him apart there and then. She'd done it before. Cian had told her that.

But it's Oisín.

She let him go. He slowly slid down the wall until he hit the floor, cradling his bruised neck and wheezing.

She felt numb. Weightless.

"The perfect prison," she murmured. "You make the prisoner fall in love with the guard. How could you do this to me?"

He looked up at her with streaming eyes.

"When you've been raised this way your whole life," he croaked hoarsely. "When you've been told since you were a little boy that you have to do something? By everyone you know and love and trust? And if you don't, it'll be . . . the end of the world. The end of everything. It's very, very hard to see it for what it is. I was born inside this thing, Alice."

Her knees gave out and she was on the floor, shaking. Sobbing.

Part of her wanted him to hold her, another part wondered if she'd snap his neck if he tried to touch her.

"Not you . . ." she sobbed. "Not you."

"How did you find out?" he asked.

"Someone told me. The whole thing. I didn't want to believe it. But the more I heard, the memories started coming back. And I realized why. Why I've been so miserable. Why I've always felt like I have to get out of here. And the only thing that's kept me from going crazy was knowing I had you. I loved you so much. But it was you! The whole time. You knew! And you let it happen. How long, Oisín, how long were we going to keep doing this?"

He laughed bitterly. "You wouldn't believe me."

She looked up at him, glaring through her disheveled hair.

"Try me," she growled.

He glanced over at the table. "See the two glasses?" he said. "I had Conn over tonight. He's just left. I invited him over because I *told him I needed to tell you the truth and end it. He's going to give us the cloak."*

Alice shook her head. "You're lying. You decided? Just like that?"

"You and I have been talking about moving away from the island. Away from my mother. Away from all of them."

"Yeah, but now I know it was all bullshit. You were just trying to keep me happy."

"No. I've been planning this for months."

"Months?"

"I've been thinking about it for months. I've been planning for weeks. I finally did something tonight. We can go down now. I promise."

"We?" she snarled. "What, you think we just go back to being a happy couple after this?"

"No," he whispered. "I know we can't go back."

She stood up and she saw him brace for another attack. What she did next was worse.

She took off her wedding ring and threw it at him.

"I don't need you. I don't forgive you. And that goes for everyone else on this island. You won't see me again. Goodbye, Oisín."

...

Conn was already in his pajamas when he came to the door. He still wore his red woolly hat. She now remembered how frigid the cottage got at night.

"Alice . . ." he began.

"Oh, Conn," she said sarcastically. "You know I'll always be Máire to you. Or did you prefer Mary? That's a question, actually. Was it better the first or second time?"

There was a flash of pain on his face, but then it was buried under cold, steely anger.

"The first," he said. "Mary was an awful dose, if I'm honest."

"I'm sure if you woke up with no memories and found out you were married to a man who looked old enough to be your grandfather you'd be pissy, too."

"Aye," he said at last. "I might at that. 'Sorry' seems a rather inadequate word."

"Doesn't it just? How about 'here's the cloak'?"

He made to go inside and then stopped. He fixed her with a suspicious glare.

"Hang on now. Where's Oisín?"

"He's back at the house," she said coldly. "He's not coming."

"Is that right?"

Suddenly, he slammed the door shut and she heard a dead bolt slide into place. She hammered on the wood.

"Conn? Conn! Let me in or I'll . . ."

"Or you'll what?!" she heard him bark. "What are you planning to do to me?!"

She took a deep breath.

"Nothing," she said, leaning her head against the wooden surface. "I promise. Conn, please. I just want to get off the island. I just want this to stop. And I know you do, too."

"How do you know that?"

"Because," she said, and she tried to fight the tears, but they were too strong, as always. "I remember everything. All of it. Every year. Every death. Every man I had to live with. And I loved you more than any of them. And that's why I know that you are going to let me in . . ."

"I have the shotgun here," he interrupted her in a tone that was less than romantic. "If you don't step away from the door, I'll shoot you through it."

"Okay then," she said. "Cool. Cool."

She moved back. "I'm stepping away from the door," she yelled.

"Did you kill my nephew?" she heard him say.

"No!" she shouted back. "I promise."

"Prove it!" he yelled. "You bring him here. Then I'll give it to you both. That was what we agreed. You can't go changing the deal."

She wanted to argue. No, she wanted to fight. She wanted to break the door down and take what she needed so she could finally be free.

She had an idea. "Phone him."

"What?"

"Phone the house. He's there. He'll tell you to give me the cloak."

There was a silence as Conn mulled it over. "Stay there," he called. "No messin' now."

"Fine," she barked.

Alice turned and looked back up the beach. A gibbous moon, not quite full, but so bright it might as well have been, made the white sand glow silver.

Out of the corner of her eye, she saw a sudden movement.

Up the hill, she saw a torch flit like a firefly and a dark, heavyset figure retreat back along the line of the cliff.

With a shudder, she realized that her conversation with Conn was being watched. Probably not overheard, the figure was too far away for that.

But still, it worried her deeply.

Did they already know? Were they already filling the pot? Were they on their way . . .

No. She tried to reassure herself.

It's just a tourist out for a midnight stroll. You're just being paranoid . . .

"There's no answer," she heard Conn call through the door. "He's not picking up."

She didn't respond. She just ran.

• • •

It was not so far from their house to Conn's cottage. The path ran through the narrowest point on the island, the knot of the bow tie.

It certainly should not have taken long for a woman running pell-mell, sprinting faster than she could ever remember, like she was in a nightmare and the monster had her scent.

And yet the moonlit path before her seemed to stretch and leer and lengthen.

She could hear trees and brambles hissing, as if the whole island was mocking her efforts.

Did you really think it would be that easy? Did you really think we would let you escape? Silly little girl.

There was the house, the front door as open as a wound, bleeding yellow light into the night.

She ran into the hall. She could hear movement in the kitchen, as if someone had been startled.

"Oisín!" she screamed. "OISÍN!"

Next, the kitchen.

Stopped.

Fell to her knees.

She did not scream.

She did not have the breath to scream.

Oisín, her husband, was on the floor.

Oisín, her husband, was on the couch.

Oisín, her husband, was on the table.

His head stared down at her.

MARA ALICE

The neck had been cut too unevenly to form a flat base, so the head rested on its side, the left cheek flattened by the tabletop. The eyes were open and he stared at her like a man paralytically drunk.

From this angle, the head and the table formed a single body, some awful four-legged creature.

She realized that she was not alone.

Cian was standing in the center of the kitchen, wearing a thick layer of Oisín, her husband.

He gently swung a fire axe through the air to hear the thrum of the blade. The axe and the arm that wielded it were so coated in red that it was hard to see where the one ended and the other began. It looked like a continuous, hideously elongated limb.

He smiled at her, a single tuft of blond hair that had somehow escaped the splatter glinted gold against the crimson.

"Mara Alice," he said softly. "What have you done?"

52
Cian

He felt drugged, honestly.

After the razor-sharp anxiety leading up to his visit to the house, and the rather sickening euphoria of the kill itself, and the hacking of the body into pieces, Cian had crashed.

He felt like he was moving in molasses, dimly aware that he was in great danger. By letting himself be discovered like this, he risked becoming an actual example of what he had gone through such great lengths to fabricate.

But he couldn't feel fear right now.

Instead, he ambled toward her.

"It's not as bad as it looks," Cian assured Alice. "I didn't, like, hack him to pieces while he was still alive or anything. I showed up at the door, asked if I could talk to him about you. I mean, he was very trusting, letting a strange man into his house at this time of night. I know you do things differently in the country, but still . . . and then I just, I just, I just bopped him on the head. When he turned away. He felt nothing. I don't think he felt anything. You need to go."

She was still staring at the head of her husband on the kitchen table.

CIAN

"No, for real. You need to go. I've put the call in. They're on their way. It was lovely knowing you, Mara Alice. And I'm pretty sure that whoever you become next . . ." He leaned in and whispered. "We are going to know each other much better."

Too late he realized his mistake. He still, fundamentally, thought her a slender woman in her twenties. Short. Petite. Nothing to be afraid of.

Then she looked at him.

Her jaw stretched like a python, her ears flattened, and her eyes seemed to expand in her head, becoming merciless and predatory. Her whole body stretched and sharpened, fingernails grew inches, additional teeth sprouted from her gums.

She gave a feral scream and sprung. Cian fell back with a yell and tried to weakly swing the axe, but she knocked it from his hand with ease.

The axe went flying and struck the microwave, smashing the glass door. The microwave sparked and flared, and a plume of flame and molten metal rose up, causing the wooden cabinets to burst into flame.

Alice was on top of him now, like a cat pinning a bird between its claws. He twisted and turned, unable to break her grip. Smoke began to fill the kitchen and flames dances across the countertop.

Cian screamed as he felt a massive maw, lined with razor-sharp needles, clamp down on his torso.

Just as he was about to black out, he heard a gunshot and felt the teeth withdrawing from his flesh so suddenly it felt like being bitten again.

"Cian! Hang on! Oh, fuck me!"

He recognized the voice. Female, with an Irish accent and just the faintest trace of Vietnamese. Sara Do. Which meant that . . .

"Stay back, ya cunt!" Martin Connell yelled, brandishing the shotgun at the nightmare that snarled at him.

Cian made a mental note to never call Martin a dry shite again. The man was a bloody action hero.

"Oh my God, Cian, are you okay?!" Sarah said, bending over him. He twisted to see the carnage Alice had wrought.

"Don't move..." Martin was growling. "Don't you fucking dare move..."

The nightmare that had once been Mara Alice Dunne froze at the sight of the barrel.

From his vantage point, his vision filling with stars and smoke, Cian lost sight of the pair.

He heard a scream and a hiss as Martin's shotgun fell to the ground.

What happened next, Cian would never be quite sure of.

He knew that Martin was on the floor, screeching piteously as he was savaged by Alice, who was trying to tear his heart out with her teeth.

Sara raised her own shotgun, and fired without aiming.

She screamed as Martin's head exploded and Alice leapt to her feet.

Behind her, the fire had spread hungrily. It was an old house, full of dry wood, and the thick curtains that covered the back sliding door were now a wall of flame.

Seeing her husband's corpse, Sara had clearly decided that the blame lay not with her poor aim but with Alice. She gave a scream and fired the shotgun again.

Alice screeched, and rolled over on the ground, spritzing blood over the tiles.

She was not even putting up a pretense of humanity now.

CIAN

Her face, contorted with a rage and pain that human beings could only feel in nightmares, seemed to burn as she looked up at them from the floor.

Cian realized that the gunshot had only wounded her, and that both he and Sara were very likely about to die.

The shotgun was double-barreled. Sara had fired twice. It was now just a large, heavy piece of junk metal.

Thankfully, Alice did not know that yet.

She hissed at them one final time and then sprinted right through the sliding door, her hair and clothes catching fire as she burst through the thick glass and out into the night.

They heard her howling.

The smell of burnt flesh and hair lingered in the room, and would remain in Cian's memory for the rest of his life.

Slowly, fighting agony, he pulled himself to his feet.

"Oh God! Oh God! Martin!" Sara howled in anguish.

"It's okay . . ." Cian wheezed, probably the biggest lie he had ever told, and he was not an amateur in the sport by any means. Gently, he pried the still-smoking shotgun from Sara's limp fingers. He knew the wound on his torso would make itself known soon, but right now he was still riding a fresh wave of adrenaline.

"We need to get out of here," he told her. Smoke had almost completely filled the room.

"I . . . I can't leave him . . . we can't leave Martin . . . and poor Oisín . . . oh my God, Martin, I killed him!"

"No. No, it wasn't your fault," he said, putting a hand on Sara's shoulder. "It was her. I'll be sure to tell them that it was Alice's fault."

"You'd . . . you'd lie for me . . ."

"It's not a lie. It's a . . . simplification. We did what we had to."

Cian probably shouldn't have said that. It put the idea in her head.

He had to give her credit. Even though she was most certainly in shock, he saw her eyes glance to the axe, still visible as it stuck out of the burning microwave. And the blood that covered him head to foot, despite the fact that he had only been bitten on the side of his torso.

He could practically see the increasingly terrified thoughts flitting back and forth through her head.

Or maybe he was simply imagining it. Paranoid.

Still, why take the risk?

His fingers clenched on the still-warm shotgun in his hand.

Just a large, heavy piece of metal.

• • •

As he staggered away from the burning house, hands pressed to his side, he hoped the rest of the Comhairle would meet him on the road before he passed out.

He glanced over his shoulder as the second story of the Dunne house began to burn.

Cian wondered what the fire would do to the three bodies.

Hopefully, it would be to his advantage.

53
Declan

He really needed to pee, but on the other hand, Declan never wanted to move from this spot.

Which was why what Natalie said next hurt so much. "This . . . was a really bad idea," she whispered sadly into his chest.

"Oh," he said, feeling a horrible sensation of weightlessness. "Was it, was it not . . ."

"Oh no," she said, her head rising so quickly an errant strand whipped him in the forehead. "I didn't mean it like that. It was good. It was really good. Like, for our first time together? No, no. Gold star."

"You were amazing," he said sincerely. "That was the best I've ever had."

"Aw," she said, kissing him softly on the lips.

She didn't, he noticed, return the compliment, but he did not have ideas above his station and refused to overthink it. It had been good. Very good. They had both enjoyed themselves. That was all that mattered.

"I just meant," she continued. "It probably wasn't the best way to deal with what we saw."

"I think it's common, though, isn't it?"

"Oh? You exhume bodies and get the ride on a regular basis?"

"No, but coming face-to-face with death, y'know? Makes people want to do things that make them feel alive? I dunno."

"Yeah. That's probably it," she murmured, idly fingering a hair on his chest.

"So?" Declan said. "You said *first* time?"

"Did I?"

"Which, I dunno if you're aware of this, would imply . . ."

"Pal, I've been waiting for round two for like twenty minutes, let's *go* . . ." Natalie climbed on top of him and for a terrible moment he thought the sight of her naked body had given him a stroke as his vision went completely white.

Then he heard the thunder and roar of rain.

Without a word, Natalie slid off him and pressed her hands against the window next to the bed, peering out into the early morning. Declan sat up and put an arm around her.

The sky over Inishbannock was usually an antiseptic gray-white. Now the morning clouds were heavy, angry, and hematoma-purple. A haze of frantic, splintering raindrops hit the windowpane, and he could see a river already flowing past the garden gate.

"I've never seen it rain like this on the island," Natalie whispered. "Except . . ."

"After the 'outbreak,'" Declan finished. "It rained like this for two days when they buried Mara."

They looked at each other.

He felt her hand, small and cold, squeeze his.

DECLAN

Beside the bed, Declan's phone buzzed. He fumbled to picked it up and saw a message from a number he didn't recognize.

> Where are you?

> I think you have the wrong number?

> Declan Burke?

Declan felt his whole body tense.
"What is it?" Natalie asked, leaning over. He didn't answer, instead he replied.

> Yes? Who is this?

> Are you still in the cottage?

> Answer the question.

> If you are you need to get out NOW.
> They'll be coming for you.

> What the fuck are you talking about?

With the next text, Declan felt a cold bead of sweat form on his brow.

> Mara's just been buried. In three days she's going to be dug up again. You're a loose end, understand?

Declan tried calling the number and was instantly blocked. Another text beeped indignantly in his inbox.

> Why are you wasting time?
> GET OUT OF THE HOUSE.

> First tell me who you are!

> Not a chance.

> Why not?

> Because if they kill you and find my name on your phone they'll kill me, too.
> Text me when you're on the road.

"Declan! What is it?" Natalie demanded.

"It's . . . oh God. It's Mara. They caught her. She's . . . she's . . ."

He was going to say "dead." No, not dead. But the Mara he knew was gone, forever. She would emerge from her grave soaking and terrified and wiped clean. A new person.

He had lost her. He only truly realized then what she had meant to him.

Declan allowed himself three terrible, bone-shaking sobs. Then he felt Natalie's arms enveloping him and holding him tightly.

Leave the dead. Look after the living.

He knew in that moment that the most important thing in the world was protecting Natalie from whatever was coming for them next.

DECLAN

He kissed her.

"Get dressed," he whispered. "We need to go."

. . .

"Declan," Natalie yelled, and even then he struggled to hear her over the torrential roar of the rain against the van's windshield. "I *really* shouldn't be driving in this."

He felt tempted to remind her that, legally speaking, she shouldn't be driving at all, but decided against it. For the continued existence of both his love life and his actual life.

"You're doing great," he said. "We just need to keep moving."

"Yeah, about that," Natalie said, as she squinted through the rain and tried to make an educated guess as to which gray blur was the road, the walls on either side of the road, and the sky. "Where exactly are we going? Considering we're on an island and I doubt we're going to get a boat to the mainland in this."

"Hang on," he said, trying to text with wet fingers as the van bumped and shuddered along the flooded road.

> We're out. Now tell me who you are.

> Meet me here.

The response took a few minutes to buffer as they crossed over to the far side of the island, where coverage was even more sparse.

A photo appeared, blurry at first, then slowly sharpened.

It was a picture of a dead tree on a hilltop overlooking the turbulent sea.

"Where is that? Do you know it?" he held his phone in front of Natalie.

She glanced at it and nodded. "That's Killroon. Highest point on the island. I've gone hiking there."

"You're a hiking girl? Oh God, this *was* a huge mistake."

"Oh yeah," she said with an evil cackle. "I'm going to have you up every morning. Six a.m. Up and down a mountain before breakfast."

"Right, just pull over and leave me here to die."

"Never." She grinned and shifted gears to get through a muddy ditch. "You know, anyone standing on a mountain in the middle of this is probably a dangerous lunatic."

"Yup. Let's go say hi."

. . .

The island looked like it was being washed away.

They passed fields full of sheep literally swimming to higher ground. A small hillock had become black with rabbits, packed in as tight as penguins on an ice floe as they watched the rising water with dull, torpid stares.

The roof of the van had sprung a large leak, and there was now a constant stream of rain pissing into the rear of the cargo bay. Declan genuinely wondered if the rusty ancient van might actually break apart.

"Oh fuck," Natalie breathed.

They were at a turn in the road. The wind was now behind them, which made the view ahead somewhat clearer than it had been. A sign pointed the way to Killroon, leading up a sharply steep country road that had become a torrential river in the storm.

DECLAN

"Do you think the van can make it to the top?" Declan asked quietly.

"If it was a sunny day? Twenty years ago? Maybe?"

"Want to get out and walk?"

"Fuck, fuck, fuck . . ." Natalie muttered a brief prayer to the god of Reagan-era Suzukis and turned the car onto the hill road. Now they were back in the path of the wind and the world before the windscreen blurred to chaos. The hill looked like a sheer wall.

"Okay, baby," Natalie said, stroking the steering wheel. "You survived the Cold War, you can survive this."

She pressed on the accelerator. The engine made a noise like a sick animal but began to climb. Declan could feel the threadbare tires weakly gripping the submerged road and instinctively reached for the seat belt that was not there.

"Come on . . ." Natalie grunted through gritted teeth.

Through the mad dance of raindrops on the windshield, Declan suddenly noticed a strange form, a massive dusty-pink blob sliding across the road.

"What is that?" Declan asked, pointing to the thing.

At once, as if a great hand had passed over them, the rain stopped.

It did not peter out. It did not quickly die off. It stopped. Totally.

Natalie slammed on the brakes.

They stared at the thing on the road as the windshield wipers cleared their view.

Declan felt the same awful hot-and-cold prickling sensation as when he had woken up to gunfire and seen a fleshy nightmare skittering away into the night.

It was not the same creature, nor the snake witch that had chased him down the hill to Conn's cottage and still chased him in his dreams.

This was something new.

The size of it was awe-inspiring. He tried to think what the shape reminded him of.

He had a faint memory of David Attenborough fending off some great gray monster with a stick.

An elephant seal, that was the rough shape.

But instead of fins, there were human hands, the size of doors. The tail was two human legs, rigid and sickeningly thin compared to the great monstrous mound of flesh that they appended. The flesh was naked, calloused, red, festooned with sores, and all over it were dead, or nearly dead, half-formed human faces. One in particular, Declan noted, seemed to be spitting and dribbling an endless stream of baby teeth.

The head, atop a massive muscular neck, seemed to be three different faces that grew into each other. The creature raised its neck and the three mouths opened and gave a horrendous, agonized wail that Declan felt in his marrow.

"Natalie," he whispered desperately. "Back up. Back up now."

She was trembling in her seat.

She couldn't move.

But he felt the van shift.

He realized that, even though the rain had stopped, the road was still a river. The wheels slipped and the whole van began to slide back down the hill. At this sudden motion, the creature swung its head round to stare at the descending van.

DECLAN

In a panic, Declan reached out and applied the hand brake, realizing too late that it was the single worst thing he could have done.

The van skidded and spun as it careened down the hill, and Declan watched in horror as the world outside the window began to tip with a terrible, nauseous slowness.

The van rolled over on its side and the back of Declan's head struck the door. Natalie's body slammed limply on top of him. Broken glass cut into his arm. His sleeve was soaked through, and for a moment he thought he must have cut an artery.

It's only rainwater, he told himself. *The road's still flooded and the cabin is filling with water.*

"Natalie?" he wheezed. "Natalie? Are you okay?"

Her body was a deadweight and he couldn't hear her breathing.

"Natalie . . . come on, love. Wake up. Please."

Awkwardly, he craned his neck and looked out the windscreen, which was now a white spiderweb of cracked glass. The Fomor lurched toward them, splashing downhill through the flowing rainwater. The three faces on the head now split apart revealing a gullet lined with great brown teeth.

"Natalie! Fuck! Natalie, wake up! Please."

"Wha . . ." she groaned and even in the midst of his absolute terror he felt a sugar rush of hope.

She's not dead. Thank Jesus.

Natalie opened her eyes and saw what was coming toward them. She shrieked and frantically scrambled to get out of the van. Declan felt her trainers stepping on his head.

"Natalie, stop! It's too late."

The thing was almost on top of them.

Declan closed his eyes and hoped for a quick death.

And then he heard a sound that cut him to the quick.

For a split second he thought it was Natalie screaming, but she had frozen on top of him, utterly still.

It was something like a violin played at the highest pitch, something like a woman's cry.

It was like wind blowing through a seashell.

It was like wire being pulled through ice.

It sounded like seabirds and rain and blood.

Declan watched in shock as the Fomor seemed to recoil from the sound.

It closed its mouth and the three faces bellowed in unison, their voices full of hate and anguish.

And then, it turned and slithered away with astonishing speed and agility.

The terrible whine stopped.

Declan allowed himself to breathe.

He felt Natalie's body moving over him.

"I can hear someone outside . . ." she whispered.

He listened. He could hear it, too. Footsteps splashing through the slowing stream of rainwater.

They heard something climbing over the side of the van.

The door yanked open, and Declan and Natalie blinked as daylight flooded the cabin.

A figure, coated head to toe in mud, stared down at them like a hunter checking a trap.

It flashed a smile, the teeth bright, dazzling and almost feral in a filthy face.

"Hi, guys," said Mara.

DECLAN

. . .

Mara took them up to Killroon, to see her latest grave.

There, under a tree, on the tallest point of the island, a hole had been carved out of the soil from the inside.

Declan stared into the grave, and then he and Natalie turned to look at Mara's hands.

"Twice," Natalie growled. "It's the fucking worst thing that could ever happen to somebody and they did it to you *twice*."

Mara gave them a sad smile. "Oh, sweetie" was all she said.

He finally noticed what was different about her. This was not his Mara. Or it was, but that was just an element of the woman before him now. He could feel centuries of experience and wisdom and loss and grief and anger and *life* in her eyes. He felt tiny before her, like a child before a mountain.

"I . . . I don't think I ever thought about it," Declan said, staring numbly at the shattered coffin, which looked like it had literally exploded. "What it must have been like."

"Weirdly? Wasn't as bad this time," Mara said with a shrug. "I knew I could get out. I knew I was strong enough."

"Wait, wait, wait," said Declan. "You know us! Don't you?"

"Of course I do, Declan," she said.

"You didn't forget us! I thought you'd lose your memory..."

She raised a hand. "You have questions and that's *perfectly fair*. But we can't stay here."

The way she said it made him instantly nervous.

"Is that monster coming back?" Natalie asked.

"No. It's the two-legged ones we have to worry about. As soon as the rain stopped, that was the starting pistol. The village will know I've returned. And they're going to come and try to put me back in the ground. Again. And, you know what? I'm getting real sick of that."

They heard the sound of a horn beeping frantically. Declan jogged to the top of the path and looked down.

A dark-blue Range Rover was idling at the bottom of the hill, unable to get past the toppled van.

"Fuck, I know that car!" Declan yelled. "That's . . ."

"Our lift," Mara said. "Come on."

The window of the Range Rover slid down and a broad face topped with curly brown hair poked out.

"What the fuck happened here?!" Padraig Dunne barked, gesturing to the downed van.

"What? What?! WHAT?!" Declan yelped. "Him?!"

"Yeah, I was surprised, too," Mara said. "Come on. I'll tell you everything when we get somewhere safe."

"Hey, Declan," Natalie asked him as they approached the wrecked van. "You really still want to be with me?"

"Course, why?" Declan fought the butterflies in his chest and tried to focus on the moment.

"Because I'm pretty sure I'm unemployed now."

He smiled and took Natalie's fingers in his.

Mara spun around and stared at them in shock. "Wait, what? I've been dead one night and now you're sleeping together?"

"We're still figuring stuff out," Declan said quickly and dropped her hand.

"Yeah, it's super, super up in the air," Natalie agreed.

"Terrific," Mara grumbled. "I'm the only monster in the friend group and now I'm the third wheel. Great." She turned and continued down the hill.

DECLAN

"You're joking right? You're not actually angry?" Natalie called after.

"Yes, I'm joking. Yes, I'm kinda angry," she called back.

"No seriously," Padraig yelled. "What the fuck happened here? How do you crash on an island with five cars?"

Declan stopped and gave Padraig a baffled look. "I'm so confused," he said.

"Be confused in the car," said Padraig. "Let's go!"

54
Mara

Padraig drove them to the western side of the island, about as far from Ballydonn as was possible without driving into the sea.

In the corner of a field, smothered in ivy and blackberry bushes, was an old abandoned feed shed, half eaten by rust. Padraig had set up a tarpaulin to replace the long-gone roof and added a few chairs, and even a portable gas camping stove. From his rucksack, he took a tinned fish pie and began to heat it on the flames. He passed it to Mara with a small plastic fork and she devoured it hungrily.

"Gives you an appetite, dying," she said between mouthfuls.

"I remember," said Declan.

"Another one?" Padraig asked.

Mara nodded enthusiastically.

"What is this place?" Natalie asked, looking around the hovel.

"It's somewhere no one knows about," Padraig said gruffly. "I sometimes bring dates here."

"Dates?" Declan said, wrinkling his nose. "What kinda place is this for . . ."

"The kind for people who like their privacy. And don't want the rest of the island knowing their business."

"Gotcha," said Declan.

"Everyone sit down," Mara said, scooping the last chunk of pie into her mouth. "We have a lot to talk about." She calmed her nerves and steadied herself.

"Fuck, where do we even start?" Declan asked. "Wait, I know. Why is he on our side? Now?"

"Actually," said Mara. "I think he always has been. Isn't that right, Padraig?"

"You were the one who told us to come to Killroon," Declan said.

Padraig gave a stiff head tilt.

"And he's the one who woke me up early," Mara said. "Both times."

Padraig nodded again, looking quite ashamed, Mara noted.

"Okay," Natalie said with the air of someone who has finally had enough. "Can you just tell us what she is? Please?"

"I thought you knew?" he said, giving Mara a confused glance.

"I do," Mara said. "Now. You tell them."

"Well, okay. She's the Maighdean Mhara."

It felt strange hearing her whole name roll off of Padraig's tongue. To be known but not despised. She fought off a shiver.

"The . . . what's that . . . ?" Declan struggled and Mara watched him mentally translate. "The Maiden of the Sea?"

"Oh my God," Natalie breathed. "A seal woman."

"Yes," Mara said.

"Around four hundred years ago, the islanders trapped me here. They stole my cloak and forced me to live on Inishbannock as a mortal. Whenever I recovered my memories or realized what I really was, they drowned me. I'd lose my memory. And the whole thing would start over."

"You're four hundred years old?" Natalie asked in disbelief.

"No, love," said Mara with a sad smile. "I was captured four hundred years ago. I am much, much older."

"How do you know?" Declan asked.

Mara felt tears prick her eyes. "Because I remember everything. All my lives. Mara, Mara Alice, Mary, Máire, Máirín, Mairéad, dozens and dozens of different women. Different lives. I remember them all. I'm whole again."

"That's amazing," said Natalie. "How?"

"Ask him." She turned to Padraig.

"We've been doing this for a long time," he said. "The islanders. And we had to learn the rules. Normally, the Maiden is drowned and buried. And then after three days she's exhumed. And we wake her."

"How?"

"You have to sing. Something about hearing someone singing wakes her up. But she doesn't remember anything. You have to . . . you have to wait three days. One time they woke her too early. She remembered everything. She even got her hands on the cloak."

"You know the story, don't you, Natalie?" Mara said.

"Yeah. You have a cloak that lets you turn into a seal. Or, you're a seal that has a cloak that lets you turn into a woman? I don't know. I don't how you identify . . ."

"As long as I don't have the cloak I'm trapped here in human form. Locked. And I bring mild weather and bountiful crops and plentiful fish," Mara sing-songed, like she was reading a travel brochure, to keep away the thick layers of hurt she felt in her core. That this even had to be her story.

MARA

"And I keep away disease. That's why they've kept me here all these years. I bring the blessing. I turn Inis Bocht into Inis an Beannacht."

"But when you're buried . . ." Natalie asked.

"Exactly. The storms. The rain. Everything that I've been holding back comes crashing in. Now. If I ever get the cloak, well, apparently it comes back even stronger. Last time was in 1839. And I almost destroyed the entire island."

"Right, yeah. The Night of the Big Wind. There's a monument in Ballydonn. The storm wrecked Inishbannock," Declan said.

"I mean, I almost destroyed *Ireland*," Mara clarified.

"My brother wanted nothing more than to help Mara escape," Padraig cut in. "He came up with a plan. He told me that, if they ever tried to drown Mara again, I was to put a phone in her coffin, with the ringtone set to a song. He knew I'd have a better chance than him because they'd drown her at the Temple. Ma would be in charge. And once she was buried, I'd call the phone. That way Mara would wake up before she lost her memories."

"But . . . that didn't happen," Declan said. "You *did* lose your memories."

Mara looked at Padraig, who glanced away again in shame.

"After that night. I . . . was the first one to find Oisín's body. Well. The second. And I had a moment where I was just . . . this is what I'm trying to set free? This is what I'm trying to help? This monster? This animal? So I didn't do the plan. Or, at least, I didn't do it the way that Oisín wanted. I called the phone, but when I knew it would already be too late. But also when I knew you'd still be in the coffin. Because I wanted to hurt you."

She stared at him. Unblinking.

"Padraig," she said. And she laid a hand on his.

He flinched, but didn't pull away.

"I understand. I think, after four hundred years, I understand your impulse better than anyone." She spun to look at Declan and Natalie. "But now he knows I didn't kill Oisín, don't you? Or Sara. Or Martin."

Padraig nodded. "Yeah. I know that now."

"But . . . Mara," Natalie said quietly. "We saw the bodies. They'd been torn apart. Crushed."

"Human beings are easy to break," Mara said. "You just need the right tools."

"It was that fucker Cian Morley," Padraig said spitting on the ground.

"Wait, Cian your boyfriend? He . . . he did *that*?!" Natalie said, shocked.

"You haven't met him, have you?" Declan asked.

"No, why?" Natalie asked, eyebrows raised.

"Because you sound surprised," Declan replied.

"You never liked him," Mara noted and felt a grin find her face.

"Never," said Declan with a hint of pride in his voice.

"Although, Padraig, when did you realize?" Mara asked Padraig. "That I hadn't done it? You haven't told me yet."

Padraig sighed. "A couple of things came together. Morley was so gung ho about being the next groom. Which, considering what you'd done to him, was pretty weird to begin with . . ."

"What did you do?" Natalie asked.

"Bit 'em," said Mara, tucking into the third pie. "Put him in hospital."

"Good for you," Natalie said.

Padraig continued: "I didn't really think of it at first because, well, *I* was supposed be next in line. That's how it works. If the groom dies and you have to be reset, the groom's younger brother is supposed to take his place. And, no offense . . ."

"None taken," said Mara with her mouth full.

"I really didn't want to be married to you. For a shed load of reasons," Padraig said. "So when Cian was putting the pressure on Ma to, y'know, skip me, I was delighted. I think Ma was, too, to be honest. So soon after losing Oisín, she wasn't ready to risk her last son.

"But then, as time went on, I started thinking that we only had Morley's word for what happened that night. See, I knew Oisín was trying to convince Conn to give up the cloak. A few weeks ago, I went down to see Conn and I just asked him straight-out. And he said that you actually came to the cottage that night to get the cloak, but he wouldn't give it to you without Oisín. He tried to call Oisín and there was no answer. Then Mara ran off.

"So I thought to myself, why would you go back to the house and kill Oisín, if you needed to bring him back to Conn?"

"Couldn't I have killed him before I spoke to Conn?" Mara asked.

Padraig shook his head. "No. Because I was there when we finally caught you. Your clothes and your hair were burnt, and you were covered with blood. And Conn said that when he spoke to you, you were as fresh as a rose. So either Morley was lying, or Conn was. And I knew which one I'd bet. And there was one more thing."

"The burglary," Declan chimed in.

Padraig frowned at him. "How do the fuck do you know that?"

"You said yourself," said Declan. "There's only five cars on the island."

"Four now," Natalie said glumly.

"I was outside the cottage when that Range Rover pulled up outside. But, y'know, points for the balaclavas. Very stealthy," Declan said.

"When Ma heard that Conn had let you two into his cottage she got very antsy," Padraig admitted. "So she told me and Cian to rob the safe. He wasn't supposed to be there that night, but out drinking in Kilty's . . . I dunno, he must have met Malachy on the way and decided to go back to the cottage with him. I think Malachy wanted Conn to shoot him. Because he was already dead when we got there."

"Fuck!" Natalie exclaimed. "Why? Why would he . . ."

No, Mara thought to herself. *Now's not the time. They can't know yet.*

"We can get into that later," Mara interrupted. "Go on, Padraig."

"And when we came in through the front door, Conn was holding the auld shotgun and . . . Morley didn't even blink. He just gunned him down like a dog. And that's when I knew. He would do anything to get what he wanted. When I saw you in the Temple that night I knew they were going to drown you again. And that, this time, I had to do right by Oisín. And by you."

Mara closed her eyes and lowered her head. "Thank you," she whispered.

"Course," he said. "After all. We're family."

MARA

"So? Where's the cloak now?" Declan asked.

Padraig shook his head sadly. "I don't know."

Mara opened her eyes in shock. This was not what she had expected to hear. "What do you mean you don't know?!"

"They didn't tell me. Sorry."

"Oh no, no, no. Not again." Mara felt the blood drain from her face.

"Mara, it's okay. We can find it. We just need to think..." Declan got up and started to pace.

"For fuck's sake, Declan, there's thirteen square miles of island and it could be buried anywhere!"

She stood up and kicked her chair so hard it splintered. Declan recoiled in fear and she felt ashamed.

"Sorry. Sorry, Declan. I just. I just need some air."

She stalked out of the ruined cottage and stood looking out at the sea.

It had never looked so blue, so welcoming, or so distant.

So close. I was almost home free.

What's left to do now?

Might as well go back to Ballydonn and let them drown me again.

She felt utterly, totally defeated.

Over the gentle breeze and the hiss of the sea she heard them talking in hushed tones.

"They must have said something, Padraig. Didn't you think to ask?"

"Of course I did. I saw Ma give Morley the box. He was very fucking smug about it, too. And I asked her where he was going to put it. And she said the fewer people that knew, the better. All she said was that Morley would hide the box somewhere Mara could never get to."

"She trusts him a lot, doesn't she?"

"Yeah. I've been thinking about that. Because she *doesn't* trust him. I know she doesn't. She thinks he's useful, but she hates his guts. I couldn't believe she'd actually give him the cloak."

Mara closed her eyes and thought hard.

Gráinne. It all comes down to Gráinne. What would she do? C'mon, Mara. You're not fighting blind anymore. You've known her since she was a baby. Where would she hide the cloak?

Out of the corner of her eye, something white moved in gentle circles.

She smiled.

Of course. She already told you.

"Padraig!" she called.

They all came running.

"What?" he asked.

"Think very carefully," she said. "Did she say Cian hid the box somewhere I'd never find it, or somewhere I *could never go?*"

He thought carefully.

"Never go," he said.

"You're sure?"

"Definitely."

"Then I think I know where it is," she said. She turned and pointed into the distance, out into the sea. There, beautiful, tall, and white as a swan, was Windmill One of the Inishbannock Offshore Wind Farm.

"Padraig," Mara asked. "How're you with boats?"

55

Gráinne

Today was supposed to be a day of rest, she thought grimly to herself. *A day to recoup. To recharge. To sit inside and listen to the rain.*

Instead Gráinne was locked in a meeting with a group of red-faced shouting islanders.

Her mind drifted idly to the big iron pot that they had filled with water only hours before to drown the maiden, remembering the first drowning she had attended. She had been a young girl then, and her brother Conn had held her hand as they had watched "Aunt Mairéad" struggling and kicking like a rabbit in a wire as their mother had held her down below the water.

Her mother had told them that it was for her own good, and that Aunt Mairéad would be better for it.

It had seemed so cruel then.

Her mother was long gone now. Not dead, but gone. Into the trees and caves and silent places of the island. Another twisted, filthy sheep eater. And the task of drowning the Maiden had fallen to her daughter.

And, like many a task that had at first seemed unpleasant or cruel, Gráinne had come to like it.

As the Comhairle meeting descended further and further into rancor, she found herself looking from red face to red face, musing on who else she would drown if she could.

She realized that, if she had her druthers, scarcely five people in the room would still be alive.

And the first in line would be . . .

"He's working with her!" Cian yelled. "That's why he asked to take the first watch! He planned this!"

"No," Gráinne said quietly.

"What did you say?" Cian asked.

A hush fell on the room. People did not use that tone with Gráinne.

"I said no," Gráinne repeated. "I know my son."

Cian scoffed, and that detestable grin broke out on his face, like a rash of boils. "Do you now? I don't think you know the first thing about him."

Gráinne stood and looked Cian in the eye. "Mr. Morley," she said. "I do not know what you are implying. But I'd advise you not to imply it again in my presence."

"We're wasting time," Stiofán interjected. "Look, I went up to Killroon with this cunt." He gestured to Cian. "Now, I don't know if Padraig had anything to do with it, but he wasn't there. And the grave was open. She's out and about. That's the important thing."

"Did you see anything else there, Stiofán? Like, I dunno, blood or anything?" someone asked nervously.

"We saw Pajo Kilty's van," said Stiofán. "Completely wrecked."

"What?! Ah for feck's sake!" a voice was heard from the back of the room.

"You know what this means?!" Derbhle, the librarian, piped up shrilly. "It's too soon! She'll remember everything! She'll be coming here to get us!"

"Good," said Gráinne. "That would be good, Derbhle."

The whole room turned to look at her.

"You always forget. All of you. She doesn't have the power. We do. We have the guns. We have the numbers. And we have the cloak. It's our island. Ours. She's trapped here with us, not the other way around. She has nowhere to hide. Sooner or later, she'll make herself known. We'll find her. Go home. Rest."

The room began to empty. One stayed behind. Of course.

As Cian looked at Gráinne she had a brief flash of her hands gripping his neck and feeling it tense as she pushed him down under the water.

"You have something to add, Mr. Morley?"

"You know . . ." he began.

He stopped, and winced in pain. She watched him scratch savagely at his side and she noticed a slight pinkness on his white shirt, as if he had a rash and his frequent scratching had drawn blood.

"I've worked very hard for you," he continued after having apparently killed the itch.

"Is that so?"

"I have suffered a great deal. I have risked a great deal. For you. For the island. I want that to be recognized."

"There isn't a performance review, Mr. Morley. You know that, don't you?"

"I mean," he pushed on. "That business with Conn alone . . ."

"Considering what happened to my brother, that is a strange way to try and curry favor."

"I did what you wanted."

"What I wanted was for you to bring the cloak to me. I never intended you to . . ."

"See, I thought that, too. But . . . I started thinking, what was the follow-up? When Conn came back home and found the safe open and the cloak gone. Was he just going to quietly accept that? Wasn't he going to beat a trail right here to the Temple and demand you give it back? And if you didn't . . . well, he might have done anything. I mean, that was why you needed to get the cloak away from him in the first place? You were worried that he was soft on Mara."

Gráinne simply gazed at him, as impassive as a stone.

"And then of course there was the whiskey. Fresh bottle of thirty-year-old whiskey on his table. Barely touched. I mean he couldn't have gotten that anywhere . . . no, no. There's only one decent bar on the island. And we're standing in it. So why would he go out to drink whatever piss Pajo Kilty's selling when he could stay home and get drunk on that? Fuck. I wouldn't want you as an enemy, Gráinne."

"Well . . ." she said modestly.

"So. Yes, actually. I think I've worked very hard for you."

"And what is it you believe you have earned?"

"I want your word that when Mara is drowned again," he said. "She stays with me."

She said nothing for a few moments.

"Here's a thought," she said. "Let's have that performance review. You see, when I think of the men who have held your role. Well, I think of Oisín obviously. Who was married to her for eleven years. And of course, I think of my brother Conn, who lasted fifty. If you can believe it. And then there's you who . . . well, you didn't even last the summer, did you? And do you know what the difference between you and Oisín or Conn is? They actually loved her. Deeply. Truly. They understood love. They understood family. They understood sacrifice. They were men of the best kind. And you, well . . . you're just a small, scared, selfish boy who saw Mammy die and has been running away from death ever since."

She saw the flash in his eyes.

"Go on," she said. "Hit me. You're the least frightening thing on this island. Padraig will be the new groom. As he was supposed to be."

Cian smiled. "Either Padraig's helping her, or she's killed him. Either way, you're fucked. Who else is going to sign up for that job? I'm the only option you have."

She folded her arms and shook her head.

"It's true what they say about handsome men, isn't it? You never learned to be charming."

"Whatever," he said. "Call me when you need your dirty work done. Like you always do."

She stood in the doorway and watched him go, only to notice Stiofán barrelling toward the Temple. He slammed his hands against the entrance of the bar. "HE TOOK IT!"

Gráinne glared furiously at him. "What the fuck are you talking about, you mad eejit!"

"Your fucking son! He took it and left your car on the jetty!"

"What?! What did he take?!"

"What do you think?! ME FUCKING BOAT!!"

Gráinne stood in stunned silence.

And then she smiled.

56
Mara

"Jaysus, you're writing a novel over there," Natalie leaned over.

Mara looked up from her notebook and flashed her a smile.

"Just putting my thoughts in order," she said, shouting to be heard over the wind on the beach.

"There he is!" Declan called.

They looked up to see Padraig rounding the headland on Stiofán's boat.

Declan ran into the sea to help him pull it to shore. Padraig tossed a life jacket to him, and another to Natalie.

He strode toward Mara.

"Alright," he said. "Sit tight here. We'll be back before you know it. Hopefully with . . . y'know, yourself."

She gave a sad smile that instantly gave her away.

"What? What is it you're not telling me, Mara?" Padraig asked.

"You know what's going to happen when I get the cloak, don't you?" she asked.

He nodded and looked away. "I know . . . I don't have the right to ask you this . . ."

"I'll give them fair warning," she promised. "But I don't know if they'll listen. I don't know if Gráinne will listen."

He took a deep breath. "Fair warning. That's more than they deserve. Thank you."

"I'm going to need you to do something for me in return," she said. "Something very important. Two things, actually."

"Name them," he said.

She gave him her notebook, and told him what she needed.

"*Slán, a Mhaighdean*," he said softly.

"Padraig," she said, laying her hand on his cheek. "I give you my blessing. May you live a long happy life, and find your heart's fondest wish."

. . .

Mara and Padraig followed her two friends down to the boat.

My friends. Did I ever have friends before? Lovers and children, yes. But they may be the first friends I had in four hundred years. Worth the wait, both of them.

Padraig said nothing as he got in the boat, and Mara noticed he refused to meet either Natalie or Declan's gazes.

"Everything alright?" Declan asked.

"Come here to me, the two of you," she said, her throat tight, and embraced them awkwardly in their bulky life jackets. "Be careful out there. Promise me. Promise me you will."

"Course we will," said Natalie.

"If anything happens . . ."

"Whoa, that's bad luck. For a voyage, isn't it?" Declan said, half seriously.

MARA

"Just listen. I love you both. I can never repay what you did for me."

"You don't have to," Natalie told her. "Because we love you, too."

"If anyone was going to crawl out of a grave and break into my house and eat all my mayonnaise, I'm so glad it was you." Declan leaned his head against Mara's.

She laughed and kissed him on the cheek and then kissed Natalie.

"Padraig," she said. "Could I borrow your phone?"

. . .

Mara watched the boat speed off, carrying the only three people in the world that she trusted, and waited until it was almost halfway to the great white windmill in the distance.

Then, she turned, and stalked toward the heart of the island.

57
Declan

"Where's she gone?" Declan called over the roar of the engine. "She's not on the beach."

Padraig made a gesture to show that he couldn't hear him.

The sea was rough this far out from the island, and when they finally pulled up beside the base of Windmill One, the combination of the tossing sea and the sheer, mind-boggling size of the structure made Declan feel quite sick.

"Y'alright?" Natalie yelled before giving him a peck on the cheek.

Jesus Christ, she's enjoying this, he lamented to himself.

Padraig tied the boat to a minuscule dock at the base of the windmill. Declan and Natalie had to work their way across, gripping the dock's handrail tight and trying not to slip on the tiny, sea-foam-soaked walkway.

He made the mistake of looking up, and for a moment, felt certain that one of the massive blades was descending on his head.

Finally they reached the hatch.

DECLAN

Padraig had provided them with a few tools, including a good, sharp fire axe and, thankfully, the engineering hatch was thin enough that Declan was able to cut the lock off with a few strong swipes.

The wind immediately caught the now-open door, which smashed into Declan's face. He felt his nose break and his vision go white.

Then he was falling backward, rolling and plunging into the freezing cold sea.

He couldn't breathe, and he felt the fear rise.

But, perhaps because of every mad and hideous thing he had seen since coming to the island.

Perhaps because he knew Mara was counting on him.

Or perhaps because he knew Natalie was up there, searching desperately for him, waiting and praying to see his head break the waves . . .

The fear receded and he felt very calm.

He closed his eyes, and the life jacket did its work, bringing him safely to the surface of the churning cauldron.

The boat was eight meters away.

Fighting the asthma attack that he could feel building in his chest, Declan swam to the boat and held on, trying to gather enough strength to pull himself over the lip. He looked up, wheezing, and blearily he could make out Natalie, shouting wordlessly over the roaring wind.

He gave her a thumbs-up and smiled.

Blood ran from his nose over his upper lip as he smiled and he could feel it coating his teeth.

She nodded, and vanished into the hatch, avoiding the madly swinging door.

"Come on," Padraig yelled to him, extending a hand. "She'll need your help getting the cloak out."

• • •

Somehow, Declan managed to drag himself into the boat and, heavy with water and lightheaded with pain, climbed back onto the walkway and followed her inside the hatch.

"Natalie!" he called out, his voice echoing up the inside of the giant wind turbine.

He looked up and swore.

A tightly winding staircase stretched up to the very top of the metal tube. He thought about scaling it, soaking wet, and then down with the heavy box.

"I can't do it," he said aloud. "I can't do it."

"Don't worry," he heard her voice say. "Neither could he."

As his eyes adjusted to the gloom, he saw Natalie kneeling on the floor, yanking at something in the gap behind the stairs.

She stood up to revealed what she had found.

"Bastard was too lazy to drag it up there," she said with a grin. "He just hid it under a pile of blankets."

As they emerged from the hatch with the black wooden case braced between them, Declan saw Padraig give them a proud smile. Getting the box into the boat without anyone, or it, falling into the sea seemed impossible, but somehow they managed it.

Barely.

They laid it on the deck of the boat. Natalie laid her hands on top, as if making sure that it was solid and real.

DECLAN

Padraig fired up the engine.

It took Declan a few minutes to realize that they were not heading back to Inishbannock. Already the ocean was calmer farther from the island.

"Padraig!" Declan shouted. "Padraig!"

There was no trace of joy or triumph on his features now. Padraig looked like someone doing vital work while in great pain. His jaw was set, his eyes focused on a point in the distance.

"Padraig, where are you taking us!" Natalie screamed.

With a furious gesture, Padraig shut off the engine and glowered at them.

With the roar of the engine gone, the silence was overpowering. Declan thought he could hear every drop of seawater lapping against the hull of the boat.

"We're not going back to the island," Padraig said quietly.

"What the fuck did you do?" Natalie asked, her eyes practically glowing as she hurled the accusation.

"What I was asked to do. By Mara," Padraig replied. He reached into his pocket and passed the notebook to Declan. "Last page."

Declan read.

Declan,

If everything's gone to plan, you're off the island. Hopefully, you found the box.

Yeah, notice I said "the box" and not "the cloak"?
Sorry.

The cloak is not in the windmill. The cloak can't leave the island, any more than I can. It's part of me. So when Padraig said that Gráinne had given Cian the box to hide, I knew the windmill was the one place it <u>COULDN'T</u> be. Gráinne hid it somewhere she felt I can't reach. And I knew you and Natalie would try to go with me to get it.

And you would have died.

Padraig is going to take you to Dingle. I need you to get as far inland as possible. When (if!) I get the cloak, every storm I've kept from this island for four hundred years will hit Inishbannock. There'll be nothing left. Don't worry, I'll give the islanders enough time to evacuate. This is not for them. It's for the Fomor.

We called them monsters, but they're not. No more than anyone else. Before my first drowning, I put a curse on the islanders. A living death that warps their bodies and keeps them alive on this island, trapped with me. The Fomor are the old islanders. Today, I'm going to sweep them into the sea. This is not revenge. I already had my revenge. I'm done with revenge. This is mercy. And that's why you three needed to leave.

Because I love you.

I owe you everything.

We won't meet again. Every cell in my body is begging to return to the sea. But I will never forget you for as long as I live. I'll keep your memory alive within me until the oceans dry up and the sun dies.

I hope you found the box. If it contains what I think it contains, well . . . Hopefully it will explain a few things.

About you, and me. And how much you mean to me.

Look after her.

DECLAN

Be good to each other.
All my love.

Mara

PS: My weird bullshit wins.

Declan skimmed it over and over. He passed it to Natalie, who read it in shocked silence.

Padraig fired up the engine again.

"Padraig!" Declan yelled. "We can't leave her here!"

Padraig said nothing.

The boat carried on its way.

58
Mara

This would be the last homecoming.

Already, she had returned to Conn's cottage. She had walked among the ashes of the home she had made with Oisín. And all around the island, no doubt, there were houses where she had lived and been kept. In some, she could admit, she had been happy for a time.

But not this place.

In the middle of a field on the northern side, buried in ivy, stood two walls that were all that remained of her first home on the island.

She regretted that there were not two walls less.

This was the house of Donn.

Nothing here, but memories of misery. No less bitter for being ancient.

She stood over the remains of the well. There had been a recent attempt to seal it off. The metal fencing lay twisted and broken on the ground, as if some great force had erupted from the well and torn through it like paper.

Mara looked down into the hole.

The cloak was down there. She could feel it. She could sense water lapping against her skin even though she stood on dry land.

Gráinne hadn't lied to her. Gráinne wouldn't lie to her.

To Cian? Absolutely. She would lie to him as a matter of principle.

But Gráinne had told Mara to her face, as a challenge.

And Donn, being a cunning and a clever man, took the cloak and put it in a box, and dropped it down the well beside his cottage.

Gráinne had not hid it where no one would ever think to look. She had hid it where no one could look for it and survive.

Mara stared into the bottomless black. And let herself fall.

She dropped through darkness absolute and landed in water so cold that it felt like being struck by lightning.

As always, when her body struck water, her limbs seemed to turn to stone.

But her prohibition, her taboo, her *geas*, did not seem quite as strong here. Maybe it was because she was still on the island, or in it. While the water was brackish, it was fresh spring water. An underground lake, not the sea.

Desperately, painfully, Mara managed to swim to solid rock and pull herself up. Mercifully, Padraig's phone had survived the swim and she was able to use the screen to light her surroundings.

She was in a cave that seemed to stretch out for all eternity, endless shadowy cathedrals of wet rock that honeycombed beneath the island.

The hole of the well's opening; a pale white Eucharist hovering above her.

Gráinne would not have had a lot of options. She would have weighted the cloak down and dropped it straight through the well to avoid the Fomor.

Mara shone her light into the water.

There, impossibly far down, she could make out a black form resting on the lake bed.

She set the phone down, steeled herself, and dove.

Every muscle in her body screamed in agony as she tried to swim to the bottom.

A migraine began in her forehead and grew like ivy throughout her body until every nerve was on fire.

Too much, too much.

She broke off and kicked her way to the surface. Pulling herself onto the rock, Mara howled in pain and frustration.

She turned at the sound of rustling behind her. The shadows twitched and rolled with a leprous vileness.

They had come. They had all come.

Her hideous children. Her monsters. Her Fomor.

The part of her that was still Mara felt a shudder of panic and revulsion. But the older part of her, the true part, saw them for what they were and felt nothing but pity.

She took a step toward them and the shadows flinched.

I'm in a nightmare, she thought. *But I am not the dreamer. I am what the dreamer flees.*

They were mad, tortured things, but they knew enough to know their maker and recoiled in terror. All but one.

The largest form rolled toward her, its rage overcoming its fear.

At last, here was a creature for which she had no pity.

"Here we are," she said, through clenched teeth. "The two of us. Back here. Didn't we know it?"

MARA

The beast opened three mouths and roared its hate at her.

She screamed hers back at him, and the whole wretched cohort snapped and gibbered through a million malignant, suppurating maws.

His mouth opened and she felt his jaws cage in around her.

Mara's arms shot out to catch them. She felt teeth digging into her palms and the hot air of his bilious stomach, the stink of dead sheep and dead men. It fell on her head in deep, heaving breaths.

They held each other there, in that terrible embrace.

He was too strong to break free. She was too strong to be devoured.

Same as it ever was.

She heard herself speak, and the voice that came from her mouth terrified her.

"If you're still in there," she hissed into his slavering, slithering throat. "I want you to know that I hate you. I could hate you for another four hundred years. For four thousand years. For four million years. I could fill an ocean with the hate I hold for you. And I know you feel the same. We destroyed each other. We turned each other into monsters, and everything that came from us was twisted by our hate. And for the first time, I think I have the strength to end it. If you help me. I can't offer you forgiveness. But I can give you peace. We can give them all peace. We can stop. We can stop."

For a moment, nothing changed. And then she felt the terrible weight pull away and the beast retreated and closed its jaws and looked at her expectantly.

And for a moment, just a moment, she saw his body. And imagined the centuries of torment, of living trapped in that heaving mound of agonized flesh, a mad mind in a mad body.

And yes, she felt pity.

The Fomor had fallen deathly silent. Waiting. Perhaps, even daring to hope.

And she turned, and dove into the water again.

It was not that she no longer felt the pain. It was that a fire had burned everything in her that could be burned. All that was left was stone.

Her hand reached out through the water and touched fur.

Mara could feel the cloak, the cloak could feel her.

They were one and the same.

It had been wrapped around a large stone. With a final, desperate burst of strength, she shook it loose.

As her vision faded, she felt it wrap itself around her.

Like an arrow shot from the bottom of the lake, she burst up through the water.

She stood before them, woman and cloak. Nature reasserted.

She was whole at last, mind and body.

The darkness screamed.

And then was silent.

59
Gráinne

She could feel a chill in the air.

She was standing in the doorway of the Temple, making sure that the whole village could see her. Calm. In control.

She had lived through times like these before, the Maiden on the loose and running wild and everyone half a second from mad panic.

You had to show them that this was all part of the dance.

And yet, that chill in the air. She knew that Mara could not have found the cloak. The very fact that Padraig had stolen Stiofán's boat showed that Mara was as clueless as always. She would be caught, and drowned, and reborn. But something felt different this time.

Some menace carried on the sea air.

She started as the phone behind the bar rang.

Slowly, calmly, not wanting to seem flustered, she went inside and picked up the handset.

"Hello?"

The line was fuzzy. She thought she could hear the sea in the background.

And then she heard a voice that sang to her, cold and clear:

"*Tá mé 'mo shuí*
Ó d'éirigh an ghealach aréir
Ag cur teineadh síos gan scíth
'S á fadú go gear
Tá bunadh a' tí 'na luí
'S tá mise liom féin
Tá na coiligh ag glaoch
'S tá 'n saol ina gcodladh ach mé."

Gráinne listened in silence until the song was done.

"Mara," she said.

"You owed me a story," said the voice on the other end. "I owed you a song."

"Well. We're even now," Gráinne noted.

There was a laugh at the other end. One that brought Gráinne not the slightest joy.

"Smart woman like you knows that's not remotely true."

"Let me speak to Padraig."

"He's not here right now."

"Have you killed my other son, too?"

"No. And I didn't kill the first one, either."

"Don't lie to me."

"I'm not. One of us has spent her whole life lying and it's not me. I'm sure you're smart enough to figure out who really killed Oisín."

Gráinne felt her blood run cold. "No," she said. Not to Mara but to herself.

Yes. Of course. She didn't even have to think twice.

Cian.

Obvious. Of course he did.

"That doesn't change anything," she said at last.

"Mother of the year, you are."

"Oh, it'll change things for Cian. Oh yes. Oh yes, it'll change things for Cian. But not for you."

"No?"

"No. We're going back to how it was. You can come back here and we can do it easy. Or you can make me come and get you, in which case I promise you will drown for *days*."

"Ohhh . . . you thought this was a negotiation?" Mara asked.

"No, that would imply you have something to bargain with. And you don't. It wasn't a bad guess," Gráinne said into the phone. "But it's not there. That's why you stole the boat, isn't it?"

She had hoped that she would hear shock and pain in the voice on the other end of the line. She was disappointed.

"No," Mara said. "I just needed to get the people I care about off the island. Cian didn't know, did he? That you took the cloak out of the box?"

"Of course not. But you know men, they like to feel important."

"So you've hidden it somewhere on the island?" Mara's voice crackled through the bad connection.

"Sure, where else could it be?"

"Somewhere secret. Somewhere I'd never think of."

"Stop fishing. You'll get nothing from me."

"Somewhere I'd never think to look," Mara mused. "Well, well, well."

Gráinne's face froze. Outside the Temple, the sky darkened and a chill ran through her bones.

"Did you really think I would be afraid to go down there again?" Mara asked. "Did you think your fears were mine? Did you think me so small?"

"Alright," Gráinne whispered. "If you have the cloak, what's keeping you here? Swim away."

"Little thing," Mara answered. "You think you can just take, and take, and take until there is no more. No. The sea remembers your debts. And I will collect. I am going to take the thing you most love from you."

Gráinne felt a stone in her throat.

"My son?" she whispered.

"No. This island. It'll sink beneath the waves, drowning every filthy thing still on it."

Gráinne closed her eyes. She had failed them. She had failed them all.

"So you have three hours."

For a second, Gráinne felt sure she hadn't heard right. "What?" she said.

"Call the ferries. Warn the people in Farvey. Get everyone off the island that you can."

"What if I don't?" Gráinne asked.

"Woman, for the first time in four hundred years, I am trying mercy. Don't test me."

"And what do you want in exchange for your mercy?"

"There's someone I don't want you to warn."

As if on cue Gráinne heard a car, driving far too fast for Ballydonn's narrow main street, pass the bar. Through the open door she saw a glimpse of golden hair in the driver's seat.

"Done," she said.

"I'm sure that was very painful for you," Mara remarked.

"Awful man. What did you ever see in him?" Gráinne replied.

Mara laughed. Long and hard and then she abruptly stopped. "Gráinne. I am going to tear you limb from limb and eat you alive. I want you to know that."

"I'll be waiting for you, *a chroí*," Gráinne answered. "I'm not going anywhere. And I will stop you. We've been here before."

"Even if you did, it would be too late. This island is no longer blessed."

60
An Maighdean Mhara

Mara stood on Killroon, the highest point of the island, the site of her final grave. She tossed Padraig's cell phone into her coffin. There would be no more burial tides.

From here, she could see all of Inishbannock, at once immense and only a speck. On the horizon, the storm swelled and rolled toward the tiny spit of land, black as death, vast as an eternity.

In that moment she had a sense of the smallness of everything.

The island.

The people on it.

Her time here.

Her joy.

Her suffering.

Her.

Atoms, all of it. Before the immensity of this storm, Mara finally felt how insignificant she really was. And it filled her with peace.

She wanted to be back in the ocean. She wanted to be tiny again. A dot in the great blue forever.

Soon.

The seal cloak whipped faster and faster in the wind.

Here it comes.

The light died.

The rain came.

Less like droplets of water, more like an ocean being poured from above.

The wind moved like muscle and flesh.

She opened her mouth to catch the storm on her tongue and howled with glorious, joyous rage.

She turned and began her last walk across Inishbannock.

Lightning snaked across the sky like Chinese dragons, casting the wretched landscape in harsh bright light. In the fields around her, Mara could see movement. Hideous, misformed shapes writhed and screamed in terror as they followed her final march.

The Fomor knew what was coming, and they had crawled to the surface like maggots rising from carrion.

Ahead of her, a yellow light was barely visible through the curtain of rain.

She was almost home.

She thought about her friends on that tiny boat who she would never see again.

It saddened her that she had said goodbye with a lie.

I already had my revenge. I'm done with revenge.

Well. Not quite.

Not quite.

61
Cian

The bite was still there.

Cian had almost forgotten about it. The last trace of scar tissue had vanished from his skin weeks ago.

And yet now, as he sat in his armchair finishing Conn Rowen's whiskey and watching the world outside get washed away, he could almost feel her teeth in his flesh. There was a line of pain, burning bright like Christmas tree lights, in a long loop over the side of his torso.

He scratched his side, rubbing the flesh raw and pink. The itch receded, but he knew it would be back soon.

He really would have to get that looked at.

By who? he asked himself sardonically.

After the council meeting, he had returned home from Ballydonn, and searched the house with a shotgun in his hand, on the off chance that she had been stupid enough to come back. Once satisfied he was alone, Cian had put on some music and waited by the phone for the call to battle.

When the storm began he had called the Temple.

Gráinne had answered.

"What's going on?!" he had yelled. "Are you seeing this?!"

CIAN

"Calm down," she said. "We caught her again. We've already drowned and buried her. This always happens."

He looked out at the madness outside of the window. He had lived through two drowning storms now. This one made them look like a summer squall. This one felt murderous. The house seemed to be shaking apart.

"You're sure?" he said.

"Of course," she replied calmly. "Stay put. It'll pass in a few days."

"A few days of THIS?"

"Oh, it'll ease off. Nothing this bad lasts forever."

He nodded, a little reassured.

"What about Padraig?" he asked. "Was I right?"

There was a long, acidic pause, so long that he was worried the line had gone dead.

"Yes," Gráinne said at last. "Padraig betrayed us."

Ah, poor heartbroken mother. Obviously he did, you stupid bitch.

He resisted the urge to gloat. This was time to be the bigger man. "I'm sorry," he said, moving in for the kill. "So. I guess that means the wedding's off?"

"Yes, yes, Mr. Morley. Your kind offer is accepted," she said.

And the strangest thing was, she sounded liked she was smiling. He must have been imagining it.

"Don't worry," she told him. "You and Mara will be reunited very soon."

She hung up.

After half an hour he tried calling again, but this time there was no answer.

He considered leaving the house and driving to Ballydonn. He knew that there was absolutely no way any boat would be able to get him to the mainland in this storm, but he had a vague idea that the side of the island facing the mainland might be more sheltered, and the old stone-and-mortar buildings would be more durable than the glass-and-steel art installation piece he had decided to make his home in.

He quickly dismissed the idea of driving in the storm as suicide, even without knowing that his car was currently floating out of his driveway.

He poured another shot of whiskey, and stood in front of the huge dining room window that overlooked the garden.

A doubt, cold and venomous, slid into his mind.

What if she found it?

He dismissed the thought at once.

She couldn't have. She literally can't leave the island. Even if she was smart enough to figure out it was on the wind turbine, it wouldn't do her a fucking bit of good. You could have told her to her face where it was, and she'd be no closer to getting it.

That was why Gráinne had trusted him with the cloak. Because she knew he would get the job done.

Even though she hated him, she needed him.

They all needed him.

Fuck!

His whole side was aflame now, it felt like itching powder had been spread onto his side an inch thick.

He scratched.

His fingers found a lump on his side.

What was it? A weal? A boil?

He found another, and another and then . . . *oh fuck.*

He felt something move. In his flesh. Like a baby in the womb, announcing its presence with a tiny, insistent kick.

CIAN

He ran to the bathroom, switched on the harsh light, tore off his shirt, and stared in utter horror at the image in the mirror.

A great, deep seam had opened in his side, right along the line where Mara had bitten him. It looked like he'd been cut open, but there was no blood.

Moving slowly, very slowly, he explored the seam with his finger.

The flesh around the seam felt tough and dry, like the sole of a foot.

His fingers slipped between the two edges as he pushed in, farther and farther, and he felt something smooth and hard there.

For a moment he thought he might be touching a rib.

And then the seams pulled apart and a great maw opened in his side and he screamed and screamed as he saw teeth, rows and rows of razor-sharp baby teeth.

The massive shark mouth in his side snapped shut.

The tips of his finger severed instantly.

He could feel the chunks of flesh fall farther inside him. Inside *it*.

He shrieked as a massive tongue emerged from inside his torso and looped around his wrist. His hand was pulled inside the mouth and its teeth pierced his palm and knuckles.

Howling, he ran from the bathroom to the kitchen.

The kettle was on the counter, still half full of water.

Barely thinking coherently, he turned it on with his free hand and desperately searched in the cutlery drawer for a weapon.

All the while, he could feel his hand being eaten inside him.

He found a large, brutal-looking carving knife.

The kettle boiled and the switch snapped up. He grabbed it and sobbed as he poured the scalding water over his possessed side. He could swear he heard the mouth gurgling in pain as it shot open, releasing the shredded stump that had been his hand.

The tongue emerged like a serpent, whipping around wildly. With his last remaining hand, Cian cut through the tongue with the carving knife.

He felt every second of it.

He passed out, and when he woke up, he was lying on the kitchen floor in a pool of his own blood. The massive tongue lay severed beside him. The side of his torso hung open like a kitchen cabinet.

He was dimly aware that he was bleeding profusely.

Get to the living room. Douse the wounds in whiskey. Use a throw or something to stanch the bleeding. Probably fail. Wait for help that won't come. Die in the living room.

Not the best plan.

But the best under the circumstances.

He crawled, he crawled.

Every inch agony.

The blood seemed to adhere him to the floor, making it even harder to move, like a snail in glue.

Cian reached the living room and raised his head to stare out the window.

Was the storm dying down?

He needed so desperately for that to be true, to believe there was a chance someone might be able to reach the house.

So he convinced himself.

Yes, yes, the wind was definitely weaker than it had been.

And then he saw it.

A flash of lightning illuminated the dark sky and a familiar shape soared majestically through the air, its elegant blades turning even now. His jaw dropped as he witnessed all one hundred and twenty meters of Windmill One flying like it was weightless.

It was impossible. It was madness. But there it was.

"Shoddy workmanship," a voice said. "That's what that is."

His head snapped around and he saw it.

A figure, standing in shadows that seemed pale compared to the blackness of the cloak it wore.

In some ridiculous way, it reminded him of the woman he had lived with.

But this was not Mara.

This was something that he had never seen before.

He screamed weakly and began to crawl away.

"Where are you off to?" she asked.

His head struck the glass. There was nowhere left to go.

She was coming for him.

He felt himself being lifted as easily as a piece of paper and then he was slammed hard against the glass.

He felt lips and teeth brushing against his ear.

"Hey, babe," said the voice. "How was your day?"

He struggled, but her grip only tightened.

"Not gonna lie. Mine was really rough. But it's all worth it to come home to you."

He screamed as he felt her nails growing inside the small of his back and nestling sharply into the muscle. She beat him against the reinforced glass until his nose and teeth broke and his skull cracked.

At last, with one final blow, she shattered the window with what remained of him and he emerged, cut, half blind, and bleeding, into the howling black void of the storm.

She held him up with one hand, and through his one eye that had not been pulped, he looked out on the garden. His garden, drowned in her rain.

It was now under a foot of water and the frequent flashes of lightning painted landscapes of hell in pure white. The whole field before him writhed with the bodies of hideous, cursed things. The nightmares howled against the storm, though whether it was in rage or a plea for mercy, no one could know.

As she raised him up above them like a trophy, Cian could make out a massive, shambling form coming toward him. He had the vaguest impression of a giant seal-like body and then the head of the creature opened up.

It's going to eat me.

That was the last coherent thought Cian Morley's brain ever made.

He heard the words she whispered in his torn half ear, but he could not understand them.

"You never met my first husband, did you?" Mara hissed. "You two should talk."

62
Gráinne

Ballydonn was gone. All that was left were hard black lines breaking the surface of the now perfectly still water.

On the roof of the Temple, Gráinne stood and waited.

When the floodwaters had poured into her tavern she had been ready to die. She had thought it oddly fitting. Drowning in the Temple. She could see a poetic justice.

But as the water had risen even higher, she had swum up to the ceiling and discovered the storm had loosened the slate tiles.

Gulping down a last lungful of air, she had broken through the roof and pulled herself through. She had sat crouched on the tiles, watching as Ballydonn was drowned around her.

But then the rain had suddenly ceased. Already it seemed the waters were receding. The church spire was already fully above the surface.

As the night sky turned salmon pink and the morning sun began to warm her drenched bones she had felt a strange joy.

Gráinne had survived. Her world had ended and she was left standing.

It was strange. She had lost so much. Her sons. Her brothers. Her home. Her very way of life. Her whole family's legacy, centuries of sacrifice paid in the wages of blood and fear, all drowned now. She'd had so much taken from her that she could scarcely even be considered the same woman she had once been. She was not Gráinne, mother of Oisín and Padraig (even if he was still alive, he was dead to her now). She was not Gráinne, sister of Conn and Malachy. She was not the landlady of the Temple or the leader of the Comhairle. That Gráinne was gone, swept into the sea.

And yet, she felt no real sense of loss. She felt happy. She felt free.

She heard a buzzing drone glinting white in the air, circling the flooded village. She waved to it, slow, dignified.

The drone moved on, but she felt certain it had seen her.

It's not the end, she told herself. *We'll survive. We'll return. We'll build something new.*

A wave lapped against the roof and she realized that the water was not as calm as it had been. She saw a flicker of a shape. At first she guessed it was a chair, or some other piece of furniture floating in the water, but then a slick form emerged. Black. Huge. And there was another. And another.

A scalloped tail broke the surface of the water and she saw sunlight reflecting off the whiskers of a doglike muzzle.

Seals.

There were hundreds.

She took a stumbling step away from the edge of the roof. Beneath her heel, one of the slate tiles suddenly shifted and fell into the water.

She saw a flash of razor-sharp teeth.

One of the seals had swum into the flooded tavern below.

GRÁINNE

Gráinne shrieked as the seal hit the roof, hard and fast, and more tiles vanished. There were now two great holes in the roof, including the one she had made during her escape.

She felt more motion below her and leapt just in time, before another hole was punched through the roof, right where she'd just been standing.

She took a deep breath and crouched on the last part of the roof still whole enough to support her.

She had thought that she would be drowned in the Temple.

But that was not the death promised to her.

She felt the blow, and then the fall. Water enveloped her.

She screamed as she felt razor-sharp teeth slitting her left palm and seawater filled her mouth as something bit deep into the bone of her right wrist.

She felt two bites in either calf and then suddenly she was being pulled in all directions.

Ah, what was it Mara had said? Tear you limb from limb. Eat you alive.

Through the reddening water a great animal form swam furiously toward her, eyes and teeth flashing white in the dark.

Through the agony, Gráinne managed a smile.

Hello, Mara.

63
Natalie

Dingle always had too many people and too little street in the summer, but now it was truly overflowing.

Emergency services, Civil Defence, and the media—local, national, and even a few from abroad—had descended on the small seaside town in the wake of Inishbannock's sudden, unprecedented drowning.

Natalie had watched the news on and off as the media frenzy unfolded. The talking heads said that, without any warning, the most intense, powerful tropical cyclone in half a millennium had suddenly arisen in the Atlantic Ocean and made a beeline for the coast of County Kerry. One island in particular had been right in the path of the storm.

Thankfully, due to a quick call put in by the islanders to the mainland, the hasty mobilization of Inishbannock's fishing fleet, and the fact that the Irish Navy just happened to be conducting patrols around the coast of County Clare, it appeared that almost the entire population had been safely evacuated before the storm hit.

Even more fortuitously, the storm did not proceed farther inland, and had exhausted itself by morning. They had faced

NATALIE

the worst storm in Irish history and, while a head count still needed to be done, early impressions were that casualties had been extremely light.

Natalie knew that, in time, the crowds would clear. Most of the tourists who had been evacuated from Farvey had, in fact, already gone home, having had a far more interesting trip than they had expected. As for the islanders, Natalie didn't know what would become of them and found she didn't particularly give a fuck.

Right now, all she cared about was ferrying the three large coffees, which she had finally acquired at exorbitant cost down on Green Street, without any of them being elbowed out of her hands by the throng.

She pushed her way through the packed pub, and quickly made her way to the table, hoping that the bartender wouldn't see her bringing in outside drinks or, if he did, wouldn't care. Declan was in a corner seat.

She placed the coffee in front of him. "Sorry about the wait. I had to go to three places. First two were sold out."

Declan was holding a photograph in his hand. She couldn't see what it was, but could tell it was yellowed with age. He put it away quickly so she decided not to pry.

She looked around. "Where's Padraig?" she asked.

Declan spoke, and immediately she heard in his voice he'd been crying.

"He . . . he went for a walk. We . . . sit down, Natalie."

She felt panic rising in her chest. "Declan? What's wrong?"

"It's fine," he tried to reassure her.

She sat down and noticed the box. It was where she had last seen it, lodged under Declan's chair. But the padlock was missing.

"Oh my God, you opened it without me?!" she hissed angrily.

His wet eyes, black and bruised from where he'd been struck by the hatch door, looked at her apologetically.

"Sorry," he said. "We did. The bartender had a bolt cutter."

"You could have waited!"

"You were taking ages!"

"I had to traipse over half of Munster and then I had to queue for . . . !"

"Sorry," he said. "Sorry. You're right. We should have waited."

He looked so crushed that she didn't have the heart to continue the fight.

"It's fine," she said. "So come on. What's in it?"

With a heavy sigh, he stood up, slid the heavy box out from under his chair, and set it on the table.

Natalie opened it.

Inside were stacks and stacks of papers. Photographs. Marriage licenses. Certs of birth and baptism. Letters. Children's drawings. Enough not for one life, but dozens.

"What is all this?" Natalie asked.

"This is . . . her. It's Mara. Everything they needed to keep secret. All her past lives."

She remembered carrying the box into the boat. The weight of it. So many memories. So much taken from one woman.

She noticed Declan was trembling. He took out the photograph, which she realized now must have come from the box.

"Do you know why I came to the island, Natalie?" he asked quietly.

"Yeah," she said. "Artist's bursary, right?"

NATALIE

He smiled sadly. "That's the how, not the why. My grandmother came from there. Her name was Caithlín. She grew up on Inishbannock, and she decided that she wanted to leave. Her ma, well, her ma wasn't having that. And they had this massive screaming row. And so my gran, she decided to run away from home. At seventeen. She runs as far as Dublin, gets a job working in a biscuit factory, and meets a fella named Kevin Rooney."

"Your granddad."

"The very same. And they get married and they have my mam. And, the way my granny told it to me . . . when my mam became a teenager, because she was such an absolute fucking dose . . ."

Natalie laughed, and Declan did, too, but through tears.

"She realized, y'know, how hard she'd been on her own mam. And she decided to go back to Inishbannock and patch things up. This is years later, now. Years. And she goes back. And she meets her mam . . . who doesn't recognize her. Who acts like she's never met her. Who drives her away. Who tells her to get off the island and never come back, spreading lies and . . ."

He broke down and Natalie held him tight.

"She never knew," Declan sobbed. "Gran died and she never knew why."

Natalie buried her face in his shoulder and felt him shake. Looking down, she could see the old photograph in his hand, clutched so preciously that it had begun to crease.

It was a picture of a beautiful dark-haired woman. In her arms, she held a little girl tightly, herself in miniature with long brown ringlets.

They look perfectly content together.

Natalie knew the face of the woman, she knew it very well. And for once, her eyes were as happy as her smile.

• • •

They found Padraig out on the waterfront, sitting on a bench looking out at the sea.

"Jesus, another sad white boy," Natalie said with a grin, giving him his coffee.

He took a sip and grimaced. "Is that some fancy iced coffee or something?"

"No, just cold. Sorry."

They sat down beside him.

"You tell her?" Padraig asked Declan.

He nodded.

"You okay?" Natalie asked.

"No," Padraig replied. "Just seeing it all in one place. How much. How long it lasted. Knowing I was a part of it. I don't think I'm supposed to be okay, honestly."

"You helped end it," she reminded him. "That counts for a lot."

A thought occurred to her. She sat back on the bench and glanced from one man to the other.

"You realize you're cousins, yeah?"

They both looked at her.

"Yeah," she said. "Definite family resemblance."

"Feck off," they said in near-perfect unison.

She cackled wickedly.

The sun dipped over the horizon and a mild chill descended.

NATALIE

Declan saw Natalie shiver and took off his coat and draped it over her.

She snuggled under his arm. "Thanks, love."

He smiled.

"What?" she asked.

"You've never called me that. 'Love.' That's the first time you . . ."

"Don't make it weird. It's not like I said, 'I love you,' or anything. And I call you 'love' all the time."

"No you don't."

"I do. Just . . . that was the first time out loud."

"Do you two want to get a room, or what?" Padraig groused amiably.

She did. She wanted to get a room and lie with him and not have to think about troubling things like how far Dublin was from Cork, or the success rates for relationships formed in stressful situations. And then she felt his hand stroking her hair and realized that, compared to the feeling that gave her, geography and statistics were pathetic indeed. He was a good guy. He was a wonderful guy. And she loved him. They'd make it work.

"Do you wonder . . ." Natalie asked.

"Go on?" Declan said.

She decided it was too soon to ask what she had been going to ask, so she changed tack.

"If . . . like, we just got really, really, really high? And none of that was real?"

"So high that we somehow called down a storm and drowned an entire island and made hundreds of people homeless?"

"Those were some good drugs," Padraig said.

Declan chuckled.

"I can't believe we'll never see her again," Natalie said softly.

Declan nodded, pecked her on the cheek. Natalie turned her gaze out over the sea. In the far distance, she saw a head break the surface, black as night.

The seal tipped its nose, a friendly salute, and then vanished beneath the waves.

She smiled.

She couldn't know it was her.

But she chose to believe.

EPILOGUE
An Mhaighdean Mhara

She swam. Soaring in an ocean that was endless. That had no walls.

The four hundred years she had spent on the hard rock were already melting away.

What were they compared to the millennia of the sea, and the millennia to come?

A brief ache.

An uneasy sleep, woken from now, and already half forgotten.

She turned her head and saw hundreds of her sisters swimming alongside her as they always had.

Had something happened?

Had something caused her to leave them?

She couldn't remember.

It didn't matter.

She was here.

She was home.

She was free.

She had the only thing she needed to be happy.

She had the sea.

Acknowledgments

Heartfelt and sincere thanks:

To Hayley Wagreich, TJ Ohler, and the team at Zando for all their skill, enthusiasm, and hard work.

To Jennie Goloboy, agent par excellence.

To T. Kingfisher, Alex Grecian, Clay McLeod Chapman, and Nick Medina for their kind support.

To Bex, for the live-blogged beta read that was as entertaining as it was useful.

To Aoife, the greatest wife and the hardest-working editor who works for cups of tea and smooches.

And to you, reader. Yer a good egg.

About the Author

NEIL SHARPSON is an Irish Writers Centre Novel Fair–winning author and playwright living in Dublin with his wife and two children. He is the author of *When the Sparrow Falls* (one of *The Times*' 10 best science fiction novels of 2021) and *Knock Knock, Open Wide* ("a high-water mark for the Irish horror novel"—*Publishers Weekly*). He is also the author of the picture book *Don't Trust Fish*, illustrated by Caldecott Medalist Dan Santat.

For timely updates, follow his comedic review blog, *Unshaved Mouse*.